Accidentally Compromising the Duke

Wedded by Scandal Series

Accidentally Compromising the Duke

Wedded by Scandal Series

STACY REID

Copyright © 2016 by Stacy Reid. All rights reserved, including the right to reproduce, distribute, or transmit in any form or by any means. For information regarding subsidiary rights, please contact the Publisher.

Entangled Publishing, LLC
2614 South Timberline Road
Suite 109
Fort Collins, CO 80525
Visit our website at www.entangledpublishing.com.

Scandalous is an imprint of Entangled Publishing, LLC.

Edited by Alycia Tornetta
Cover design by Erin Dameron-Hill
Cover art by Period Images

ISBN 978-1-68281-214-3

Manufactured in the United States of America

First Edition May 2016

For Dusean: I love you

Chapter One

England, 1817
Pembington House, Wiltshire

The cold press of keys in Lady Adeline's palm, and the knowledge of why they had been so surreptitiously given, made her feel decidedly wicked, a state she was experiencing for the first time in her twenty-one years. Anticipation and nerves cascaded through her in equal measure at the notion of acting in a manner that was improper, potentially ruinous, and without any doubt, utterly scandalous.

Tonight she would decide her own future—an acknowledged extraordinary feat—and take a very bold step to ensure the gentleman she would marry was the man she deeply cared for and respected—Mr. James Atwood, and *not* the man who had attacked her, taking liberties he had no right to—the Earl of Vale.

"Thank you," Adel said softly to her dearest friend, Lady Evelyn—Evie to her close intimates. Adel was grateful she had someone assisting her in this escapade; surely her nerves would have deserted her if she acted alone.

Evie leaned in close. "Remember, I will arrange for mother to enter his chamber very soon."

Adel nodded. "How will you convince her to intrude on Mr. Atwood's privacy?"

"I urge you not to worry about the *how*. I know Mamma, and with a few whispers, I will make certain the chamber doors are opened at the opportune moment," Evie said, her voice trembling with excitement. Or mayhap it was trepidation?

Adel buried a groan, flicking an invisible piece of lint from her light green gloves. "This plan of ours smacks of recklessness."

An unladylike snort sounded. "Do you *want* to be the Countess of Vale?"

Not even if she was to be drawn and quartered. The earl was a repugnant reprobate, and a conceited ass. She would much prefer a quiet life in the country with a man she liked and respected, than the pomp and ceremony of being a countess to a man she loathed. Adel was in possession of two exquisite younger stepsisters whom she adored, who would benefit at their debuts, if Adel was a countess. Even with that added incentive, it was distressing to imagine a life as Lady Vale.

"No, I want to be Mrs. Atwood." Though Adel felt no shivering excitement at the prospect, there was a distinct appeal of being the lady of her own home. She'd no longer live by the capricious whim of her stepmother, and best of all, never have to endure another year of a failed season.

"Then let's dispense with the fear," Evie said with an encouraging smile.

Adel cared little for society's censure and opinions, being so far removed from the heart of the *ton*, spending most of the year in Somerset at her father's modest but well-kept manor. However, Mr. Atwood had remarked on more than one occasion, the value he placed on high society's opinion. "What if Mr. Atwood is outraged at my lack of propriety? When I suggested we elope, he adamantly and most earnestly refused."

Evie gripped her hand. "He wants to marry you, very much, and if you do not act, you will endure a lifetime of pain as the earl's wife. I would daresay you and Mr. Atwood will be the only love match of the season, and a few gossips should not prevent such a union. It is not as if you have any intention of making your permanent abode in London. From my experience gossip in the country is nonexistent. I implore you, though, to ensure you are not in a terrible state of *dishabille*. We want a bit of a stir, not a full blown scandal."

Adel scowled. "Now is not the time to use 'full blown' and 'scandal' in the same breath. And I have no intention of moving from the door. We only need a hint of impropriety to convince Papa, and I daresay the very notion of me being on the threshold of Mr. Atwood's chamber is enough. I am a bit anxious at how my actions will affect Helena's debut."

Evie plucked two glasses of champagne from a passing footman and handed Adel one. "Your sister is fourteen. She has two more years before facing the gauntlet of the marriage mart. Even if there is a slight stir, it would certainly be squashed by then. With her beauty, the *beaux* of the *ton* will be very agreeable and forgiving."

Adel sighed. "Very well. Onward with our plan."

Evie gave her an approving look, then with a wink, she darted away.

Adel turned toward the large potted palm to her left, and with the utmost secrecy, slipped the keys into the neckline at her bosom. There was no chance of them being jostled loose, for it was unlikely she would partake in any of the night's frivolities.

She strolled along the edge of the ballroom, humming

softly to the lively music of the quadrille. She hadn't been asked to dance all evening, though she had worn the most lavish silken high-waisted gown she owned. Her underdress of palest blue silk had the bodice decorated with tiny forget-me-not flowers embroidered with seed pearls. The three rows of ruched ribbon showed beneath her simple white gauze overdress and she thought she looked particularly fine. She also wore her mother's pearls in her ears and around her throat, and had caught her hair in a loose chignon with a few loose tendrils cascading in a becoming manner down her neck. A few admiring glances had drifted her way, but none of the young men had made any overtures for even conversation.

With a soft sigh she directed her gaze to the dance floor, an ache building in her chest. When was the last time she had been asked to dance at a ball? Adel was fully cognizant of only being passably pretty without much distinction to recommend her for marriage. But surely the gentlemen of the *ton* could be courteous enough to dance with the young ladies without obvious partners.

She straightened her spine, refusing to dampen her spirits. By this time tomorrow, her engagement would be announced, and she would be free as much as it was possible to be unencumbered as a man's wife. She suppressed the uncharitable thought, for Mr. Atwood was a dear friend, and when they wed he would treat her with respect and gentle regard, not as property.

She lifted the champagne to her lips and sipped. She had been wondering if she should make Mr. Atwood privy to their plan. Evie had been adamant it be a secret in the event things went awry, but Adel wanted some reassurance from the man she intended to thoroughly compromise.

Compromised.

Nerves erupted in her stomach and her hands trembled. What if the resultant scandal was so vast, she was unable to return to society? And Mr. Atwood's ambitions of being a successful barrister were destroyed in the aftermath? And Helena was tarnished by association?

You are being a ninny. Only Lady Gladstone will know, Adel sternly reminded herself. The countess was very discreet. After all, she had already spied Evie in a shocking embrace with the scarred and aloof Marquess of Westfall, and none in society had been any the wiser. The countess had swept it under the rug, no doubt because of the man's dastardly reputation.

Adel mentally ticked off all the scandals of the past season.

Lady Sophie was seen kissing her father's valet. That young lady was now being welcomed back into the drawing rooms after only a few short months. Of course, she was now the Viscountess of Rayburn.

Lady Thornton had cuckolded her duke, and she was somehow still a powerful force in society.

Lord Brunel, it was whispered, had been seen with Miss Elizabeth, in a far worse situation than that which Adel had planned, and they were still widely admired and respected.

They also have much to recommend them.

She ignored her flutter of doubt and scanned the ballroom for the young man she was intending to secure. A man who had professed his admiration several times and desperately desired to wed her, despite her shortcomings. Adel stiffened when she espied Mr. Atwood bowing over Lady Daphne's hand, one of the season's reigning darlings. She was pursued in earnest because she had everything to recommend her. Her father, the Earl of Leicester, was well known in parliament and lauded for his reform speeches. Her dowry was rumored to be thirty thousand pounds, and added to the pot was Lady Daphne's fashionably blond beauty.

Mr. Atwood ran his fingers through his curly brown hair,

a sheepish smile blooming at his lips. What was Lady Daphne saying to him? Adel frowned at his besotted mien. Had she been mistaken in his affections? Surely not. It was only last week he'd approached her by the lake bordering her father's property and informed her he would again ask for her hand. Not surprisingly, Papa had refused. He had a higher prospect in mind for her, than Mr. Atwood. Papa did not care this was Adel's *fourth* season and no titled gentleman thought to make her an offer.

Mr. Atwood was mild mannered and affable. He had never been the sort to ruffle feathers nor would he even dare stand toe to toe with her father and plead his case. The only time he seemed passionate was when he'd declared his love. A smile tugged at her mouth, and she willed him to glance in her direction.

His gaze was firmly stuck on Lady Daphne's pouting lips. "Lord Vale!"

Adel flinched as the man whose clutches she was desperate to escape appeared on the landing above the staircase. What was he doing here? The annual Gladstone house party was considered one of the most exciting events of the season, but Evie had promised that her mother had not issued an invitation to the earl.

Adel's wrists tingled, and the fading bruises his punishing grip had left ached. Bile rose in her throat and she gulped the remainder of the champagne to wash away the unpleasant taste. Her father and stepmother had accepted an offer for her hand from the slimy toad. His presence was dangerous. What if he announced their engagement? Extricating herself from such a disaster would be impossible.

His gaze had unerringly found her. Not that it was much work, as she was one of three young ladies standing on the periphery of the room with their dance cards virtually empty. A pleased smile appeared on his face and her throat tightened.

It would be a catastrophe if he singled her out. The bile she'd tried to banish resurfaced, and the crush of the ballroom she'd found exciting an hour ago was now suffocating. She remembered the nasty words Lord Vale had whispered against her lips as he forced her to kiss him. He had mockingly laughed when she had slapped him, saying he liked it rough sometimes. She'd been bewildered as to what *it* referred to, only knowing she had to be afraid. Adel had fled to her father despite Lord Vale's threat that she keep quiet. The bodice of her dress had been torn, her lips swollen—evidence of the earl's loss of control. She had expected her father to protect her, not *give* her to the man.

Panic attempted to freeze her limbs, but she scampered away as if she had not seen the earl. She scanned the ballroom for her father. He and her stepmother typically made a concentrated effort to ingratiate themselves with other lofty guests, and she could spy Lady Margaret's high purple turban with its peacock feathers making the rounds. But where was Papa? Adel had seen him leaving the card room earlier. He had slipped through the terrace windows. Surely he should have returned by now?

Adel pretended she did not see Lord Vale fighting the crush to reach her. With quickened steps she followed the path her father had taken. There were several guests on the terrace, laughing and chatting. She ignored them and spun to the hot house in the distance. He was a secret botanist and instinctively she knew to where he had escaped.

Oh, Papa. How she wished he would not bend so easily to the demands of his wife. Never would Adel believe it was her father's wish to rub shoulders with the finest of the *bon ton*. When her mother had been alive they had been so happy. Life had been wonderful, and they had lived in Somerset, rarely traveling to London or Bath. Her father had remarried only a year after Adel's mother died, and everything had changed.

Do not dwell in the past, Adel, look to the future.

The gardens and the grounds were well lit by gas lamps and she hastened to the hot house, stepping carefully along the cobbled trail. She slipped in through the entrance, her heart squeezing when she spied him with a magnifying glass, peering at some plant. "Father," she said softly.

He lowered the glass and faced her. For a wonderful second, pleasure suffused his face, before he became guarded. With a pointed glare behind her, he spoke, "Why have you traveled this far without a chaperone? Where is your mother?"

Stepmother. She bit back the instinctive rebuttal. "It is a short journey here, and I urgently needed to speak with you, Papa." She moved farther inside. "Lord Vale arrived a few minutes ago and I—"

"Excellent," her father said, with a wide smile. "I must go and greet him. Come along, I am certain he will want a few dances with you."

"No!" She gritted her teeth. "Though I miss the pleasure of dancing, I cannot consent to—"

A heavy sigh filled the air. "You are to wed the earl, Adel. He has secured an invitation to Lady Gladstone's house party solely to court you. It shows me how much he esteems you and wishes to secure your affections."

"Have you gone mad?" she demanded faintly. Surely her father couldn't be so cruel? He knew of Lord Vale's licentious character, of the atrocious way he had behaved toward her. "He attacked me, Papa." She winced at the pleading note in her voice. Squaring her shoulders, she lifted her chin and stepped forward. "I cannot marry a man who has so little regard for my welfare. He left bruises on my arms. He is a despicable cad."

Her father, Sir Archibald Hays, glared at her. "You will accord the earl the respect that is indeed due to him, young lady."

How could he have forgotten her tears and fright? It still lived with her, though days had passed. "Papa...Lord Vale *attacked* me." It was not that she desired her father to do something frightful like challenge the earl to a duel, but she expected some outrage on her behalf. She expected him to protect her, and his stance now shattered the naive belief she'd held onto that she was the most important person in his world. Her stepmother now had that honor, and as a viscount's daughter, Lady Margaret's wish was to see their family's meager social connections strengthened. It seems Adel's father was willing to sacrifice his daughter's happiness to please his wife.

His face flushed in what might have been discomfort, before scrunching into a frown. "Pish... Passion...you are very beautiful, Adel, you look very much like your mother." For a second his features softened and regret gleamed in his gaze. Then he cleared his throat and continued, "It is expected that as your intended, Lord Vale may have gotten a bit carried away. I visited his estate yesterday before traveling down and he explained to me, apologized for his slight indiscretion. I accepted his generous offer for your hand."

Slight indiscretion? "You are trivializing my pain."

He gently placed the magnifying glass on the table. "You are twenty-one, Adel. This is your fourth outing, our coffers are nigh empty and we cannot afford another season for you. The earl is making amends for his actions by offering marriage. I only want what is best for you, my dear."

She stepped forward, searching his face. "My happiness would be in marrying a man that esteems me...much like you did Mamma. Mr. Atwood has been my friend and our neighbor for years. He has offer—"

"No."

"Papa, please. If you would meet with him again, you would see what a kind, sensitive, and amiable gentleman he is—"

"Mr. Atwood's only prospect is a distant baronetcy with little income to support a family. When you marry Lord Vale, you will be a countess," he said forcefully.

Adel was too stunned to point out that *he* was only a baronet. In desperation she gripped his fingers. "Papa, if you do not agree on Mr. Atwood. At least give me a few more months to secure another suitor. If I've no offer by the year end I will…I will marry your choice." She almost choked on the words.

"You had a late coming out because of your mother's passing. I regret that deeply for I feel with her guidance you would have garnered an attractive offer. You've attended three seasons and no man wants you with the small dowry I can provide. Five hundred pounds is not enough to tempt any man."

She flinched and released his arm. She heard what he had not said. Her dark, unfashionable hair, too-rounded hips and bosom did not tempt a man, either, nor the fact that she could read and write in several languages, and cipher.

"You are not to partake in any dances with Mr. Atwood or partner him in any of the parlor and outdoor games. Lord Vale will announce at tomorrow's ball the news of your engagement, and it would not do for his fiancée to make a hash of things by being silly with another man."

"Papa—"

"Do you understand me, young lady?"

She pressed a finger to her forehead, and it did nothing to stop the sudden ache pounding through her temple. "Papa, society will speculate on the sudden engagement. He has not been seen escorting me in the country or in London. As far as society knows, we have not been introduced. It is best the earl courts me for several months before there can be talks of an engagement." Her stomach tightened in knots at the very idea of being in the earl's presence, but she must do something to discourage her father. Then she would have at least some weeks to figure out how to extricate herself from the earl's grasping and lascivious clutches if her scheme tonight failed.

"I've already given Lord Vale my blessings. It would be dishonorable of me to importune him to change his mind because of your feminine nerves. I expect your obedience or you will gain my severe displeasure."

Severe displeasure? "And I fear you have lost my good opinion," she said hoarsely, fighting the urge to cry. "You are supposed to protect me, Papa."

"I am protecting you," he said stiffly. "I am doing all in my power to secure your future since you have little thought for it or for your sisters' and brothers' future. A connection with the earl will go a long way toward establishing their prospects."

Of course, my life is not my own. "Mamma would never have pledged me to man who has no respect or affection for me."

He blanched, but she turned away, and hastened into the night.

She could no longer afford to possess the doubts she had in her heart. She had to act, and it must be tonight.

Chapter Two

"It's the mad duke."

The *ton* was nothing if not predictable. The lone whisper was the indication the rest of the throng needed to take it upon themselves to revisit his past.

"He confessed to his good friend, the Marquess of Westfall, that he killed his wife. It was the talk of the town a few years past."

Edmond Elias Rochester, the Duke of Wolverton, ignored the gossip that erupted in his wake and moved with purpose toward the corridor that would lead him to the Gladstone library. The *ton* normally watched him like a hawk, searching for a reaction whenever they whispered too loudly of his supposed insanity. Would he lash out and prove his affliction? They were sorely disappointed every time.

"He lost his heir as well."

A too-loud gasp sounded.

Though he ensured his countenance was cold and uninterested, their words were like a dagger to his heart. He had certainly been responsible for the death of his wife and son. The guilt and pain was always waiting to strike, reminding him that he had no right to peace or happiness. It was a pain he lived with every day, and it was this rabid interest and speculation in his life that had seen him largely shunning society for the few years since their deaths.

He'd only ever traveled to London for the opening of parliament when he had been careful to avoid the balls and entertainments of the season. He had little interest in such affairs. House parties, in particular, struck him as tedious, even though his experience of them was limited. His sole purpose tonight for being at the Gladstone country home was to finalize some settlement negotiations. When not rubbing reluctant elbows with the *bon ton*, Edmond was fairly content to bury himself at his estate in Hampshire with his daughters.

Sarah and Rosa. Rage and regret kicked him in the gut, hard and brutal. He had been so damnably blind to their needs. His daughters had been going through governesses like sand through a sieve. The tutor he'd resorted to hiring also seemed at his wits end. No one could tolerate their antics for long, and it had taken him too long to realize they required the comfort and guidance of a mother, and the stability of a normal family life. After losing Maryann, Edmond had vowed never to take another wife. What a damnable ass he had been.

Memory had finally pierced through the cold fog of his misery. He did not need to engage his heart with his next duchess. There was certainly no need for him to ever risk the torment of loss that still haunted his sleep and waking thoughts. The *ton* mocked any hint of tender emotions between man and wife, thinking it very unfashionable. He'd broken the mold once and married for such sentiments, this time he would do it for very sensible and pragmatic reasons. Many in the *ton* had such uncomplicated marriage arraignments, and he would simply seek a similar situation for the benefit of his children.

Ignoring the eyes of the multitude of guests and returning a few nods from other gentleman, he made it to the entrance hall and headed directly to the library. Lord Gladstone, the man he was visiting to negotiate with, acknowledged his presence with a nod, then the earl made his way from his guests towards Edmond.

"Wolverton," Lord Gladstone greeted, falling into step beside him.

"Gladstone, pleased to see you." Edmond wanted to waste no time with inane pleasantries. He had corresponded with the earl and had made an offer for his daughter, Lady Evelyn. He remembered her vaguely from a few years ago, and she had appeared a likable young lady, a bit too cheerful, but she had a pleasant countenance. The reports from her father also boasted of a young woman of sense and intelligence. She spoke three languages fluently, was adept at painting and playing the pianoforte.

A hard smile twisted Edmond's lips. She was perfect. She would fill the void he needed, without overtly tempting his baser needs. Female companionship was a comfort he had eschewed since the loss of his wife. In fact, the reason Edmond had even made an offer for Lady Evelyn was because he was certain he would feel nothing physical for her.

They entered the library.

"Brandy?" Gladstone asked, strolling to the sideboard.

Edmond inclined his head and the man prepared two glasses. Discomfort was evident in every line of the earl's posture. Awareness stirred, and Edmond gritted his teeth in denial. "Is your daughter aware that I am here?"

The earl handed him the drink with a sigh. "No."

"I made arrangements to return to my estate in a few days' time."

"I would urge you to stay for the duration of the house party. There will be a game of croquet on the lawn tomorrow.

We plan hunting on Friday, and a ball tomorrow night. I've also heard my daughter mention a few parlor games and tricks. Take this as an opportunity to get to know her," Gladstone urged.

Edmond took a sip of his brandy, considering the earl. The man already knew Edmond's terms. "No," he said flatly. "If you have changed your mind, say so, and I will do what needs to be done and find another."

Gladstone grimaced. "Do not be hasty. My countess has summoned Lady Evelyn."

There was a guarded note in the man's tone that had caution settling in Edmond's gut. He studied the earl and he did not like the guilt he saw on the man. *Hell.* "Is Lady Evelyn even aware of my offer?"

A tic appeared on Gladstone's forehead and grew more pronounced as the silence lengthened. "No," he finally muttered, tugging at his cravat.

Edmond lowered his glass of brandy slowly. "We have been negotiating the terms of the marriage for two months now and you have not seen fit to inform her?" Never would he have acted with such callous disregard for his own daughters' emotions. *You have done worse,* his conscience reminded him, and he ruthlessly repressed the guilt.

Before Gladstone answered the door burst opened, and in swept Lady Evelyn.

"Father, is all well? Mother—"

Dark green eyes widened when they landed on him and she inhaled audibly. A blush climbed her cheeks and Edmond wondered if he'd ever seen a more becoming young lady.

"Forgive me, I was not aware you had company."

She was a beauty with her gold spun hair and elegant carriage. Why was she in her third season without any offers? Could it be the *ton* was aware of her father's impoverished state? The earl thought the knowledge well hidden. If not for the thorough investigation Edmond had launched into the background of the families his mother had suggested for a potential alliance, he would not have uncovered their state.

He admired her beauty as one would a stunning jewel, but she roused no feeling of passion in him, and *that* was what he wanted. Swift introductions were made, and she dipped into a graceful curtsy.

"Your Grace, it is a pleasure to make your acquaintance."

She paled after her father exited the library with vague murmurings. The man was careful to leave the door open a crack.

"Your Grace, I…I…" She took a deep breath and pasted an obviously uncomfortable smile on her face. Knowledge and distress gleamed in her eyes.

It was his turn to tug at his cravat. "Lady Evelyn." *Blast the man.* Her father had certainly made a hash of things. Edmond had not envisioned the evening like this. He had expected the young lady to have been informed of his generous offer and be eagerly awaiting his presence. Where was he to start? The earl should have already laid the groundwork and prepared her for the responsibilities she would soon assume.

Lady Evelyn watched him with an air of anxiety. It was impossible for him to sprout the required foolish sentiments and artful flattery. Sudden impatience bit at him, and he wanted the encounter over. "I have asked your father for your hand in marriage, and he consented," he said without any finesse.

She paled alarmingly and swayed.

He stepped forward with a muttered curse, alert in the event she swooned. Now *he* was making a hash of things. His mother would be appalled at his distinct lack of care for the lady's sensibilities. There was no doubt she would blame his conduct on his deliberate and frustrating absence from the whirl of polite society.

Her throat worked on a swallow. "You wish to marry me?"

"Yes."

Her lids lowered, shadowing her expressive eyes. "Why?"

"I am in need of a wife, and you are desirous of a husband."

Her head snapped up and a startled laugh escaped her. One of her hands fluttered to her throat. "Forgive me, Your Grace, but I have no *need* for a husband, and I am certain I can choose my own."

He shrugged, unconcerned with coddling her delicate sensibilities and unable to pretend otherwise. He'd never been the one to be hypocritical. *But I could be caring.* "Then your father is in need of money."

She flinched, but offered no protest. The lady was indeed aware of her father's precarious finances.

"I see," she said quietly. "And if my affections are otherwise engaged?"

Edmond took a swallow of his brandy and regarded her closely. "Your father told me you were without attachment for any young man. Are you saying your affections are engaged?"

Her throat worked, but she remained muted.

"You can refuse, Lady Evelyn," he said softly, though he would hate for her to reject him without some thought. Edmond loathed the very idea of entering the marriage mart, wading through a gaggle of females and their ambitious mammas, the eventual speculation and gossips, the weeks of empty courtship, and then the plans for a wedding of the season. He had done it all with Maryann, and he would rather walk through the bowels of hell than repeat the experience.

But remember you would traverse any challenge, even slaying the devil himself for your daughters.

He closed his eyes briefly. Yes, he would. If the lady was so averse to his offer, he would reach out to the other lords with unmarried daughters on his mother's list, or steel himself to immerse himself in a world full of artifice. It had taken him several weeks to decide on the top five families from the list his mother had provided. All had responded to his initial query with enthusiasm, but he'd selected Lord Gladstone because the man's daughter was the only one above eighteen. Edmond already felt jaded and empty at thirty. He would loath to be aligned with a young lady he would constantly have to reassure, and one who would long for the outings and glamour society had to offer. He'd hoped for a young lady who had at least experienced several years of balls, picnics, and outings to the theatre and gardens, who would not weep uncontrollably at the thought of spending most of the year, if not all in the country.

"Is Mamma also aware of your offer?"

"Yes."

She bit her lower lip. "I see. And how long is it since you made your intentions known to my parents?" Her eyes were wide and pleading for information.

Apparently Lady Evelyn was not swooning with joy at the prospect of being a duchess, as his mother had informed him any sensible young lady would do. "Your father and I have been in negotiations for eight weeks. I was led to believe you were aware of my offer."

He walked to the sideboard and poured himself another generous splash of brandy. "Would you like something to drink?"

Surprise widened her eyes. "I…I…no. Your Grace, how long do you need until I give you an answer?"

"I depart in three days' time."

"Does your offer expire when you leave?"

"Yes," he said flatly. He'd promised Rosa he would be home in time for her birthday. The hope and excitement that he would be there, had shone brightly in her eyes. He would not disappoint her. Though he could very well travel back to

Wiltshire after. There was no need for him to disclose that to the lady, the more time she had to ponder, the more solid objections she would have for her father.

Lady Evelyn offered him a wobbly smile. "You shall have your answer by then. If you will excuse me?"

She turned hastily, but not fast enough to hide the tears glistening on her lashes.

"Lady Evelyn," he said softly, disturbed to be an unwitting party to her distress.

She stiffened, but remained faced away.

"Yes?"

What could he say? He needed her? Not just any wife. That would surely be a lie. It flummoxed him that he wanted to offer soothing words, to reassure her that their eventual marriage would be a success for her. He gritted his teeth until his jaw ached, and the entire time she remained rooted. Possibly waiting for words that would free her from the hell he wanted to consign her. "Sleep well," he finally said. Inadequate words, but they were all he had to give.

With a firm nod, she departed, closing the door with a soft *snick*.

Devil take it all.

Chapter Three

Adel now understood why men imbibed for liquid courage. She certainly felt braver and more confident. She tipped the glass, swallowing the last drop of the delicious tawny brown liquid.

"Would you like another glass?" Evie asked tremulously.

"Hmm," Adel murmured noncommittally, feeling pleasantly languid. She gave the decanter of Sherry a considering glance. Before she had been a wreck, nerves rioting through her veins, and she had worn the priceless carpet in her chamber to threads pacing like a caged lion. Now she was warm, relaxed, and a bit tingly. "I believe someone needs to bottle and sell this as courage. They would make a fortune."

Evie laughed and Adel hiccupped.

"Oh dear," her friend said softly. "How many fingers am I showing?"

Adel frowned. "You are being silly, Evie, and we have no time to waste. While I feel decidedly relaxed, I assure you I am not foxed."

A snort sounded. "And what would you know about being soused?"

"I saw enough of drunkenness from papa after mother died."

All the merriment wiped from Evie.

"Forgive me for dampening your happiness," Adel said softly.

Evie rushed over and clasped her hand. "Never," she said a bit hoarsely. "You could never dampen my spirits."

Adel smiled. "Do you think I should change into a simple dress?"

Evie shook her head. "Your nightgown is perfect. Remember to go no farther than the door, and leave it cracked."

"I will. Now wish me good fortune."

Her friend's throat worked. "Adel wait…I…I…do not believe it is wise after all, I—"

"Shush!" Adel said with a soft laugh. "Do not try to drain my hard-worked-for courage. Remember only you and your mother are to come. We want enough ammunition to encourage my father to feel obliged in accepting Mr. Atwood, not gossip fodder for your mother's guests." With a quick kiss on Evie's cheek, Adel tumbled from her room, consternation biting deep. She did feel a bit wobbly? Or was it giddy anticipation of finally being free of Lord Vale?

With swift and somewhat sure feet, she followed the directions Evie had provided. The hallways were empty, but she could hear the faint din of laughter and clinking off glass from below stairs. The last time she checked, it had been half past three in the morning, but it seemed the house guests were determined to be merry until the crack of dawn. Even with such a dire assessment, no anxiety seared her. Selfish, selfish men. Ordering women to stay away from liquor fully well knowing the wondrous properties it possessed.

Footsteps sounded along the corridor, and she made a

mad dash toward a linen closet and ducked inside giggling. She waited until the loud steps passed, then opened the door and peeked through the slight crack. Adel spied Viscount Ravenswood, Evie's brother, standing at a door, looking left and then right. He knocked once and it was flung open to reveal another guest clad in a very sheer and provocative nightgown. A blush reddened Adel's cheeks when the lady hugged him and her hand slid down to cup Lord Ravenswood's backside. A husky laugh slipped from him, and as he kissed her and they tumbled into the room. *The rogue!*

Adel moved cautiously out of her hiding place and hurried along the hallway. After turning left, she counted until she arrived at the fifth door. With a quick glance each way along the hallway, she uncurled her clenched fist and retrieved the keys. A faint stirring of unease tried to rear its head. She closed her eyes and recalled the heavy and frightful press of the earl's body against hers, his sweaty palms that had dug into the soft flesh of her thighs as he struggled to raise her gown. That, and perhaps much worse she had to look forward to, if she did not succeed tonight. Grief lay heavy on her heart. How she wished her father had listened to her pleas to wed Mr. Atwood. Firming her shoulders, she inserted the key and twisted. The door opened on a soft *snick* and she entered.

She leaned against the door. *I've done it!* The fire on the hearth had burned down to orange embers and there was a distinct chill in the air. She lost precious seconds standing by the door, wondering what next to do. Adel curled her feet into the expensive carpet, seeking warmth. Why had she not thought to slip her feet into slippers?

The bed creaked slightly.

She frowned. "Mr. Atwood?"

Maddening silence. Then a soft rumble rose from the bed in the far corner and she muffled a startled squeak. Swallowing a nervous chuckle she peered, trying to make out his form in the darkened room. Drifting closer, she muttered an unladylike curse as she stubbed her toes on something hard. She stooped and felt around.

It was the bed. How had it moved from that corner to here? Confusion rushed through her and she lurched upright. The sudden move made her dizzy and she stumbled, landing on the bed in an undignified heap onto a very hard body.

Good heavens!

• • •

Edmond was roused to full consciousness by the lightest caress. There was a soft weight on his shoulder, the heated press of a palm. The delicate tips of a single finger skimmed over his naked chest, the touch was tentative, curious even, a gentle foray that spoke of inexperience, yet his cock surged to life with painful immediacy. The betrayal of his body froze him, and he remained still as the caress became firmer, even more seductive, causing his length to flex, his heart to jerk, and his mouth to go ridiculously dry. *Impossible.*

He subtly inhaled. Her fragrance was clean and sweet. No cloying perfume, simply the fresh scent of lavender soap and roses. His reaction to this stranger was thrilling and unpardonable in equal measure.

"Are you awake?" The voice was raspy, seductive, and a bit fearful. Before he could respond she spoke, "Your body is harder than I imagined it would be."

The awe in her voice was evident, and a fleeting smile touched his lips.

"Why are you sleeping without a nightshirt?" The pique in the tone was glaring.

Delicate fingers glided over his chest, dipping low, skimming over his tensed abdomen to stop at his hip. Edmond frowned as everything in him reacted. His cock twitched, his heart raced even more, and hot and urgent desire coiled in his gut. He savored the barest of touches, not realizing how desperate he'd been for a woman's enticing embrace. Warring needs swirled inside of Edmond. He wanted to push away this unknown woman that smelled like temptation, but the need was also there to sate this surprising hunger—a hunger he had long denied.

Three years and seven months.

It was the desperation that grounded him, and allowed him to tamp down on his sudden lustful urges. He would never allow such emotions to hold sway over him again. He shifted with all intention of leaving the warm confines of the bed when the figure tumbled forward. A warm kiss pressed into the hollow of his throat, and soft feminine curves arched into him.

Edmond couldn't help it. He groaned. Breathing slowly, he calmed himself, willing his body to relax. *Who would be so bold?* Lady Evelyn? Damned unlikely. The light glowing from the embers of the fireplace were too low for him to ascertain her features. Hell…was he even truly awake?

"I missed you today. Why did you not ask me to dance at all tonight?"

Ah, so this was a dream, the result of imbibing a few more glasses of brandy in the cold loneliness of the library before retiring. A dangerous need rode Edmond, and the temptation to slake his hunger in her willing warmth was overwhelming.

A gentle nip at his throat as if punishment for being absent, then a kiss soothing the sting. A whiff of her sweet breath teased his nostrils. Sherry. So his intrepid seducer had consumed liquor to shore up her fortitude. Was the lady drunk?

A sigh wafted from her on a soft moan. "You smell different… I like it, very much," she whispered almost shyly.

As if they had a will of their own, his hands searched,

found her hips and tugged her closer. His body hummed with eagerness and desire heated his blood. Edmond drew her up to him, and dipped his head. He lightly grazed her cheek with his lips, and pressed a light kiss down to her neck. *So damn tempting.*

"I believe I want you to kiss me," she gasped, astonishment rife in her tone.

She nuzzled into his chest and his control began to fray, thread by thread. Edmond pressed an open mouth kiss to the tiny pulse flickering wildly above her collarbone and inhaled her scent into his lungs, wanting to trap the refreshing fragrance. As he nipped at her tender flesh with his teeth, she shivered violently, and a soft moan slipped from her.

"I…I feel…warm, and there is a strange feeling fluttering in my stomach."

His body was rebelling at his self-imposed celibacy and his cock was leading the charge. With a muttered epithet he drew her closer, wanting to dip his fingers beneath her gown to find out how passionate a woman she was. Through the fog of lust shrouding his logical thoughts, common sense reared its head. He'd never had a faceless liaison, and he was not about to start. But devil take it. He felt something other than blinding pain and emptiness for the first time, in what felt like a lifetime. Before he could decide how to handle his unexpected companion, the softest of lips settled on his. *Sweet Christ.* Rational thought told him to push her away, but everything burned under the tide of excruciating lust.

This must be a dream…a hidden fantasy bourgeoning to life from abject misery, seeking something new and wonderful. Never had Edmond felt such an intensity of desire. This was an aberration…a distressingly enticing one.

She parted her lips on a sigh, and he took ruthless advantage. He allowed his tongue to stroke inside of her mouth, to twine with hers as he slanted her head, deepening an already far too intimate kiss. Her flavor exploded on his tongue, and he bit back the deep groan wanting to erupt from the cold place inside him that seemed to have thawed to molten lava. The taste of her was indescribable—sweet, warm, *carnal*. She whimpered, and then the timid slide of her tongue met his.

It took all of his years of discipline, not to tumble her onto her back, and take her. He worshipped her mouth, giving her no chance to retreat, and it distantly resounded that she did not want to flee from his embrace. She arched to him, her breasts unconfined beneath the nightgown she wore, and he itched to cup her breasts and feel her nipples stabbing into his palm.

She pulled from him, trembling. "I…I…between my legs…*aches*…Mr. Atwood, I…you've never kissed me like that before."

Mr. Atwood?

"This is so wonderfully reckless, but kiss me again," she breathed, sounding dazed, and if he was not mistaken, a bit tippled. "Kiss me again," she demanded fiercely.

Yes, Edmond's body shouted. But he wouldn't. He called himself all sorts of foolish names. But he couldn't allow it to go further, not when she clearly thought he was someone else. He would be more than a despicable cur to press an advantage. No matter how much his cock ached. "No," he groaned, tempted beyond measure, pulling fully from her clasp.

As expected she froze at his voice. A tremor ran down her taut spine, and then she burst into a flurry of movements, twisting the sheets around her body in her haste. Unfortunately rubbing the soft pad of her ass into his lap. "Be still!"

"Please, no. No! This cannot be so…" Her whisper of dread and frantic movements only served to inflame his ardor. She twisted and he bit back a groan, as she rubbed at his aroused length.

His hips surged against his will, pressing harder into her, and she became motionless at the evidence of his desire.

He heard her gulp. Then she shivered. "Please let me go."

He complied immediately.

As if afraid to make any sudden movements, she took her time sliding from his lap. Edmond wanted to curse, as the sinuous shift caused him to throb. He hissed a sigh of relief when her body was away from him completely.

Her erratic breathing was loud in the chamber.

"Who are you?"

Chapter Four

I am ruined by the wrong man.

Adel had suspected something was wrong from her dizzying reaction to the man's closeness. Mr. Atwood had never made her feel such wanton heat from a mere touch. But she had foolishly dismissed the warning clangs away, thinking it was the fright and exhilaration of doing something so wickedly forbidden…and the mystifying power of the liquid courage.

There was a shuffle. Then a tinderbox was struck, and the candle on the nightstand was lit.

Her breath caught audibly and unknown sensations erupted below her navel. He was savagely beautiful, and nothing like her Mr. Atwood. The bold angles of this unknown man's face hinted at restrained power. Cynicism and sensuality combined in the hard lines of his mouth. As she recalled the sublime taste and the feel of those firm, sensual lips, she trembled, noticing eyes that belonged to a hawk sharpen with interest. He continued to stare without speaking and a curious tightening sensation clenched deep inside, rooting her.

It made her feel very uncomfortable. In fact, he had a quality of stillness that she found unnerving. But it was his eyes…they were empty and devoid of the passion and intent she had certainly felt in his touch. Suddenly her heart ached for this man, whoever he was.

His expression was impassive. "I will ask again, who are you and why are you in my bed?" His tone was rough, and devilishly sinful.

Devilishly sinful…oh… She read too many romantic novels. Adel's mortifying response must be on account of the few glasses of sherry. "Surely you do not expect me to own to my identity?"

He chuckled, the sound full of dark challenge. "Yes, in fact, I insist upon it."

She blinked. He was most assuredly serious. The glow from the candle was very weak. If she could barely ascertain his features, surely he might not recognize her in the light of day. "I bid you good-bye," Adel said.

She made to launch from the bed, and swifter than she tracked, a firm hand clasped her wrist. Sudden fear sliced through the false relaxation she had been lulled into by her liquid courage.

"Tell me your name before you leave," he demanded, sounding earnest and mystified in the same breath. Then he scowled and released her, as if he had been stung. "Go," he bit out sharply. "Before I do something foolish in my desire to find out who you are and how you had the means to enter my locked chamber."

Who was he? And why was she in *his* chamber? There was a niggle of uncertainty, and she frowned, wading through the haze, the steps she had taken to arrive at this particular chamber. "*Oh, God* someone is going to come soon!" Adel scrambled from the bed, tripping on the sheets in her haste.

A spasm of fear coursed through her at the realization Evie would have her mother barging in at any moment. "I thought you were someone else, and I must leave immediately. Please, sir, I beg of you do not repeat this story to anyone!"

There was simply no time for her to ascertain his intention, and to extract a promise of silence. On the heels of her proclamation the door was flung open and everything inside of Adel collapsed in dread. She would *never* recover from this.

Oh, God, Mr. Atwood.

She had lost him, and the hope of freedom.

The man's hand darted with a speed she almost missed and his forefingers pinched the flickering flame of the wick, plunging the room into darkness. Only the light spilling in from the hallway offered some sight.

"Upon my word, Miss Adeline!" Lady Gladstone gasped, clearly able to still recognize Adel.

Her breath rasped and her heart pounded. *No…no, no.* She clenched her eyes shut. She couldn't credit what was happening. Everything had been so perfectly planned. She couldn't have been found in bed with a stranger. She hurried forward, praying she would not stumble. "I swear to you on my honor, Lady Gladstone, this is a dreadful mistake and there is a very reasonable explanation. If you would quickly close the door, I will—"

Heavy footsteps sounded and Lord Vale appeared in the doorway, and the hopes Adel had to extricate herself diminished by the second. What was he doing here? Confusion bubbled inside her. Where was Evie?

"Lady Gladstone, is all well? I received a note to meet you here most urgently. Decidedly odd, if I may so say."

The earl's gaze homed in on Adel and his eyes widened then narrowed in awareness. He glanced to the bed and rage lit in his eyes. "Who in the devil are you and why are you in a chamber alone with my fiancée, you blackguard?" Lord Vale demanded, storming into the chambers with his fists clenched at his side. "I will demand satisfaction for this!"

"My lord! I am not your fiancée." The words slipped from her involuntarily and the room went deathly quiet.

A gasp sounded, and she looked past the earl and spied Viscount Ravenswood. His shocked eyes raked over her, before swinging to the darkened bed. Panic clawed at Adel's throat. The situation was worsening by the second.

This was a humiliating spectacle.

The man in the bed said nothing. Was he in shock? *Oh Lord*, he must be. Certainly he was analyzing the dreaded implications of her *foolish, foolish* plans. What if this unknown man was married, or promised to another? The scandal would be horrifying. The light from the candles in the corridor was meager, and she was grateful his identity was protected. What if he had a wife?

He kissed you, a small voice reminded her. Surely a man who already held the affections of another woman would not behave so?

Please say something, she silently urged him, tears prickling behind her lids. As surely as she had ruined her life with the eyes of the *ton* looking on, she had compromised his. The most heartbreaking and alarming conclusions Adel realized, was that this had all been orchestrated by her dearest friend. The haze from the sherry was already lifting, and it was becoming clear what had transpired. After all, it was Evie who had snuck Adel new keys saying she'd made a mistake earlier. Evie was the person who had encouraged Adel to take a few sips of sherry, to bolster her nerves, and had been there when Adel consumed three full glasses.

Shocked murmurs spilled in from the hallway, and several footsteps sounded along the corridor. Seconds later Lord Gladstone framed the door, with the Viscountess of Marriot, one of the most notorious gossips in society. On a defeated sigh, Adel crumpled into the lone sofa in the chamber and buried her face in her hands.

Why, Evie?

• • •

I thought you were someone else. Edmond ignored the harsh gasp of those gathered in the doorway. His host and hostess, their son, the Earl of Vale, and Lady Marriot spilled farther into his chambers. Edmond supposed he could be grateful there was not a greater audience. He directed his attention to the young lady he had been seconds away from ravishing. He was much used to scandal and rabid speculation, but Society would not be kind to the unknown lady and they would shred her to pieces. Although she *had* known they would appear. Perhaps she was more mercenary in her thoughts, and not as fragile as many of the young misses of the *ton*.

Though pale with fright and mortification, she was hauntingly lovely with a heart-shaped face dominated by enchanting almond shaped eyes, which were a stunning shade of hazel. Her hair was black as the deepest darkness of night, and her lips were wide and pouting.

Her loveliness was heart jerking. She had tested the mettle of his control and he had failed. An unusual occurrence as he had never before been so consumed by passion. She had tasted delectable, her flavor one of pure addictive temptation that had tempted him to sink his cock into a woman he had never seen. *Madness.* Utter reckless madness.

What had possessed him? The only thing he was sure of was that a prayer, even when muttered hastily, on occasion seemed to work. He had braced himself to enter the dreaded marriage mart, after surmising Lady Evelyn would reject his offer. And now a young lady was fortuitously dropped into his lap…into his *bed*.

He would need to be swift and decisive in order to stem the tide of scandal that would surely follow. She was irrefutably ruined. Edmond had become accustomed to the worst that Society could offer in regards to malicious gossiping. This young lady would be destroyed in the most absolute sense. Honor demanded that he wed her, yet he hesitated. She had roused his body before he'd even seen her, and now looking at her dark exotic beauty, the craving only stirred with more turbulence. The last thing he wanted was a wife he would desire, after all, intimacy between a man and woman always led to greater sentiment, and to love was surely the path to irrevocable heartache. *Bloody hell.*

What the hell was he to do? With the scandal that had embraced him following his wife's death, he could walk away unchallenged from the gossip, but it would be unconscionable to leave this young lady to the vultures. Edmond would crush any man who would even think to treat his daughters with such callous disregard. Yet he could not take a woman like *her* to be his wife. Even now, with an audience, he was in the shadows fighting the lust pounding through his veins, and fervently willing his damn cock to subside. "Everyone out," he said, rousing from the bed.

Lady Gladstone swayed and recognition dawned on her face. "I…I… Wolverton?"

Before he could confirm his identity the countess's rounded eyes slashed to the frozen young lady and a sneer curled the countess's lips.

"How could you, Miss Adeline? I will see you ruined for this."

Adeline…beautiful, an inane thought to have at this very moment, but he thought her name as comely as her face and figure.

The young girl jerked to her feet. "Lady Gladstone, I

entered the wrong room. I never intended—"

"You knew full well whose chamber you were crawling into, you wanton tramp!"

Lady Marriot gasped and Miss Adeline sucked in a harsh breath. Red bloomed on her cheeks, and he detected the slight tremble of her frame.

The countess, righteous in her fury, marched farther into the chamber toward the young lady. "I will see that your family is not welcomed in any drawing room in all of London. How dare you come into my home and—"

"You forget yourself, madam, and you will hold your tongue," Edmond said with icy disdain, sudden fury pounding through his veins at the uncalled for attack. It was evident to all Miss Adeline was already mortified. What did the countess hope to gain from besmirching her further?

His hostess flushed and tried to stammer an apology, which he waved off, impatient to be alone so he could dress and deal with the matter before it turned into a circus. "I would be obliged if everyone departed. I will be out shortly," he said in a far milder tone.

"Miss Adeline is my fiancée, and I demand satisfaction for the insult," Lord Vale hissed coldly. "I demand your full name so I may have my seconds call on you. This is a matter of honor."

Edmond did not even acknowledge Vale's asinine demand for a duel. From what Edmond knew of the earl's character, he wouldn't know honor if it strolled up to him and bit him on the ass.

A visible shiver went through Miss Adeline. "I am not his affianced lady."

The earl glowered and she straightened her spine, looking past him. The spark of fire intrigued Edmond and he suppressed the flare of interest. He should not care to know why she had recklessly thought to compromise someone, and why she was not twittering with excitement at the hope of being Lord Vale's countess.

Voices rose from in the hallway and footsteps moved closer. The vultures were already swarming. "Close the door," he ordered flatly. Things were already beyond the pale.

Lord Gladstone flushed and complied. "Wolverton, this is insupportable," he growled.

As if he were just hearing Edmond's title, Lord Vale stiffened and he peered closer into the dark. Edmond did not move from his shadowy corner. He was naked. The gossip would turn into something much harsher and vindictive if they were to realize his state. "I urge everyone to depart my chamber. I would caution silence."

Immediately the young lady took a step toward the door.

"We must repair this damage. Whatever happened must never leave this room," young viscount Ravenswood said with a heavy sigh.

"I agree," Lady Gladstone said, pressing a palm to her stomach.

"Surely you do not believe such a thing possible," Lady Marriot interjected, looking too pleased. There was no doubt she was eager to depart and provide fodder for the throng. "All of society is in the hall, and they will not depart until they see who has left the chamber."

Miss Adeline's throat worked as she attempted to swallow. Eyes glistening with tears scanned the room, not fully settling on anyone.

The countess inhaled. "What are we to do?"

Edmond stifled a curse. "Gladstone, I will meet you in your office shortly. I will also speak with Miss Adeline's parents if they are here. It may not have any weight, but I would like to at least assure them their daughter's virtue is intact. You entered this chamber quite shortly after her."

The silence was heavy. Several eyes settled on the young

lady, noting her apparel, her bare toes peeking from the hem of her night rail, and the tumbled mass of beautiful silken hair. It did not escape Edmond that Ravenswood, Gladstone, and Lord Vale narrowed in on her obviously swollen and thoroughly ravished lips.

Hell. Edmond could walk away and remained unscathed. Society was ridiculous enough where all blame for this mishap would be placed wholly at her feet. He noted the pained awareness glimmering in her eyes, a quiet desperation that hinted at her position in society.

If he walked away, she would be crushed. There was no choice but to marry her. With ruthless will, Edmond rebuilt the walls she had cracked and doused his desire. He would make an offer, but never must he allow her intimacy. He would have to be resolute in keeping away from her bed until he was ready, *if* he was ever ready.

But his daughters would have a mother.

Chapter Five

Adel's cheeks blazed as she held her head high and rushed from the chamber and faltered. It seemed all the guests were outside. There was a moment of shocked silence in the hall as they regarded her. Belatedly she realized only about a dozen people were there, but two well-placed ladies were all that would be needed for society to learn of her folly. She identified the Countess of Livingston, the Marchioness of Deerwood, and several influential society matrons. Adel fought the tears burning to spill as the voices rose, overlapping one another so rabid they were, scenting fresh blood. The scandal sheets would be burning for weeks with this debacle.

She squared her shoulders and pushed past the many eyes heavy with speculation, some with pity, and others with scorn.

"Whose chamber was she in?"

"I do not know."

"The duke's."

Her knees weakened, and she stumbled. Good Heavens! *He is a duke?* She was caught in flagrante with a duke. *Oh… oh…oh!* They were ruined. The Viscountess of Sheffield's daughter had claimed the Earl of Maschelly tried to seduce her. The family had not been able to bring him up to scratch and their daughter had fled to Scotland to avoid the outrage of society's derision. The earl, of course, had been unruffled by her humiliation. What would the duke do to Adel and her family after this disgrace? Would Mr. Atwood still wish to wed her?

"Which one?"

"Wolverton."

"The mad duke?" Equal fascination and shock was implied.

Dread sat heavy in Adel's stomach. How had this happened? Lady Gladstone had called him by his title, but somehow in Adel's distress it had not truly resounded. Even she had heard whispers of Wolverton. The duke was reputed to be influential with other lords, coldly distant, frighteningly uncivil, and shockingly handsome.

"He has said he would never remarry. There is no hope for her if she was thinking to force his hand."

"It is far more likely she succumbed to his shocking handsomeness and virility."

A few voices laughed, though it was hard to identify who, as they all had their fans poised demurely in front of their mouths.

"Perhaps she is already with child, and it is her he attended the house party for. We know of what goes on behind closed door at these gatherings."

"Scandalous!"

"Indeed, remember many say the true objective of a well-organized house party is to provide ample opportunities to engage in that sort of dalliance."

Desperate to escape the unkind whispers, Adel headed for her chamber without looking behind her. With every step she felt the awful weight of their eyes boring into her back.

Never had she imagined the night would end like this. Unable to walk at a sedate pace, she gripped the folds of her gown and ran down the hall until she reached her chamber. She wrenched the door open, then slammed it closed. She leaned against the frame for support, pressing the heel of her palm on her forehead.

What am I to do? She tried to marshal her thoughts and reason around the panic rearing its head. First she needed to alert her father, then speak with Mr. Atwood, Evie, and then...

The door pushed, and Adel lurched around.

"Oh, Evie," Adel gasped, and shocked herself by bursting into raw ugly tears. "Oh, forgive me. I fear my nerves are shattered."

Evie's eyes were red rimmed, and she looked broken and guilty. "Dress quickly. Mamma is coming."

Then she hurried to the armoire and selected a pale yellow high waist gown that had already been pressed for tomorrow's croquet match. Responding to Evie's urgency, Adel shrugged from the voluminous nightgown and slipped on her underclothes and the dress with Evie's aid.

The door to her chamber crashed opened once again.

The countess stormed in, lips flattened, eyes pinched in fury. *What is it?* When Adel had concocted her plan, she understood she would have earned the countess's disapproval, despite Evie's assurance her mother would understand. But the rage in her hostess's steps spoke of something more.

"Sir Archibald and Lady Margaret will see you in the library. I have informed them of the situation."

Adel was unable to imagine her father's distraught. "Lady Gladstone, I—"

"Do not speak. We invited you into our life, and by association you and your family were greatly elevated and this is how you repaid Evie? By stealing her fiancé?" Lady

Gladstone's voice was sharp and accusatory.

Adel's heart skipped a beat, and then another. A deep sense of foreboding traveled through her. She glanced at Evie. Guilt darkened her eyes and tears tracked down her cheeks.

"*Forgive me*," Evie mouthed.

Adel was too numb to react. She was herded to the library despite Evie's plea to her mother that she needed to speak with Adel. The countess all but shoved her out of the chamber, and she was grateful to see the guests had gone. A minute later Adel entered the room and the countess slammed the door on her exit. *Oh*. It did not take long for loss and betrayal to scythe through Adel's heart. Surely the countess would prevent further association with Evie...and what had she been thinking?

Adel paced, waiting in dread for her father to arrive and voice his displeasure. How could it have gone so wrong? The door creaked and she lifted her head. Her father and stepmother entered. Lord Gladstone strolled in behind them and gently closed the door. He gave her a reassuring smile, but Adel's stomach dipped, and fear coated the back of her throat. She had never seen her father so livid and so embarrassed. "Papa, I can explain, I—"

"Be silent," he roared, a bit of spittle flying from between his lips. He advanced and she retreated, her hips hitting against the oak table positioned in the center of the room. "I was in the card rooms with your mother when I was summoned. Your mother is appalled at your reckless disregard—"

"Stepmother," Adel snapped, the agitation of being reminded of how easily he replaced her mother loosening her tongue.

He continued as if she had not spoken. "I have spent the last few minutes reassuring your fiancé this must all be a dreadful mistake, and you would never act with such wanton impropriety. Lord Vale has agreed to announce the engagement immediately. Now to stave off any further scandal the wedding will be proceeded with urgency. No time for banns to be posted and Vale is in the process of using his considerable influence to procure a special license."

Somehow she never imagined her father's reaction would be to foist her off even faster onto the earl. She glanced at Lady Margaret, and was met with a similar resolve in her gaze. Adel swallowed the laugh bubbling forth. She was found in the bed of a powerful duke who would certainly crush her for her temerity. The humiliation to come was enough to encourage her to flee to Derbyshire to her godmother. Why would Lord Vale still insist on marriage?

She hugged her middle, caught up in a vice of fear. As she thought on her life so far this season, Lord Vale's constant veiled insinuations and repulsive pinches, a hot tide of rebellion stirred inside. "I have been compromised. Surely Lord Vale would not wish for a wife that is—"

Her father shook his head. "He understands that the blackguard James Atwood must have forced you to come to his room, and that young man will be dealt with. You are fortunate, Lord Vale is still willing to marry you and—"

"Young Mr. Atwood?" Lord Gladstone asked, from the mantel where he been watching the entire exchange.

Adel's cheeks burned at the humiliation. The countess had not revealed with whom she had been caught. But why would Lord Vale pretend it had not been the duke? *Of course*, he was correctly thinking her parents would eagerly seek a forced match with Wolverton. Why would they settle for an earl when they could snag a duke? Lord Vale must have been hoping, they would have shepherded Adel from Pembington House and straight into his arms immediately.

Her father's expression bloomed with ire at the interruption. He enjoyed listening to his admonishing sermons, which he had been delivering quite often ever since

Adel could remember. *No…*since her mother died and he remarried.

"Yes," he snapped. "Mr. Atwood has been hounding me for my daughter's hand, and I have refused him several times, and this ploy of theirs is nothing more than their attempt to circumvent—"

"Forgive me, Sir Archibald, but your daughter was not found with young Mr. Atwood."

She had never thought her father could be rendered speechless. He spluttered, then swung a wild-eyed gaze to her, while her stepmother affected a swoon and wilted on the chaise, sobbing.

"Your daughter was found in the bed of the Duke of Wolverton," Lord Gladstone said with some measure of satisfaction. Why was he pleased? It was his daughter that had been set to marry the man. Why was he not as angry as his lady?

"I was not found in his bed," she said hoarsely.

"The Duke of Wolverton?" Lady Margaret whispered, disbelief rife in her voice.

At the pronounced silence in the library, Lord Gladstone excused himself, leaving Adel alone with her father and stepmother.

Lady Margaret glanced at Adel, eyes wide with apprehension and was that a glimmer of excitement? She was no doubt envisioning the lofty circles their family could be mingling with. "My dear," she turned to her husband, her fingers laced tightly together. "You cannot insist Lord Vale marry our daughter if she was found in the bed of a Duke. She may even be with child as we speak. We must insist the duke to do the honorable thing."

Heat burned Adel's face. With child? *Good heavens.*

"Yes, yes, of course," her father muttered.

Adel rushed forward. "Papa, this is ridiculous. The duke is

innocent in this matter and it was all a dreadful mistake on my part. I do admit I did intend to compromise Mr. Atwood, who most ardently desires to marry me despite the shortcoming of not possessing a sizable dowry or being a fashionable beauty. It would be beyond cruel to even think to make a demand of the duke, when an hour ago he had no knowledge of me. I am sure he will be expecting to marry a young lady of great fortune and impeccable breeding…and that is not me."

Lady Margaret threw her a glance filled with incredulity. "All of society is now aware he stole your virtue."

Adel blushed furiously, thinking of their kiss. "He did nothing of the sort!"

"You are a grave disappointment to your family," her father said. "To act with such…with such…" He closed his eyes as if pained.

"It was ill-judged of me to concoct such a plan, but what was I to do when you refused to listen to reason, Papa? Lord Vale attacked me, left bruises on me, and you were still insisting that I wed him. I had little choice but to protect my virtue, for certainly he would have tried to steal it before we were even married," she said, her voice roughened with unshed tears.

Lady Margaret's lips flattened. "You are failing to understand the import of your actions. You will be forced into seclusion, and we will not be able to show our face in society because of the shame. No one will accept us." Her lower lip trembled and tears glistened on her incredibly long eyelashes.

Papa tenderly held her hand, muttering soothing nonsense. "It shan't come to that, I won't allow it," he said.

"We *will* have to go into exile," Lady Margaret said and closed her eyes. "My darlings Helena and Beatrix will never recover from this. How do we survive it? I fear after this dreadful development, only Mr. Atwood may want her and he will just not do."

Before Adel or Papa could respond, there was a sharp perfunctory rap on the door and then it was opened. The duke strolled in, fully dressed in a dark coat and trousers, looking shockingly handsome. His shrewd gray eyes took in the scene in a sweeping glance, then settled on her. Though so coldly aloof, he was quite magnificent, her addled mind realized.

"May I present you to Sir Archibald and his wife, Lady Margaret, Your Grace. Sir Archibald and Lady Margaret, may I introduce His Grace, the Duke of Wolverton," Lord Gladstone said, entering behind the duke.

Lady Margaret surged to her feet and dropped into an elegant deep curtsy.

"Your Grace," her father said standing and bowing. "I have read many of your wonderful articles championing better treatment for the invalided soldiers. Very admirable and not unexpected of a man of your exceedingly eloquent stature."

Her father was much adept at flattery. He did nothing in this instance but lay on thick praise to the duke, even going as far as to quote him on some article he had recently written for the *Gentleman's Magazine*. Lady Margaret's head bobbed with every word uttered from Papa. The duke looked on with chilling tolerance, and Adel was too weary to be embarrassed on behalf of her father and stepmother, but she was most assuredly filled with rioting nerves.

"We understand there was a slight incident earlier, and we apologize for our daughter's behavior," Lady Margaret said, after Papa finally took a breath.

"Entirely my fault. It seemed I occupied the wrong chamber," the duke said dryly, with the slightest quirk of his lips.

Adel inhaled at the flutter of warm sensations that erupted in her stomach and her heartbeat quickened uncomfortably. That barely-there smile had rendered him charming, approachable.

"You are so kind and *honorable*, Your Grace. I…we…" Lady Margaret inhaled.

Adel winced at her stepmother's emphasis. Nothing in the duke's mien indicated he was aware of her subtle pressure.

"Thank you for receiving me on such short notice." His tone was so bland and polite; Adel struggled to guess what he was actually feeling.

His wintry gaze scanned the room and settled on her father. "You are no doubt aware of why I am here, Sir Archibald. Shall we speak alone?"

Anger stirred in Adel. She was mightily tired of her life being decided for her. "No."

The caress of his eyes slid over her like a sharpened blade, then he lowered his lids and dismissed her.

It stung.

"By all means," her father said.

"You will have to bodily remove me, Papa. It is my future we are discussing and I should be a part of it," she announced decisively.

Chapter Six

"Are you here to offer for our daughter?" Lady Margaret asked, no doubt anxious to get to the heart of the matter.

Adel gasped, and all eyes swung to her. This was all going dreadfully wrong. Of course the duke would not offer for her, she had nothing to recommend her for the lofty title of duchess. She'd had her first come out the year after her mother died, and in the three years since, only two young men had called on her and only Mr. Atwood had remained constant. Lord Vale was an anomaly and he'd not courted her. He'd stared, accidentally grazed her breast when no one looked, made suggestive whispers, and then attacked her. What made her stepmother believe the duke would do something so utterly implausible?

"Yes," he said.

Shock stabbed through Adel. "What?"

"You will do the honorable thing?" her father asked faintly.

The duke strolled to the sidebar and lifted the crystal from the decanter. He poured a golden liquid into a glass, then faced her father. "Most assuredly. In fact, I believe it wise if Miss Adeline and I were to wed as soon as possible, Sir Archibald."

This was so unexpected she felt faint. Adel's mouth went dry, and she was certain there was some misunderstanding. "Your Grace," she finally said very carefully, "You wish to make *me* your duchess?"

It seemed as if everyone in the library braced for his response.

"Yes."

"Good heavens," Lady Margaret breathed and gripped her husband's arms, as if seeking support from swooning. "A very sensible arrangement, Your Grace. Your sense of honor does you credit." She bobbed her head so vigorously the high purple turban with the plume feathers attached was in the precarious position of falling.

Adel was too stupefied to do anything but stare at the duke.

"Leave us," he commanded to the room at large. "I wish to have a few words with Miss Adeline."

Irritation bubbled in her when her stepmother and father bowed and scrambled out. Lord Gladstone nodded and he too made to depart.

They were leaving her alone with the man?

"Your Grace, please—" Her teeth snapped together at the gentle closing of the door. She closed her eyes for precious seconds. "You cannot wish to marry me." For some reason she had believed he would refuse her father's demands, not that he had even given Papa the chance to bluster. The duke did not seem like a man easily intimidated.

His eyebrow lifted slightly. "I do."

She searched his gaze frantically, and found nothing but sincerity. "But why?" she spluttered.

"You were found in my bed, and I had been seconds away

from drawing you underneath me and stealing your virtue," he said so dryly they could have been discussing the weather.

Embarrassment heated her cheeks. "There is no need to be so explicit," she countered staunchly. "And my virtue was never in any danger."

"Even if our encounter has somehow slipped your memory, I am sure you remember our host and hostess discovering us."

He said it as if they had conspired to have a clandestine rendezvous. She narrowed her eyes. "I feel compelled to point out I was in the middle of the room when Lady Gladstone entered."

Provoking amusement lit his eyes, then disappeared so swiftly she wondered if she had imagined it. "We are compromised and therefore we must marry. I will not tarnish my honor by walking away."

Though he said the words lightly, instinctively she recognized that being honorable was important to him. But how could he commit to something as permanent as marriage for honor? How could Adel consent when a man who loved her was probably eagerly waiting to speak with her? She was clasping her hands so tightly together her fingers hurt. "You do realize I believed you were someone else."

He prowled closer, his expression inscrutable. "Did you?"

She swallowed, taking small retreating steps away from him, desperate to maintain a particular distance between them. "Yes. A Mr. James Atwood. We are close in temperament and age, not that I am saying you are old, Your Grace." Heat burned her and she was sure her face was as red as the lobster she had eaten earlier. "Mr. Atwood… Ahh…he offered for me, but my father said no. It was his chamber I had intended to enter."

The duke frowned briefly. "I have a clear memory of you telling me I felt harder, *tasted* sweet, that you felt hot and wet.

I put forth the argument you knew I was not your young Mr. Atwood, Miss Adeline."

The bloody scoundrel! It was not the mark of a gentleman to so baldly and arrogantly remind a lady of her lapse in judgment. Worse, she was alarmed at the possibility that he was right. "You are mistaken, Your Grace," she said frostily.

The dratted man smiled, though it did not reach his eyes. "You knew I was not Mr. Atwood the instant you touched me."

Her head swam with the humiliating truth of his words. She hadn't been sure. But he couldn't know...*could he*? The minute she had tumbled into his powerful frame, the masculine fragrance of sandalwood and a cologne she had never smelled before had wrapped around her senses, confusing her. In desperation she had reached out, feeling and caressing, and had been met with a hardness that surprised and enthralled her. She had wondered how it was possible for the very slim and elegant Mr. Atwood to feel so male. Awareness had bloomed, but she had ignored the doubt, insisting it was nerves and too much liquid courage.

Evie and Adel's plan had not even intended her to kiss Mr. Atwood, only to be caught standing in his chamber. But she had kissed this man, and she had known without a shadow of doubt she had sneaked into the wrong bed. The curious desire that had blazed in her blood had been alarming and wonderful. How utterly foolish she had been.

"I have no notion of what you speak. You are kind in making your generous offer, but I cannot marry you," she whispered, sickened with the awareness of how easily she had been inconstant. She needed to see Mr. Atwood right away.

The duke's mien shuttered even more. "You are ruined and your current state can only be rendered respectable by marriage."

Ruined. She trembled and his silver gaze sharpened. In

that moment he looked like a predator and her heart started a slow thud. Why did he want to marry her? He was not even offering a token of resistance. Shouldn't the duke be insisting he would not bind himself to a lady with so little to recommend her?

"Why do you wish to marry me?" *It's the mad duke.* The whispers from the hallway crowded her thoughts. "Are you the man the *ton* calls the mad duke?"

Anger flickered in his gray eyes, and a chilling smile formed on his lips. She was at a loss as to how she had thought him charming and approachable. The man before her stood cloaked in cold ruthlessness. Uncertainty gripped her in a powerful hold. "Forgive me for being thoughtless and impertinent."

"It is one of the names I've been called."

He was clearly not afflicted.

"Why?"

"Does it matter?"

"If we are discussing marriage, yes." What was she saying? Surely she was not even thinking on his ludicrous proposal. She knew nothing of this man but a sobriquet, and was certain Mr. Atwood awaited her.

The duke's brows lifted and irrationally she wanted to step closer to him, tip on her toes and trace his slashing brows. Maybe even massage the lines on his forehead that indicated he had cause to frown often. She couldn't do this. "You know nothing of my character, nor I of yours."

"I value honesty above all else."

"I…I…" She frowned. She had simply been making a point, not seeking his finer qualities.

"Whatever right I have to happiness I receive from being in my daughters' presence."

Her heart lodged in her throat. "You have children?"

"Yes."

"I...I...what are their names, their ages?"

"Lady Sarah is six years and Lady Rosa is nine."

It was impossible for Adel to speak. When had their mother died? Who was now caring for them? Were they happy? The crushing pain and loneliness she had endured when her mother passed reared its head.

"I will have your answer, Miss Adeline. I do not have all night to linger over your indecision and lack of concern for your reputation."

The retort strangled in her throat. He was insufferable, but it seemed the duke truly wanted to marry her. "I am sure, Your Grace, you see how shocking your...your...offer is. You are a duke and I..." She swallowed past the lump that had somehow formed in her throat. What was she? A simple lady with simple pleasures not made for the grandiosity of being a duchess. "I have nothing to offer you, no dowry or suitable connections."

"Once again you are overlooking the obvious, we must marry."

Adel winced. She had little option *but* to say yes to his proposal. "I never imagined I would have a grand love story. But I at least thought there would be some affection between me and my husband. Some common interest...a spark of something deeper than duty and obligation to society's judgment," she said softly.

The man before was so aloof, she wondered fleetingly if it had been someone else in the dark. She did not believe he even *liked* her.

"It is tempting to offer you false flattery to save you from your foolhardy actions, but I despise deceit. I will not promise you tender sentiments. All the love I had to give is buried six feet beneath the earth, in the family vault in the churchyard of our parish church." His tone was autocratic and unrepentant. "People marry for duty, for material considerations and for offspring. If you are naive enough to want a marriage based on love, please walk away from my offer and face society's derision and scorn with your Mr. Atwood. I have endured torment and loss, and its bitter taste is one I have no wish to suffer ever again. The false illusion of love I will not offer you."

The slow thud of her heart was painful. The duke's words were so cold and emotionless. Adel firmly believed a couple closely aligned must fall deeply into tender romance. Even her father and Lady Margaret appeared besotted at times.

"It must be terribly lonely to have such beliefs."

"Yet I am quite contented."

Was he not at all affected by her impulsiveness? Did he not rail that he would no longer wed Evie? "And Lady Evelyn?"

He arched a brow. "I have already surmised Lady Evelyn is the reason you entered my chamber in error."

Adel could not refute the truth of his words. They were standing distressingly close, yet Adel was unable to withdraw from his false comforting warmth. "Then what do you offer, Your Grace?"

"I offer you your own home and my name, Miss Adeline."

Yearning struck her in the stomach, thick and undeniable. A family…of her own, and she would be a *duchess*, more powerful than a countess and be positioned to aid her younger sisters. But surely Wolverton must think her beneath his ilk.

"I offer you power and wealth. I will promise you faithfulness, the protection of my name and title."

"But not the more tender sentiments."

"Yes."

"You would consign us to a cold union."

"I would save your reputation, give you a life of privilege you can only imagine, and in turn you will provide a comforting presence for my daughters."

Oh. "And will you allow me to comfort you when needed?" She had no idea where the provocatively bold thought came from, but he seemed too reserved. She felt a fleeting sense of triumph that she had pierced his armor when shock flared in his gaze before he lowered his eyes...to her lips.

A curious heat filled Adel. Was he perhaps thinking of kissing her? As if he had heard her wanton thoughts he dipped his head even further. The duke visibly shuddered and the reaction was quiet enthralling. "Why do you tremble?"

A soft curse hissed from him, and she blushed at the vulgarity.

Chapter Seven

"Your utterances, Your Grace, are ungentlemanly."

"Censure from a young lady that climbed into a man's bed with flagrant disregard for society's expectation... *bloody hell*," Edmond incised quite deliberately.

She stared at him in ill-concealed shock. "You disapprove of me."

Earlier he had spoken at length to his host and hostess, and despite Lady Gladstone's anger, she had previously thought Miss Adeline a sensible young lady, a good friend, and companion to her daughter. A better man than he would have felt guilty for taking advantage of her embarrassing situation, but he'd never deluded himself as to being good. "Forgive my rudeness," he said, stepping even farther away. "I do not."

Her eyes were widened, and her face was flushed becomingly. *Too becomingly.*

He would have to be ruthless in guarding his response to this female. If he were to marry her and keep his sanity, there would be no more kisses or talks of her providing comfort.

Though he had belatedly realized she had not meant the comfort of being buried deep inside of what he knew would be the tightest sheath.

Her spine snapped straight, stretching the thin muslin of her dress across her ample but well-shaped breasts. He gritted his teeth and turned away, disgusted with his lack of restraint. He strolled to the door and braced his forehead against its frame. What was he doing? The feelings she had stirred inside him, the spark of interest to learn her likes and dislikes was bloody unwelcome. So why was he still pressing his suit? *She is unwilling.* He should let her go to face the consequences of her actions.

His heart twisted. It startled Edmond to realize he cared. The idea of society cutting her had fury surging in his gut. Miss Adeline had no notion of what it was like to walk into a ballroom and know that everyone present whispered about her. A simple stroll down the street or a ride in Hyde Park would have onlookers desperate to gawk. Then a flurry of voices would rise, as they rehashed every perceived infraction, until whatever they gossiped about traversed embellishment and became laughably ridiculous.

It's the mad duke of Wolverton. The whispers had been unceasing. He doubted many even knew why he'd been given the moniker, and it had taken very little for it to be assigned. After all, the *ton* could not comprehend a union made because of genuine sentiments. Edmond had loved his wife, and he had been mocked for making a rare *love match*. He'd doted on her…and even his friends had tried to encourage him to take a mistress. He'd retreated to the country with Maryann to raise their children, and it was hinted that he had departed his common sense.

Dukes and duchesses did not raise and nurture their own brood. Nursemaids and governesses did. Yet his Maryann had refused all offers of assistance, bathing her own babes and even insisting on feeding them herself, which had scandalized Edmond's mother.

When his wife had died, because of *him*...how he had grieved and railed, how the pain had tormented him for months, which is why he had shunned society and frivolous diversions. Because society and his friends had not been able to understand, they insisted he was mad. Vapid insufferable fools. A mockery of a smile twisted Edmond's lips. Mayhap he was indeed a madman to even contemplate taking a woman so scandalously bold and improper, yet so frustratingly enticing.

Perhaps he should enter the marriage mart and try his hands at wooing some blushing debutant once more. Bile rose in his throat as his heart instinctively rejected the idea. It would be hypocritical to go through all that smiling, caressing, and dancing to court another woman. He would never let that be a part of him again. That part was long dead, and he hardly believed it could be resurrected. The pain of losing Maryann and his son had been gut wrenching and inescapable.

Perhaps despite her appeal it was damn fortunate Miss Adeline had climbed into his bed and saved him from the farce of the marriage mart.

"Your Grace?"

He pushed away from the door and faced her.

"I would speak with Mr. Atwood first."

Edmond bit back a short oath. "I would not dream to stand in the path of true love," he said with sarcasm.

Her expression grew cautious. "Then I may leave?"

"If you insist you would prefer to wed Mr. Atwood, I urge you to go to him. Your father will be eager for you to form any alliance, to stem the tide of gossips that will swirl around your name for months to come. A hasty marriage will be in your best interest."

She looked briefly disconcerted at that pronouncement, and then she smoothed her features. "Thank you, Your

Grace," she said softly.

He inclined his head and she rushed from the library as if the devil were nipping at her heels. In truth, Edmond had to admit he must seem quite like the devil right now. He knew very well what Mr. Atwood's reaction to the rumors already spreading like wildfire would be.

In the short span of time it had taken him to dress and meet Lord and Lady Gladstone in the drawing room, from the whispers he gleaned Miss Adeline had long been his mistress and might now already be carrying his child.

Good God, the lady had no idea what he had tried to save her from.

No notion. She would be made to suffer the humiliation of vicious gossips for months, and the simplest act could revive it for years to come. But with him…there would be no intimacy or opening for sentiments. In fact, Edmond was resolved to stay away from her bed. But she would be a duchess.

Edmond grimaced. Was he truly the better choice?

$$\cdot \; \cdot \; \cdot$$

Adel's eyes were gritty, and she was unable to stop yawning. She had fled from the duke to her room but had been unable to sleep. Nor was she feeling brave enough to venture downstairs. She could not marry Wolverton or Lord Vale. She'd scribbled a hasty note and entrusted it to the maid assigned to her, to be delivered to Mr. Atwood with utmost discretion. The clock outside in the hall chimed, and she glanced down at the small pocket watch that belonged to her papa. It was almost time to meet Mr. Atwood in the orangery, if he had indeed received her directions. She was resolute in the way forward—they would have to elope.

There was a knock on the door but before she answered it was opened, and in strolled Evie.

Hurt tightened Adel's throat. She had been unable to dwell on her closest friend's betrayal. To see the ravages of tears and torment now in Evie's eyes did not soothe Adel in any manner. Evie deserved to feel wretched, no matter how uncharitable it seemed. Adel forced herself to take a deep, steadying breath. "I never knew the Duke of Wolverton had offered for you."

Evie already had red eyes filled with tears. She rushed forward and Adel jerked away. Evie faltered, then clasped her hands together. "I became aware of his offer only last night," she said hoarsely.

"And you acted with wanton selfishness. Instead of rejecting his offer, you did everything to derail my chance at happiness."

Evie flinched. "In my fear and panic I was thoughtless, and now I must suffer the consequences of losing the affections of my dearest friend. Please forgive me."

"No."

She gasped, but Adel remained unmoved. "I know why you did it."

Evie paled.

Adel clasped her fingers together at her front to stop them from trembling. "You have been in love with the Marquess of Westfall since I made your acquaintance these two years past. The prospect of marrying anyone else must have been terrifying. But did you not see that you robbed me of the same opportunity of wedding the man I held affections for? Though I rail against it, I fear deep in my heart I must marry the duke, or my family will never be able to recover from such a mess. He is so unlike Mr. Atwood, I cannot see how we will have a happy—or even a slightly happy—situation. The duke's charms upon closer acquaintance are sorely lacking. He is severe, cold, Evie."

But his kisses are divine. Adel ignored the traitorous

reflections.

Evie's face crumpled and silent tears streamed down her cheeks. "Westfall and Wolverton are the closest of friends."

Adel closed her eyes. That would have been unbearable, but it could not excuse Evie's action. Adel had trusted her friend absolutely.

Evie's throat worked. "I could not bear to wed the duke, knowing as his duchess I would have cause to entertain his closest friend. I tried to speak to Mamma and all my pleas fell on deaf ears. I cannot imagine a world without belonging to Westfall...and I thought since you had no such similar affections for Mr. Atwood, I..."

Adel stiffened. "I would not wed a man I have no regards for!"

Evie shook her head, her green eyes pleading. "You care for Mr. Atwood, but I *love* Westfall. At the crest of each dawn I think of him. He is my friend, my confidant, but I also yearn to be his lover. He makes me ache, and my heart belongs to him. He kissed me once, and I still feel the press of his lips against mine, the heat of his body, and the strength of his arms."

Heat climbed Adel's cheek. Mr. Atwood never roused such longing in her; but surely in a few more years it would bloom? *But the duke did make your blood stir.* It was as if the very devil himself whispered the traitorous thoughts to her.

Evie moved farther into the room. "I own to the love I have for the marquess, but it does not excuse my behavior, Adel. I was rash and so foolish. I am not sure what I imagined would happen, but it was not this. All the guests are speaking of you being in the duke's chamber. Mamma says by next week all of London will know, and the tattle sheets will speak of nothing else for months," she ended on a harsh sob. "I wish I could go back in time and undo my thoughtlessness," she said with heartbreaking sincerity.

Tears pricked behind Adel's lid. For as long as she knew Evie, she had been in love with the marquess who mostly treated her as the younger sister of one of his closest friends. The marquess seemed like he had no thoughts of considering marriage, and Evie was not sure if it was on account of the mysterious scars that roped half of his face, or just the general contempt that seemed to leak from him whenever he mingled with polite society. Though it pained her to acknowledge, Adel was filled with relief that Evie did not have to marry Wolverton and be consigned to such a distressing situation. But Adel would not say so; the sting of the betrayal was too fresh and deep.

"Have you seen Mr. Atwood?"

Evie shook her head.

"I must go to him," Adel said glancing on the watch. "I hope he has not heard the rumors."

Evie exhaled softly. "Will you marry the duke?"

Did she have a choice? "If Mr. Atwood is willing to elope, I…" Adel swallowed the sob rising in her throat. "I do not know what I am feeling or thinking. Only a couple hours have passed since I entered the wrong chamber. I do not want to see my family ruined beyond all measure. If I were to elope with Mr. Atwood would that not be the outcome? Would I not be compounding the disaster? Yet I cannot imagine my life with a man I have no knowledge of, one who has said I should not entertain the notion of future love between us. One who looks at me with nothing but emptiness in his eyes? I see no admiration…only a resolve to be honorable. We are ill-suited."

Evie gasped and sympathy filled her eyes. "I sincerely sympathize with your distress, and I am so very sorry," she whispered.

So am I.

It took a lot of courage and ingenuity on Adel's part to enter the orangery unseen. It was barely eight in the morning, but several guests were already up. She was grateful most were still abed, no doubt tired from the late night's entertainment. Adel colored, remembering how she had added to their amusement.

She pushed open the glass door and espied Mr. Atwood in the far left corner. Her heart soared. Surely it was a good omen he had made the effort to meet with her. At the sound of her footsteps he spun to face her, and Adel was distressed to realize the exhilaration she normally felt at seeing him was decidedly absent. Images of the duke's cold mien filtered through her thoughts, and she gritted her teeth until they ached. "Mr. Atwood, I am so relieved you were able to slip away. Thank you."

He nodded stiffly, his normally smiling face stern with disapproval.

Her heart sank. "I am not sure if you've heard—"

"I did!" he snapped. "And I will be made to be a laughingstock for it was known I courted you."

"Mr. Atwood, I—"

"It is on everyone's tongue how *you* compromised the duke. I must admire you for setting your cap so high."

A pang shot 's heart. Surely he didn't believe her capable of such wanton social climbing. "I most certainly did not. I thought I was slipping into your room, Mr. Atwood," she said honestly. She had thought such a confession would have soothed him, but instead he stiffened.

"Did he take your virtue?"

She blushed. "*Nothing happened.*"

The smoky taste of lips flavored with the hint of brandy, the feel of his throbbing heat…had been incredible, but instead she focused on what she would lose today. Mr. Atwood's face was becoming more mottled, and disappointment was settling into her stomach. Every instinct was shouting that if Mr. Atwood truly had genuine feelings for her, he would have acted upon them, and they would now be making plans on how to weather society's scorn. "I could not have been in His Grace's chamber for more than a few minutes before Lady Gladstone entered." Adel was still unsure of how long she had actually been in the chamber. The sherry had muddled her thoughts more than she realized.

"A few minutes are all it takes," Mr. Atwood growled in obvious agitation. "To think of that mad bloody scoundrel touching you, kissing your fair lips is enough to make me want to call him out."

Mad bloody scoundrel?

Her heart lurched. "Don't be silly. His Grace is innocent in all of this. Everyone seems to be forgetting I thought it was your room. Don't you see, Mr. Atwood? I thought if we were caught in a compromising position, father would make us wed." She took a deep breath. "There is no avoiding all that has happened, but the question is, do you still wish to marry me?"

A sharp pang of loss cut deep into her heart. If she were to marry James, the chaotic need the duke had aroused in her body would never be experienced. She angrily pushed such thoughts aside. She had already betrayed James with her body's reaction to the man; she would not do so with her thoughts.

He froze, his Adam's apple bobbing as he seemingly struggled to swallow. "We cannot, Adel, I—" He thrust fingers through his hair in obvious frustration.

She firmed her lips to prevent their trembling. "I see. I never realized society's opinion was so very important to you. You were so eager to wed me, and Papa was so against our union, I thought if the countess knew I had been alone in your room even for a second, she would encourage Papa to see us wed. Entering the duke's room was a horrid misfortune."

A florid flush climbed his face. "I cannot even think of continuing to press my suit! Everyone knows you were in his room, and it has already been suggested you may be *enceinte*. If we were to still wed, I would be forced to defend your honor at every instance."

Forced to defend my honor…yet a stranger was willing to place the proverbial noose around his neck to save her reputation. Adel's heart fluttered at her assessment. "Why should we allow the whispers of small-minded people to dictate our lives?" she demanded, though her heart kept plummeting.

He looked away from her, steadfastly refusing to meet her gaze. "They are crucial to my success. The house is already rife with talk of the duke having had you," Mr. Atwood muttered. "I should not be speaking to you of such delicate matters, but it seems it is unavoidable."

What delicate matters? "What are they saying Wolverton made me do?" It should not be important, but she strangely cared.

Red splashed across Mr. Atwood's face and Adel was nonplussed to realize he was blushing.

"They are saying you have been his mistress," he said harshly.

Mr. Atwood must know such a ridiculous assertion could not possibly be true, but the facts would not be believed. Once society spoke of it, he would find it an affront.

"I see," she said softly, distressed and annoyed in equal measure to feel tears rising once more to the surface. "I feel as if I have aged a decade in just a few hours," she gasped, fighting the urge to cry. "I feel so ridiculous. Society's opinion is far more important to you than I am. I have been silly enough to willingly take steps that might bring ruin to my name, because I thought the *tendre* we had formed was worth so much more than a cold union."

Perhaps the duke was right; sentiments in marriage were for the fool-hearted. She had been so certain Mr. Atwood adored her as he'd professed on several occasions.

He grimaced, and then turned soulful eyes to her. "You are so beautiful, Adeline."

Her eyes widened. Never had he referred to her with such intimacy before, or referred to her as a beauty.

He continued gruffly, "For a long time I felt undeserving of you. That someone as wonderful as you would want to marry me. You enjoy fishing, you listened when I spoke of my work and my dreams of becoming a barrister."

Regret settled on his face and Adel felt a tight knot forming in the pit of her stomach.

"I cannot marry you, not after you have been caught with the duke. I do not even believe we can be friends. The duke has sworn off marriage, and everyone speaks of the fact that he will abandon you. Your reputation has been irreparably damaged, and you may tarnish mine by association."

She flinched and he tugged at his cravat. Before she could inform him that the duke had done the honorable thing, Mr. Atwood hurried past her.

"I am sorry," he murmured as he darted away.

Adel was too stunned to even turn to watch him leave. Years of friendship and expectation had been reduced to a hasty dismissal and good-bye. She closed her eyes. What was she to do now? Would the duke even still want to marry her, after her earlier rejection? She did not have to marry him, she could flee to the country and use her modest inheritance from her mother to try and open a bookshop after the scandal died away. Although her infamy might very well cause patrons to flock to her establishment. She wondered if she should change her name and hope for anonymity to hide her from society's censure.

And what of your sisters? Though Helena and Beatrix were her stepsisters, Adel loved them wholeheartedly. If she were ruined, the scandal would follow her for years, her sisters would also suffer the consequences. With stiff movements she turned around and walked from the orangery toward the main house. She would have to marry. The idea of wedding Lord Vale was unbearable, and certainly no other man would be interested. She would have to wed the duke…if he would still have her.

Chapter Eight

The rousing strains of the orchestra did little to soothe Adel's nerves. Life had continued for the guests of Pembington House, and it was only her world that had been shattered. The ball was in full swing, and her stomach was in knots as she descended the wide staircase. Adel had worn the turquoise muslin gown trimmed with gold embroidery for tonight's ball. She'd not wanted to attend, but Papa and Lady Margaret had been firm, they would not hide as if they were ashamed. The *ton* was quicker to smell blood when in retreat. Adel became the focus of several pointed stares, and though she had stoically prepared herself for the chatter, the swell that rose in the ballroom was shocking.

"There she is!"

"She has some nerve showing her face. I thought her family would have bundled her away by now, for the shame."

"She is quite beautiful isn't she? It is easy to see what tempted the duke."

The assessment so startled her, she glanced in the direction of the voices and witnessed three gentlemen staring at her.

She recognized the Marquess of Westfall amongst them. He insolently caressed her length with his tawny golden eyes, and a smile tugged at his lips, drawing her gaze to the mess of scars running from his forehead down to his chin on the left side of his face. His manner was so bold and outrageous Adel flushed. She had no idea what Evie saw in the reprobate.

"Beauty?" The marquess drawled. *"I doubt Wolverton touched the chit. She was simply being a mercenary bitch, and will no doubt expire from shock when he ignores her."*

A sob clawed from the depths of her being and spilled from her throat at the blatant insult.

Mercenary bitch.

His eyes flared and gleamed with something similar to regret, then an expression of icy disdain settled on his face. The men with him appeared so shocked by his vulgarity that it left them silent.

"That is very unsporting of you, Westfall," one of the men muttered, looking discomfited. *"Perhaps Wolverton will offer for her."*

"Why ever would he do such a ghastly thing?"

Tears pricked behind her lids, and she gave Westfall her back and walked away. Westfall was Wolverton's closest friend. Had the duke shared with the marquess his true opinion of her mistake? Adel so badly wanted to scamper away and plead with her father to depart the house party. Surely her presence would only fan the embers of scandal more. Surely out of sight would be out of mind.

"I wonder if he will take her to be his mistress."

"I've been told she was already his soiled little dove."

With false calm she waited near the terrace windows. No one greeted her, and dance after dance were announced and no one had approached her. They only stared. Even Mr. Atwood made a concentrated effort to direct his attention elsewhere and those of society in the Gladstone ballroom took note. She sucked in a breath when Lady Margaret entered and instead of coming over, chose to make the rounds. Adel had just decided to leave when a sudden ripple of conversation washed over the assembled throng. The too loud murmurs began at the far left side of the ballroom and crested in Adel's direction.

"It's the duke."

"Wolverton?"

"Yes…it seems as if Viscount Eldridge has won the wager. He swore the duke would make an appearance tonight and Lord Westfall bet twenty guineas he would not!"

Several ladies actually turned so they could see as he descended the stairs. He looked handsome, clad in black trousers with a matching jacket and silver brocade waistcoat. His dark hair was tamed, and Adel fancied she could see the piercing silver of his eyes from where she stood.

"Will he go to her or cut her?"

Adel felt sick at that whisper. She had rejected his offer. And he had no notion that she had tried to speak with him earlier, but had been told he had been out riding. What if he ignored her for the duration of the ball? That would cement in society's eyes, that she was soiled and unworthy. Firming her jaw and straightening her spine, she scanned the crowd. Satisfaction curled inside her that many were unable to meet her gaze for long. It was a small triumph but she welcomed it.

Many greeted him as he came off the final steps. Lord and Lady Gladstone were one of the first to approach him, and they smiled and chatted as if nothing were amiss. After a few minutes the duke inclined his head and walked away. The crowd parted as he moved with purpose not toward her, but away.

Adel's heart pounded and in desperation she went to the refreshment table and collected a punch glass.

"He is cutting her." A whisper to her left reached her ears.

Tears pricked her lids. Should she stay? Or should she try to slip away unnoticed. It did not take her long to realize that such an endeavor would be impossible. The attention of the lords and ladies at present was split. Some ogled her and the others were craning their necks, making no attempt to not be obvious as they watched Wolverton.

If she left they would know she was fleeing in shame, and the slander would be worse tomorrow. She dreaded reading about her own escapades in the scandal sheets. Although Adel stood in a sea of people, she had never felt so desperately alone. It was quite evident she was at this moment, a pariah. No one moved close, even Lady Margaret was carefully nearing the terrace door, her eyes wide with apprehension as she watched the duke. As if on cue, Adel's cheeks smarted where her stepmother had slapped her earlier, when she'd informed them she rejected the duke and asked if they could arrange an audience, so she could correct her error.

It seemed as if she could do nothing right.

Another wave of titters crested through the ballroom, and her gaze unerringly landed on the duke's broad shoulders. He was beside the orchestra. He bent to say something to one of their number. The musicians nodded, and he sauntered away, bold and graceful…right toward her. Adel's hands shook, fearing she would spill the punch she had yet to sip, she placed it on the refreshment table with a soft clink.

He stopped in front of her, and it was as if the entire room held its breath.

A few seconds later the violins sounded, and the scandalous strain of a waltz filtered on the air, shocking her. The duke bowed, then straightened and held his hand out to her. "Miss Adeline, would you honor me with a waltz?"

From the periphery of her vision she saw her stepmother wilting in relief, and even Evie smiled, her eyes filling with tears. Adel wanted to fling herself into his arms and shout for relief. His public show of support must mean that he still desired to marry her. Her sisters were saved; her family was not ruined, if she did not botch it further. She sank into a curtsy. "I would be honored, Your Grace." Then she rose and stepped into his arms as if she belonged there.

On cue the rousing strains of the waltz filled in the ballroom. Adel was painfully aware they were the only couple dancing. It seemed the members of society who were packed into the Gladstone ballroom were now content to watch them in stunned silence.

The duke held her firmly, at a respectable distance, but there was something possessive in his embrace. Her heart tripped in her chest. As she soared with him, the dozens of eyes boring into her back faded. "Thank you for being kind after my earlier stubbornness."

"Think nothing of it," he reassured her, his regard piercing and intent.

"Why have you singled me out? Not that I am ungrateful," she hastily added.

His mouth curved faintly. "You are very direct. It is a trait I admire."

"Thank you."

"My attentions to you now are a double edge sword. If I walk away without any announcement of our impending nuptials, your ruination will be completed. Yet if I had ignored you, the result would have been the same."

The slow thud of her heart was painful. Adel was only distantly aware of other couples eagerly taking their places on the dance floor. Did this really mean he still wanted to wed her? Without taking his eyes from her, he spun her into several wonderful spins, the power and grace in his movements thrilling. His eyes were truly wonderful, the harsh gray color of the sky as it heralded a winter storm. Now they were filled with a guarded awareness and cool intelligence. A surge of interest to understand Edmond stirred in her heart.

"I never thought you would have such care for my reputation. You hardly know me, Your Grace, and I thank you." It mattered to her that he had been thoughtful. When was the last time someone truly had given a fig about her? Warmth poured through her veins. "Do you still want me to be your duchess?"

Triumph flared in his gaze. "Yes."

Relief twisted through her. "Thank you, I'm very much obliged to you."

"I will have my solicitors draft the agreement and present to your father. I will also obtain a special license, and we will wed by Friday."

She gasped. "That is in two days' time."

"Yes."

Adel spluttered. "Surely that will be impossible. Would it not be best to have a courtship period of at least six months and then a quiet wedding?"

She did not want society's judgmental eyes upon them when they cemented their vows. "There are already rumors there may be a…a…child," she ended on a furious whisper, blushing profusely. "If we wait it will be evident to all, nothing of import happened."

A dark brow arched. "The only part I am in agreement with is a quiet wedding. My offer is by this Friday or we do not wed at all."

He seemed so cold and uncompromising she almost faltered. "May I inquire as to why the urgency?"

"My daughters expect me at Rosette Park by Sunday."

Rosette Park. Even Adel had heard about the beauty and wealth of that estate. "Surely after—"

"No."

Her hands tightened on his, and he glanced at their clasped palms. He shifted one of his fingers in a soothing stroke over her knuckles. The caress was unexpected, but what was even more startling was the heat that pooled in her veins. "I hardly know you," she gasped.

"Are you committed to marrying me?"

She nodded slightly.

"Then why does it matter if we wed a few days from now, or in a few months? Unless your intention is to call off the engagement, when the furor eventually dies down? Let me assure you that will make an even greater scandal."

The thought had not even occurred to her. She simply did not know him, like she had known Mr. Atwood. Adel winced. Much good that had done her. They had been friends for years and yet he had been persuaded away.

"The thought never occurred to me." She would marry this man and spend a lifetime with him. *Who is he?* Honorable. That much she knew. Though he admitted to wanting a wife for his children, he could wed any one of the beautiful, well-dowered, and well-connected young ladies of society. She had accurately assessed the envy in many of their eyes as he bowed over her hand.

"I…I am not very polished," she admitted. "I fear I would disappoint you as a hostess and as your wife. I have no doubt you would prefer a duchess of high moral character and excellent references."

"Are you by chance trying to inform me of your lack of such faculties?"

"Of course not." With a frown she added, "Surely you are not overlooking the fact I had planned to compromise Mr. Atwood."

"What could or should have happened has never interested me much. What did happen was you compromised *me*. I have decided it is fate, since I am in need of a wife. This is the final time I will ask this question, Miss Adeline. Are you certain you wish to be my duchess?"

She swallowed, forcing the lump to dispel, and stepped over the petrifying ledge she had perched on since she climbed into his bed. "Yes."

Savage satisfaction emanated from him.

"What expectations would you have of me as your duchess?" Even saying the title out loud did not diminish the surreal feel.

"I want there to be only honesty between us. It is important to me that you never lie to me." Torment flashed in his eyes and echoes of pain vibrated in his voice.

Who had lied to him? "Yes, Your Grace."

"All subjects pertaining to my previous wife are forbidden. I will care for you and protect you with my life. I will be faithful, and I will endeavor to be a kind husband."

She nodded, her heart pounding. "Thank you for your honesty, Your Grace."

"Edmond." He tugged her closer, and her heart tripped alarmingly. "I trust we have shared enough intimacies where formalities are not required between us. Please call me Edmond." Piercing eyes ran over her in a caress that was distressingly bold and intimate. "Will you honor me with the same intimacy, Adeline?" he asked with a charm that made her wary.

"I…" Why was she hesitating? The hard lump formed again in her throat. "Yes…Edmond. I know we've only just met, but do you think," she asked slowly, "that there will ever come a time when you might fall in love with me?"

He considered her, and her cheeks burned with humiliation at the prolonged silence. The waltz ended, and he drew her towards the countess and earl. Lady Margaret and Papa were waiting, both looking anxious. The duke gave a slight nod to Lord Gladstone and the man smiled. Everything next passed in a daze for Adel. She became aware of the stunned silence in the ballroom as Lord Gladstone commanded their attention.

Glasses were raised, and applause sounded as he announced the engagement of the Duke of Wolverton to Miss Adeline Hays.

She glanced up at the duke. He surveyed the throng, a cold disinterest in his eyes, his manner that of an overlord watching his subjects. Nerves erupted in her stomach. Instead of feeling relief that she had been saved from ruination, Adel wondered what she had consigned herself to. One thing she was certain of, despite the foolish hopeful sentiments in her heart, she must never mention love to the duke again.

Chapter Nine

Seven people were present in the Pembington House chapel to witness Edmond's marriage to Miss Adeline. Sitting in the pews quite somberly were the Gladstones and their two children, Lady Evelyn and Viscount Ravenswood, then his bride's family, Sir Archibald, and Lady Margaret. One of Edmond's most trusted friends, the Marquess of Westfall, was also in attendance, his golden eyes coolly mocking as he stood witness.

There was a rustle and Edmond looked to the entrance of the small chapel. His heart jolted. It seemed in the two days he had been away obtaining a marriage license and sending orders back to Hampshire, he had forgotten how truly ravishing Miss Adeline was. She walked towards him on her father's arm, in a lovely rose-colored gown, with a low cut neckline that just stopped short of being provocative. Her raven black hair was pinned and plaited into a complicated arrangement save a few wispy tendrils had escaped to decoratively cascade around her face. Someone had been thoughtful enough to provide her with a posy of rosebuds which she held in a death grip.

She reached his side and held his gaze as she faced him. The satisfaction worming itself through him made him wary.

The rector, whose parish covered the Gladstone estate, started the ceremony.

"Dearly beloved, we are gathered together here in the sight of God, and in the face of this congregation, to join together this man and this woman in holy matrimony; which is an honorable estate…"

The rector's voice faded as Edmond observed Adeline. She swallowed and her hazel eyes whispered over his face, searching. What she looked for Edmond did not know, but it was as if she had lifted her hands, and trailed the tip of her fingers over his cheek. Her stare was rousing, provoking, and in the depth of her eyes he saw the need for reassurance.

The rector continued, "Your Grace, Edmond Elias Alastair Rochester, wilt thou have this woman to thy wedded wife, to live together after God's ordinance in the holy estate of matrimony? Wilt thou love her, comfort her, honor, and keep her in sickness and in health; and, forsaking all other, keep thee only unto her, so long as ye both shall live?"

"I will," he vowed.

The rector shifted to Adeline.

"Miss Adeline Georgiana Hays, wilt thou have this man to thy wedded husband, to live together after God's ordinance in the holy estate of matrimony? Wilt thou obey him, and serve him, love, honor, and keep him in sickness and in health; and, forsaking all other, keep thee only unto him, so long as ye both shall live?"

"I will," she said with a voice that trembled slightly, then she smiled.

Damnation, she is beautiful.

He gritted his teeth and ruthlessly pushed away all such thoughts. Her eyes widened and she lowered her lids, but he saw the flash of disappointment. What the hell had she expected, for him to return her smile?

Not more than a minute later the ceremony ended.

I have a new wife.

He shook away the slow pump of disquiet and directed his thoughts to the greater accomplishment of the day. His daughters now had a woman in their life.

It was sheer torture, but it took discipline for him to only press a soft kiss to her cheeks, and ignore the temptation of her lips.

• • •

She was a *duchess*. Adel was still unsure how it had all happened. A week ago, her only thoughts had been to escape the oppressive feeling of living with her father and stepmother, and maybe, existing as Mrs. James Atwood, then eventually with his support open a bookshop.

Never had she imagined her life could have taken such a drastic turn with so little warning or preparation. Seated at the breakfast table, she did her very best to ignore the imposing presence of Edmond. Adel turned back to her half-eaten breakfast, stared at the scrambled eggs and sliced ham for a moment, then pushed the plate away with a grimace. She was a nervous wreck and unable to appreciate the thoughtfulness of Lady Gladstone, who despite everything had made the day a bit more bearable for Adel. The countess had ensured that breakfast was made available in a smaller dining room for her, the duke, and her family. She had even decorated the room with bountiful vases of orchids and lily.

"Will you be staying for the rest of the house party, Your Grace?" her stepmother asked.

Adel waited for his response. Since he had brushed his cold lips on her cheek in the chapel, he had not acknowledged her. At first she had been baffled, then hurt, then her feelings shifted to gratefulness. She could not endure any attempts at polite conversation.

She felt as if she were in a sea, drowning in uncertainty and trepidation. She was sure of nothing—the duke, his children, her wedding night, and their future. Everything was so overwhelming, she preferred to be silent and not be prodded to converse.

Thankfully, her father and Lady Margaret had ignored her as well, and they had spent the last hour, chattering away at Edmond. Adel doubted he got in more than a few words, though he seemed content to remain stoic.

"We depart for Hampshire at noon," he said.

Oh. "I know no one in Hampshire." Why had she opened her mouth? His piercing regard prompted her to force a smile to her lips. "Though I hear it is most congenial there," Adel said.

"Your sisters will be very excited to visit your new home. The country air will do wonders for their health," Papa said, already trying to ensure Lady Margaret's daughters were seen to be connected with Wolverton.

Lady Margaret gave her husband a sweet approving smile.

"It does you credit, Your Grace, that you would have your family to the famous Rosette Park for a visit in short order."

It took Adel several moments to realize Lady Margaret spoke to her. She was now *Your Grace*. Good Heavens! A visit to Rosette Park? Not that Adel minded, her stepsisters were good natured, even if a bit silly at times, but it was certainly too soon to have every one descended on them. "With Edmond's approval you will all be welcome to visit for a spell, however, Papa, I think it is best that the duke and I have the first few weeks alone so we may learn each other. Remember we hardly even got a chance to converse properly…and here we are, wedded."

Her stepmother's eyes pinched in irritation and her father frowned, and then nodded. "Of course, my dear. We will take to the waters in Bath for a few weeks. We've leased a house at Camden Place and the girls are looking forward to traveling down."

The duke said nothing, taking too long before he removed his unnerving regard from her back to Lady Margaret.

Good lord. When will I be comfortable with him? But the better question was, had that been admiration she saw in his eyes?

Adel was filled with relief they would be departing in two hours' time. The journey to Hampshire would take the better part of the day, and they might very well arrive at Rosette Park tomorrow. She lowered her napkin. "If you will excuse me, I must oversee the packing of my belongings." She pushed back her chair, as the duke stood. After dipping into a shallow curtsy, Adel hurried from the dining room, able to feel his roving stare burning through her dress like a heated caress.

Chapter Ten

Adel shifted the curtains of the carriage and peered into the dark. Under the banner of moonlight she made out the powerful form of the rider ahead. The duke. They had been traveling for several hours, and she had passed the time by reading. Now the carriage lantern was not sufficient for her to discern the words on the pages, and the passage of Theodore Aikens's latest espionage tale was thrilling and quite rousing.

The coach turned into what looked like the driveway of a lively inn despite the late hour and rolled to a stop. Edmond was the one to assist her from the equipage.

"Thank you," she said smiling up at him.

He nodded curtly and held out his arm.

"It wouldn't be amiss to smile," she muttered.

"Why would I be smiling when there is no cause?"

She stumbled slightly, not expecting for him to hear her comment. "To be polite. A smile goes a long way toward making someone feel more welcomed and relaxed, and it does not hurt to be pleasant."

"If you are looking for someone to coddle your

sensibilities you will be gravely disappointed," he said, his tone extremely dry.

He crossed the gravel pathway with rapid strides, but Adel had no difficulty keeping pace.

They entered the inn, and it was evident from the several nods that he received from patrons in the common room that he was well known. The wretched man treated them with the same cold incivility. A room was ordered and immediately they were taken to the best the inn had to offer. Adel was surprised the room was so clean and pleasant, with an inviting fire place. She strolled over to the hearth, tugged off her gloves, and held her hands over the heat.

The duke's imperious tone from behind her ordered a supper tray for their room and a bath.

She glanced over her shoulders to find him watching her with an inscrutable mien.

"You do want a bath, do you not?"

After traveling for several hours she did feel a bit travel worn, and she was painfully aware this was their wedding night. Unable to help herself, her eyes were drawn to the bed in the center of the room.

His dark brows drew together as he stared at her. "Is there something on the bed sheets?"

She felt the heat climbed her neck. Determined to remain unruffled, she pasted a smile on her lips. "Of course not, and a bath would be lovely."

His gaze flickered briefly to her mouth, and her heart clamored. Then with a curt nod, he turned and marched from the room.

Good God, would the man ever unbend and smile? Worse…had that unfathomable look at her lips meant he wanted to kiss her or that she should prepare for a wedding night? She prayed not. She understood her duty to the duke, but the very idea of completing their union at an inn was exceptionally off-putting. She would certainly say so if he were to approach her. Though she doubted he would indeed even touch her. The man treated her with nothing but chilling incivility and the awareness of it had a terrible, hollow ache rising in her chest.

It was never more apparent to her, how much she was lacking. Not that she wanted to tempt him…even though she had no idea what she should be really tempting him to! Earlier as she'd peered at his powerful and uncompromising form seated on his horse, she had felt out of her depths. How could she have formed an attachment with a man who had no interest in her? If not for her folly…Adel was certain he would never have glanced in her direction.

With a soft sigh, she pushed Edmond from her mind, determined not to dampen her spirits further. She had months…years to understand the situation she was now in. If only acknowledging such a thought did not cramp her stomach with such acute discomfort.

• • •

An hour after he'd left the room, Edmond returned fully expecting Adeline to be sleeping. Instead, she was submerged in the bath still, singing softly. Her voice was warm and rich and…sultry. Something elusive stirred inside him. He closed the door with an audible click and she stiffened.

She darted a nervous glance at him, then her eyes jerked to the bed.

"You may relax, madam, I won't pounce," he drawled, almost amused.

"I…I am naked, sir."

He didn't even bother to point out that she was almost fully submerged in the bath water in the far corner…the only part of her on display was the elegant lines of her swan like neck, and that was because she had perched her mass of curls high atop her head. "You have nothing to tempt me with, madam, you are safe."

Liar, the sensuous line of her neck, begged to be licked, nibbled…

Noting she still looked anxious, he sighed. "It will be as if I am not in the room."

His tone may have been a trifle too bland for she looked dubiously at him. He made no further overture to make her comfortable. He rose and started to shrug from his coat. She flushed and turned away. He removed his overcoat and waistcoat, and untied the simple cravat he had worn. After shedding his boots, and arranging everything neatly on the sole chair in the room, he made his way to the bed, and lay down. The frame groaned under his weight, and he closed his eyes, completely ignoring her.

She muttered something under her breath about being rude and insufferable, and it actually pulled a smile to his lips. Closing his eyes, he allowed his mind to drift. He'd sent word to the estate that he was arriving home with his duchess. He could just imagine the uproar that would cause. But he was more concerned with how his daughters would react to Adeline. Sarah was almost three years old when Maryann died, and had no memory of her. Rosa was just shy of six, but she had whispered to him tearfully several months ago that she could not remember her mother and if that made her bad.

A rustle in the room jerked him from his thoughts. He swallowed. It seemed Adeline had emerged from her bath. He waited, listening to the soft sounds she made, slightly curious as to what she was feeling. A few seconds later the bed dipped.

Knowing she was so close to him sent frissons of heat through his body. He ruthlessly suppressed the urge, not allowing it to be born. Edmond glanced at her. She herself was so stiff on the far side of the bed she could have passed for a dead body. How she was to sleep through the night he had no idea. He'd already told her she was safe, and he would waste no time providing other reassurances.

"It is strange that tonight is our wedding night is it not?" she offered somewhat tentatively.

He turned his head, and the dark, hazel eyes met his. The lady had shifted her entire body towards him, but she still maintained the ridiculous distance that would no doubt see her spilling from the bed sometime through the night. "No."

Her eyes widened when she realized he would say nothing further. "Are you always this curt?"

He swallowed the sigh. He'd spent most of the day in the saddle and was weary. "Yes."

No…there had been a time when he was a boy that he'd been happy. He had memories of sitting on his father's shoulders as they toured his estates, eating apples and listening to the soft rumble of the man he'd idolized. A man he'd not thought could fade from his life. It was at the age of twelve he tasted second-hand the first sting of death, and he'd entered one of the darkest hours of his life. Edmond belatedly realized it was as if he'd never emerged.

"Why do you think that is?"

"What?"

She sighed. "Why are you so curt?"

A ripple of annoyance stirred his blood. "Adeline."

"Yes, Edmond?"

"Go to sleep, we have several more hours of traveling tomorrow."

He smiled in the dark when her breath huffed in what appeared to be irritation.

"You are the most maddening man."

"You have no notion of my character." Though he did not think she referred to talk of him being *the mad duke*.

"No, I don't," she mused softly, her voice sweet and sensual. "But I would very much like to. Are you not at all curious about me?"

He scowled. "No."

A soft hurt gasp sounded and regret stirred. He might be disinterested, and it was quite well for him to say so…except it truly wasn't. She was his duchess for better or worse. He belatedly realized though they had no prior attachment, she must have had some expectations of him.

Hell…

It seemed he'd not thought through beyond the need to provide a mother for his children. He had nothing to give Adeline, not even the wedding night she seemed to be anticipating with such acute nervousness. He would wait until they were at Rosette Park before he informed her she would not have to dread his attentions, for he would never allow them intimacy.

Chapter Eleven

After traveling for what felt like a lifetime, the elegant and well-sprung carriage pulled into the forecourt of Rosette Park a few minutes after noon the following day. Adel heaved a sigh of relief.

The door was opened by a pair of footmen, who assisted her down. Adel almost stumbled at the splendor of Rosette Park. The estate grounds were glorious. This was not a manor, but a castle with a sweeping arched entrance, and it was situated on one of the most splendid lakes she had ever seen. But it was the rolling lawns which seemed to spread for miles which held her attention. In the far distance she could see a few children running, but they were too far away for her to hear their enjoyment. An avenue of beech trees lined the long driveway, and in the far distance behind the lake the sunlight dappled through the thick leaves.

How glorious…

And she was its mistress.

She moved closer and realized her first impression that it was a castle was incorrect although the mansion boasted several crenellations and a number of decorative towers. The house clearly was built in the last few generations, but felt heroic in the beautiful setting. Formal gardens surrounded a classical fountain in which sea nymphs frolicked around a benevolent Neptune. Behind the house more gardens could be seen and sweeping lawns leading down to the picturesque lake. Within the lake were a number of small islands which were bedecked with weeping willows and abundant greenery. Swans and other water birds swam in the waters followed by their offspring.

There was a gentle clearing of a throat, and she faced the line of servants who were dressed smartly and waiting on her. At that moment the sound of thundering hooves alerted her to the fact her husband had caught up with them. Though it had drizzled rain for a few hours, he had elected to ride his massive black stallion, instead of being seated in the carriage with her. It had slightly stung, but she spent the arduous journey reflecting on how to be successful in her new station. It had made no sense lamenting on what could have been, and she so badly wanted to eventually be happy with Edmond. Marriage was so...*permanent*. It perplexed Adel that many in society were simply content with a lukewarm attachment with their spouses. Not that she was overly romantic, but she wanted—no, needed—warmth and passion in her marriage, much like her mother had experienced with Papa.

Edmond swept inside the forecourt, and without waiting for the horse to fully stop, launched himself from its back. With a gasp she stepped forward. Was he mad? He could have broken his neck.

He tugged off his black hat and thrust fingers roughly through his hair, which was damp from the scattering of raindrops. After a few slaps to his thigh muscles with the hat, he fairly prowled towards her. A very large and powerful dog raced from beside the lake to greet Edmond who sank to his knees to tousle the dog's head in greeting. *Good heavens.* The dog seemed like a mix between a wolfhound, a Mastiff…and, well, the very devil himself. She had never see a dog so large, but his presence certainly wrought miracles. The duke was *smiling.* Edmond absently stroked its ears, and she swore the fearsome creature actually purred.

Edmond stood and came over.

"Adeline," the duke greeted, his gray eyes hooded.

She dipped into a shallow curtsy. "Edmond."

"This is Maximus, my companion."

Adeline was transfixed.

She stepped close and touched the dog's nose lightly. "Hello, Maximus, I am quite delighted to meet you."

He woofed at his name and his head lolled to the side.

A fleeting smile touched Edmond's lips. He held his hand out to her, and she gratefully clasped his arm. They strolled over to the line of servants and the housekeeper stepped forward, smiles wreathing her kind face. If Adel was not mistaken actual tears were glistening in her warm brown eyes.

"Your Graces," she said as she dropped into a deep curtsy.

"May I present my wife, Adeline, the Duchess of Wolverton," he intoned with his voice fairly bland.

What had she expected? Pride at presenting his new wife? He'd only married her because she had forced his hand. He had initially wanted the much more ravishing and well connected Lady Evelyn.

The housekeeper, Mrs. Fields was a portly, attractive woman. She took over the introductions of the staff and the names blurred together. After they had all curtsied or bowed to her and their lord, Edmond turned to the figures in the distance.

"Come," he said.

He started walking toward the lawns, and Adel stepped with him trying to bury her ire at his highhandedness. "Are you asking me to accompany you on a stroll, Your Grace?"

His lips twitched. "Would you do me the honor of walking with me? I would have you meet my daughters."

Oh. "I would very much like that." She was to meet Lady Rosa and Lady Sarah now. Raw nerves shimmered in Adel's stomach. What if they hated her as she'd hated her father's new wife? Should she insist on freshening first? They had departed the last inn hours ago, and she was a little crumpled. When she'd risen this morning, Adel had ensured she attired herself smartly. She had on a walking dress of pale blue with black stripes, a dark blue pelisse and a plumed bonnet. They strolled in silence along the pathway, and with each step her nervousness grew. "Do Lady Sarah and Rosa know you have married?"

"No."

Adel jerked to a halt, and he glanced down.

"I…I…cannot credit you would not have alerted them."

"I would not have told my children such news in a letter."

Adel recalled how stunned and distressed she had been when her father had suddenly announced he was engaged. Her throat tightened. "Did… Has their mother been long gone?"

The muscle underneath the tip of her fingers tensed and a chill blasted from the duke.

"I only asked because my father presented Lady Margaret to me as his intended only thirteen months after Mamma died. It was very hard for me to love her. In fact, I fairly resented him such happiness, while I was still mourning for my mother. I would hate for your daughters to endure such a similar heartache."

She had not forgotten Edmond had said no questions about his deceased wife, but surely he would understand why she would inquire in this instance.

"It has been almost three years."

Oh. "I see." She gave him a tremulous smile. "Well, let's proceed."

They continued on, the wind doing its best to tug the bonnet from her head. With one hand clasped on her head to keep the dratted thing in place, and the other holding onto the duke, they made their way across the expanse of lawn. One of the young girls glimpsed them, and Adel smiled at the sheer joy that suffused her face. Adel expected her to race across the lawn, but she waited with hardly a fidget, the joy on her face replaced with cautious happiness.

The laughter and the shrieks died down as they approached, and two very delightful girls separated from the others and stepped forward. Based on their heights, Adel could guess who Rosa was, and who Sarah was. Both girls had fiery red hair and sweetly rounded cheeks. Their eyes were a replica of their father's—even the cool reserve in their hidden depths was similar in manner.

The taller girl stepped forward as they stopped and curtseyed. "Father, welcome back," she said with a smile.

Edmond released Adel's arm and crouched. She found it odd, he did not hug his children nor did they seem inclined to do so. "Lady Rosa, happy birthday."

A charming smile wreathed her face. *Oh, she is a beauty.*

"Thank you, Father."

Curious eyes shifted to Adel, but Rosa asked no questions.

Edmond tugged his other daughter close, and then he rose, and prodded them forward. He stood behind them and rested a hand on each of their shoulders.

"Girls, I would like you to meet Adeline, my new duchess of Wolverton."

Rosa gasped, her eyes widening. "You're married, Father?"

"I am."

Rosa dipped into an elegant curtsy, her manners already

ladylike. "Your Grace," she said, her voice a mere whisper.

"Hello," Lady Sarah said with a shy, but very sweet smile. "Are you to be my new mother?"

Adel's heart was pounding like a hammer in her chest. She sank to her knees in the grass, uncaring that the stains would ruin one of her better gowns. "Hello, Lady Rosa, Lady Sarah, I am delighted to make your acquaintances." With a smile at Sarah, Adel continued, "If it is your wish, I would love to be your friend and new mother. However I am quite happy to be your friend until you say otherwise."

"It is our wish," Rosa said, wariness evident in her posture.

Adel frowned and Lady Rosa expounded. "It is our wish for you be our new mother. I think that is why father married you. He asked me what I would want for my birthday…and I said a mother." Awe was evident in her voice, and when she looked up at her father, tears were glistening on her lashes.

"Thank you, Father."

Adel swallowed. She was a birthday gift. A very foolish and convenient one. The duke really had not cared about her reputation; he'd just needed an urgent wife. Any lady would have certainly worked for him, because this icy distance that fairly simmered, warning her to keep away, this cool regard was not because of her being passably pretty, with no money or connection… This was simply *him*, and whatever thoughts that went on behind those beautiful but distressingly empty eyes.

• • •

Two hours later, Adel climbed the stairs behind the housekeeper. Mrs. Fields' voice rattled with animation, but Adel felt too brittle to pay her any mind. Lady Rosa had been having a tea party with their neighbor the Earl of Sheffield's three daughters and their governess. The duke had taken his seat on the blanket and Adel had joined. Edmond had sat in a chilling aloof silence, content to watch his girls play and… well, he watched *her*. It was awkward and Adel had vacillated between tears and laughter. Rosa and Sarah were so tentative with her, touching her every so often, and then staring as if she were an exotic creature. That was how Adel had felt…like she had been on display. The dratted man had hardly said a word.

The girls were now preparing for supper, and Adel desperately wanted a bath and at least an hour of rest before she must face it again. The duke had actually called for another horse and ridden away without saying anything really. She tried not to let his distance crush her. They had only been married a day after all.

"With the short notice, Your Grace, this was the best we could do under the circumstances," Mrs. Fields said apologetically as they stopped.

Adel frowned when the housekeeper opened the door to an elegant and well-appointed room. The best she could do? The chamber was well-suited to a lady. The walls were decorated with wallpaper upon which trellises of leaves climbed over a straw-colored background. The furniture and draperies were in a pale green patterned with the same straw color. The room was far larger than the bedroom she had formerly dwelled in at home and it had its own dressing room decorated in the same paper. "This is wonderful, thank you."

Pleasure lit the woman eyes. "I will ask the duke what I am to do about the duchess's chambers when he gets in."

Adel froze. "These are not the duchess's rooms?"

"No, Your Grace."

Her heartbeat quickened. "Why am I not in the duchess's quarters?"

Mrs. Fields appeared flustered. "I received no orders to clean the chambers, Your Grace. The missive the duke sent only said to prepare a chamber."

"I am certain he meant the duchess' apartment, Mrs. Fields," Adel said kindly. "I would have you direct the maids to deposit my luggage there and call for a bath."

The housekeeper's wariness grew even more pronounced. "The rooms are not ready for you, Your Ladyship."

Mrs. Fields refused to meet Adel's eyes and sudden curiosity burned through her.

"Take me to the rooms."

With a firm nod and flattened lips, Mrs. Fields continued along the corridor. They turned left and walked a few paces down before they stopped at a door. A bunch of keys jangled, and Mrs. Fields twisted one in the ornate brass door and it swung opened.

She stepped back and allowed Adel to enter. She walked in and faltered. Everything in the chamber was covered in white sheets. Cobwebs draped from the ceilings and the dust was so much, the windows that covered half of the left wall seemed covered in cinder. Adel was unable to credit what she was seeing. "Good Heavens, when last was the duchess's chambers aired and cleaned?"

"Almost three years ago, Your Grace."

She turned incredulous eyes to Mrs. Fields. "Are you saying no one has entered the rooms since the death of the last duchess?"

"Yes, Your Grace."

Adel was at loss for words. "Are the duke's rooms connected to here?"

"Yes, Your Grace."

She frowned. Were they not to have normal marital relations? She was not sure how higher lords and ladies coexisted, but her mother and father's chambers had been connected, and it was even the same now with Papa and Lady Margaret. "I see."

"Get out."

The chilling command cracked through the room like a whip, causing Adel to jerk. She spun around and faced the door where Edmond hovered in the doorway behind Mrs. Fields. Not hovered, more like he stood frozen, the harsh lines of his face more pronounced, his eyes glittering with cold fury. Adel buried the trepidation stirring inside and gave the housekeeper an encouraging smile. The poor woman looked ready to collapse.

"You may go, Mrs. Fields."

She bobbed her head, gave them a quick curtsy, and hurried away. Adel calmly exited and gently closed the door. "Please do not be irritated with Mrs. Fields. I asked to see the duchess's chambers."

He stared, his gray eyes growing more distant by the second. He appeared so...intimidating was the word that came to mind, but she would not display any anxiety. They were married, for better or worse, and she was resolved to make their situation as happy as possible. "Forgive me for intruding, I was but startled when I learned I had not been put in the duchess's chambers. Mrs. Fields was unsure if she should have the rooms cleaned and aired."

Edmond smiled tightly. "These chambers are to remain closed. See that you remember."

The words stung quite harshly.

With a sharp nod, he spun and walked down the hall with clipped strides.

Chapter Twelve

After the earlier debacle Edmond disappeared. She had spent the rest of the day unpacking and shoring up her courage for dinner. The lady's maid she had been assigned, Meg, was appalled at Adel unpacking her trunks. She had chuckled. Living with her father, they only had one upstairs maid, and Lady Margaret had monopolized her time. Adel had learned to do much on her own, and she relished the small acts of independence. Simply placing her few dresses in the armoire was soothing, and had helped to quiet the jangle of nerves.

She made her way to the elegantly appointed dining hall to a wonderful supper of watercress soup, game pie, lamb cutlets, chicken Italienne, mushroom fritters, roast beef, baked pike, artichoke hearts followed by rose water flavored ice cream, jellies in a pretty shape, fruit compote, and Genoese cake.

Conversation with Edmond was stilted and her nerves pounded through her as she fretted about whether tonight he would consummate their vows. She had eaten as quickly as possible, then excused herself and hurried to her chamber.

Then she bathed in scented rose petal water and brushed her hair with hundreds of strokes, before bundling into one of her very old and frayed white cotton nightgowns.

Perched on the edge of the well-padded mattress, Adel bit into the soft of her lower lip, her anxiety mounting as she watched the door. She had sent a note with Meg to the duke after it occurred to her that he would not know where her chambers were. That had been over fifteen minutes past.

The minutes crept away and with a sigh she went over to the wide windows that took up an entire wall of her chamber. The stars and the moon bathed the land in an ethereal glow. The gardens were brilliantly landscaped into rolling lawns dotted with oak, elm, cypress and willow trees, a topiary garden, and even a gazebo which was covered by beautiful flowering vines. Adel had never seen a view more beautiful.

She would explore it tomorrow after properly spending some time with her new daughters. She frowned, biting deep into her bottom lip. She would have to tread with care. Lady Margaret had not been very welcoming when Adel met her for the first time. In fact her father's new wife had always taken on an air of mild annoyance whenever Adel was about. She felt nothing of the sort when she thought of speaking with Sarah and Rosa tomorrow, but they had seemed so reserved today.

There was a knock on the door and her heart leapt into her throat. She spun around, pulling the edges of the gown close. "Come in."

The handle twisted and in strolled the duke, a glass of amber liquid in his hand. He was still clothed in his evening clothes and raised a coolly mocking brow, holding up her note between his thumb and forefinger. "You summoned me, Adeline."

"I was not sure if I was to make my way to your chamber," she said tentatively.

There was something undeniably disturbing in his eyes. "For what purpose?"

"I may not know the full of it, Edmond, but I am certain my duties as your wife extend to me being with you in your chamber." She fought the blush climbing her cheeks, striving to appear self-assured.

His lips twisted slightly. "Ah...so you are ready to fulfill your marital duties? I had not thought you so aware of what that entails." His tone was dry, his expression inscrutable.

"I beg to differ. I have lived in the country most of my life. I dare say I have an idea," she said teasingly. Her smile faltered when he failed to respond. How was she to pierce his aloofness? Should she even be trying? "Are we to be at odds so soon?" she asked softly.

He stiffened and then scrubbed a hand across his face. "Forgive me, Adeline," he said, regret heavy in his tone. "I am being slightly boorish."

She arched a brow. "Only slightly?"

He smiled, and she rocked back on her heels. The man was simply too handsome for his own purpose.

"Being married...though it was a decision I made in earnest, I find I am plagued with more doubts than I expected."

Oh. That bit of honesty warmed her heart. "I think it is normal to feel doubt, not that I am an expert on marriage," she said with a small smile. "And our situation was highly unexpected."

"Hmmm," he murmured noncommittally, sipping his drink. But his eyes...they devoured her, from the top of her head to her toes in a slow heated sweep. What was he thinking?

Her heart seemed to flip over when his eyes finally collided with hers. The expression of raw need in his gaze both frightened and excited her. "Should I...should I go on the bed?" She didn't have much of an idea what should happen, but she knew enough that it must happen there underneath the covers. Adel had heard enough giggled whispers from the maids at her former home.

A disturbingly sensual smile curved his lips, yet his eyes remained guarded. "While there is distinct appeal in the notion, I believe you need time. There is no rush."

This Adel had not expected. "Thank you for being so considerate, but I assure you, time would only serve to fuel my anxiety."

"I had thought you would be pining over Mr. Atwood."

Adel gasped. Edmond was blunt to the point of being distressing. A gentleman would not so willingly hint his wife might be in love with another man. Would he? What was even more startling, she had not given Mr. Atwood a thought since she married Edmond. Her heart ached with the knowledge she would have wedded a man she apparently had little or no romantic feelings for. "Mr. Atwood is in the past."

Edmond downed his drink and moved farther into the room. He placed her note on a small side table and rested the glass on it. Then he sauntered over to her, his movements so graceful and masculine she was mesmerized. There was a startling surge of heat in her veins, and a flutter wormed its way through her heart. It was an unfamiliar sensation, but not an unpleasant one.

He skimmed his fingers over her cheek, and then dragged the pad of his thumb across her lips. "Is he?"

She swallowed. "Yes."

"A few days ago you were planning on marrying him. You were so certain of your affection you took radical steps to climb into his bed and into his life. Are you saying that you did not love your young Mr. Atwood?"

A soft pain sliced through her heart. She had assuredly been fond of James. The only man with whom she had laughed, bantered. They had even exchanged a few chaste kisses.

However she would admit she had been desperate to marry him because of how strident her papa had been in pressuring her to marry Lord Vale. Without her father's ambitions, she would have waited until she and James had formed a stronger bond. "I had affections for Mr. Atwood, and I respected him. They have not disappeared despite his inconstancy, but I am now attached to you."

Cynicism twisted Edmond's lips and she hated to see it there.

"I do not need time," she insisted. "I would prefer to get it over with." Her stepmother's only advice in relation to the martial bed had been *Do not brace against the pain or it will make it harder, and if your duke is the sensible sort it will prove to be stimulating.* The mysterious *it* once again. Adel would have preferred to have had the knowledge of what she should expect in the marriage bed rather than wait in anxiety. Though if what she had experienced in his arms was a precursor she was baffled as to how it, could ever be unpleasant.

A shadow seemed to cross his face, and dark eyes watched her. "Get some rest and in the morning I will inform you of the state of our marriage."

The state of their marriage? "I would have you inform me now."

"No."

"I will not be able to sleep a wink after such dire words. I will not hesitate to follow you to your chambers for answers."

An imperious brow arched, no doubt at her audacity.

"Our marriage will not be consummated."

Adel truly appreciated his restrain but it was not needed. "Thank you for thinking of giving me a reprieve." She winced. "I expressed that poorly. It is not necessary for us to wait until tomorrow, I am ready to—"

"I do not only speak of tonight."

Bewilderment filled Adel. She searched his face, seeking

understanding. His mien was cool and distant. "I do not understand," she said softly.

He crossed his forearms across his chest and leaned against the door. Something akin to regret gleamed in his eyes. "I had thought since you were in love with another man, you would welcome such news."

She flinched. "I am not in love with Mr. Atwood! If this is the reason you—"

"Nevertheless it is best we delay. We had no knowledge of each other a few days ago. It would not be remiss if we wait until we are better acquainted to pursue the more intimate aspects of marriage. My home, my wealth, and titles are yours, let that be enough for now."

She considered him. Was this the normal way of *ton* marriages? Suddenly she felt the burning need for her mother's guidance. *Oh, Mamma, how I wish you were here.* "I do believe waiting will create more distance between us," she said softly.

Adel should have been happy he was willing to wait, for she hardly knew this severe man standing before her. But instinctively she felt if she agreed to such a separation, the fight for his heart would be much greater, and the divide would be impossible to close. She jolted. *The fight for his heart?* When had she even thought it likely she wanted this cold infuriating man to hold affections for her? Certainly a happy marriage could be achieved without any attachments?

No…it cannot. Even with her limited understanding of what a marriage should entail, without love they would be like the many lords and ladies she had observed throughout the seasons. Most attachments were cold and impersonal, with both man and woman seeking other lovers to soothe the heartache of loneliness. She couldn't endure such a union.

"I do not desire anything deeper from this union," he said flatly, piercing the disquieting silence that had formed.

Pained awareness dawned. "You are not granting me time to acclimatize myself to you…are you?"

"No."

"Are you saying there is a possibility we may never consummate our vows, even if years pass?"

"Yes."

A startled laugh burst from her. "Surely that is the most ludicrous notion I've ever heard. Why?"

He became even more guarded.

"I may be ignorant of the acts of the marriage bed, but even I know that without consummation you cannot gain an heir." And according to her stepmother and the *ton*, every titled man was in need of an heir.

"I have an heir."

Her eyes widened. "I beg your pardon?"

"I did not misspoke, Duchess."

"An heir?"

"Yes, my mother thoughtfully provided my father with a spare before he died. My brother Jackson is currently away in the diplomatic corps, but he is the heir presumptive, and I am quite content for it to remain so."

She froze, and the shock gave way under the tide of rage that filled her. "And did you hold this knowledge before wedding me?"

A shadow shifted over his face. "Yes."

"And it never occurred to you I would desire children of my own?" she said, her throat tightening with anger.

"I did not single you out for my attention, *you* climbed into my bed. You would have been ruined and disgraced if I'd walked away."

"The truth of that situation does not make your assertions now any less despicable. Has it not occurred to you I would have preferred a life disgraced in the country with Mr. Atwood or someone else, rather than be a duchess who will be denied the chance of...of...motherhood?" she growled, her heart pounding. She could not believe they were having a raging argument in such little time. This did not bode well for their marriage, and she hated the tears thickening her throat.

"No man would have had you, once society was through," he said coldly. "I daresay the turn I did you by marrying you is unmatched."

She gasped. "You are a heartless brute."

"It is better that I am heartless, than that I am held responsible for your death," he snapped, finally showing some passion.

Her death?

Edmond pushed from the door and raked fingers through his hair with force. He grabbed the doorknob.

"Don't you dare walk away from me!"

"We will finish this discussion in the morning when we are calmer," he said and opened the door.

"I beg your pardon; do you believe I will be able sleep after what you just said?"

"I assure you I will be thoroughly rested." As if to say he was not concerned about her state of rest.

Then the wretched, infuriating man walked away.

She growled under her breath and rushed after him, the voluminous nightgown swirling around her ankles. "You have been nothing to me but boorish and...and uncivil. You seem quite content that I not speak to you, and now we are not to form any intimate attachment. Surely such a state of matrimony cannot be agreeable to anyone."

His long strides took him to his chamber in short order, and she hurried to keep up.

He wrenched opened his door and seemly hesitated. "Oomph," slipped from her as she collided into his back.

They tumbled and he twisted so his back slammed into the jamb of the door, protecting her. Acting on instinct she slipped her hands around his neck and gripped him tightly. Adel could feel the thud of his heart against her body.

She tilted her face to his. "Do not walk away, Edmond."

Eyes filled with raging emotions glared at Adel.

"Tell me what you meant about me dying."

His muscles tensed, and she tightened her hands at his nape.

"My wife died in childbirth."

Adel bit into her bottom lip, hard enough to draw blood. "I am deeply sorry," she said hoarsely.

His mien grew even colder. "She was much more voluptuous than you but even so she forfeited her life."

The mad duke killed his wife. She remembered the vile whisper. How could society blame him? She wanted to ask, but the question lodged in her throat. "It does not stand to reason I would suffer the same fate, if that is your concern," Adel whispered.

He flinched. Then he closed his eyes, and tipped back his head to rest against the wall baring the corded column of his throat. The move forced her to lift herself more on her toes so that she could maintain her hold on his neck. What was he thinking?

"Edmond, I—"

His eyes snapped open and the raw torment in his gaze strangled her words. Her heart pounded ferociously, and it was as if his will pressed in on her, encouraging her to release him. Slowly, she slid her hands from around his neck and fisted them to her sides.

His dark eyes never left hers and the distress in them swelled, and spilled forth crashing over her senses. Her limbs trembled. It was as if she could feel his raging pain. *Impossible.*

Later, she would never be able to say what had possessed her. It could have been the need to wipe the grief from his eyes, or to just offer comfort, or maybe she just wanted to kiss him. Either way Adel reached up and pressed her lips to his.

The fleeting touch of his lips to hers was devastating. Adel stood transfixed for a timeless instant. His taste, his scent… Shock exploded through her. She was no longer even slightly soused, so her reaction was beyond alarming. The intensity was nerve-wracking. *Good Lord*. Then he shifted, cradling her cheeks into his large palms, and his lips parted. His touch was sinfully alluring.

He used one of his thumbs to part her lips. Then Edmond took her lips in a kiss that was at once domineering and tender, with a seductive ruthlessness. Adel helplessly responded. She gasped, and he swallowed it as she sagged against him. His mouth settled more possessively over hers, his tongue urging her lips to part wider to his wonderful assault. On a moan she surrendered and he plundered.

Glorious heavens.

Pleasure dark and stormy filled her veins. His hands stroked her jaw, over to her collarbone, down to the underside of her breast and around to her back and down to her backside, which he gripped tightly in his large hands…and squeezed. His touch wasn't considerate of her innocence, and Adel shivered in his embrace.

He drew her closer, and she gasped into his mouth at the hard length that pressed in through his trousers and branded her stomach.

"Wrap your legs around my waist," he whispered harshly, pulling his lips from hers.

She tried to comply, but the length of the nightgown tangled her legs. With a muttered curse, he swung her into his arms, his rapid stride taking them over to the massive bed in the center of his chamber. What was happening? Was he forgoing all he'd just said?

Before she could foolishly question him, he took her lips once more, tumbling with her to the massive but lush bed, careful to keep his weight on his forearms.

Oh! Her heart jerked in trepidation and excitement. The drugging kisses he pressed to her mouth were scrambling her brain. Who knew kisses could feel this wonderful? She fisted her fingers through the thick strands of his hair, and melded her mouth to his. Their teeth clinked, and he pulled from her with a rough pained chuckle.

"Easy," he whispered, dragging his lips roughly down her cheek, then neck, where he nibbled. The firestorm of sensations that peaked in the low of her stomach were surely unnatural, wanton, and gloriously unladylike.

She inhaled, trying to control the chaotic hunger that had erupted in her body, and the nerves determined to rear their head.

There was restrained power in the touch that gripped her nightgown and pushed it to her waist. His thumb dragged against the inside of her thighs creating little sparks of sensations that shot directly to the throbbing flesh between her legs.

Adel breathed raggedly. Edmond kept his face buried in her neck, his body tight with tension. What was he thinking?

The confusion bubbling inside her was enough to have tears prickling behind her lids. She parted her lips to speak and then he shifted, cupping the most intimate part of her. The breath puffed from her mouth in a painful burst and then she stilled.

It took her a few seconds to realize they were both frozen, and the furious pounding against her breastbone was not only her heart.

His hand moved and one finger slid through her alarming wetness.

He groaned, and she swallowed. Then with a virulent curse, he leapt from her. "Forgive my lapse in control, it will not happen again." Then he turned to stride from the room.

Disappointment sliced through her. "Is this not your chamber?"

He halted but did not turn around. "You can sleep here for tonight or return to your chambers. The choice is yours."

Heat stained her cheeks. He was so dismissive. Then he exited.

Adel scrambled from the bed, placing her foot onto thick soft carpeting as she stood in the center of the room, shaking. The pleasant masculine décor of the room with rich colors and dark wood furniture did nothing to ease her stormy emotions. With a great effort she calmed the racing of her heart. She inhaled, and his scent rushed into her lungs. Unable to stay any longer she hurried to the door, opened it, and rushed down the corridor to her chamber. She crawled onto the bed and buried herself in the mound of pillows.

What had just happened? With a frustrated sigh, she rolled on her back and stared at the canopy above her. She felt empty and bereft. Was this how her marriage would be? Should she accept the duke's edicts, or wait to see how their lives unfolded? It would be useless for her to fervently hope he might come to love her, and while she would not fight for a love he was not willing to give her, she would not remain childless.

She needed to understand his demons, but she knew the maddening man would not allow her close. But…he'd just responded to her with such raw force, surely that must mean he desired her. Should she try and make him fall in love with her as surely as she knew, she would eventually love him? Why would she even want to waste her time, loving such a vexing man?

His empty eyes.

No one should look so lonely and bereft.

She crushed the thoughts with willpower she never knew she possessed and drew the coverlet to her chin, before closing her eyes. Eventually she would know what to do, and prayed she would not muck it up. She was now a mother…a wife, and there was no turning back the hands of time.

In this, she would not fail. Adel had failed in her season, and she had certainly failed to be an exemplary daughter with her conduct, but she was determined to succeed as a mother…and as Edmond's wife and duchess. She lay on the bed and watched the embers dying on the hearth until she finally succumbed to sleep.

Chapter Thirteen

It was most assuredly not the scotch, but the woman herself.
Edmond had held on to the belief that without his drinking
the night he visited Lord Gladstone, Adel climbing into his
bed would not have had such an effect. It was not pleasant
learning he was very wrong. It was not only love he was
uninterested in...he wanted distance from *this* brutal punch
of pleasure to his system from a simple whiff of her scent and
taste.

He was a damned fool, God help him, for he had been
unable to stop the madness of tasting her. When last had he
felt such pleasure from a mere kiss? The front of his breeches
tightened embarrassingly and instead of withdrawing, the
vexing and bewitching lady had stretched up on her toes, lifted
her hands, and wrapped them around his neck, her fingers
combing through his hair. Her touch had been exploratory,
definitely innocent, and it had allowed him to pull back from
her when everything in him clamored to devour, to slake a
need that had been too long denied.

Thank Christ. A tiny sound of protest had caught in her

throat as he withdrew and disappointment had glowed in her eyes. The lady was purported to be in love with another man. Why would she been yearning for his kisses, when her heart was engaged elsewhere?

But what was it about Adeline that made him loose the tether on his control? Edmond had almost taken her, and without an ounce of the tender consideration he had bestowed on his first wife on their wedding night. Though he'd only been eighteen when he had married Maryann, he'd had a few lovers. She had been the shy blushing virgin, and it had taken him almost an hour before he'd been able to convince her to shed her nightclothes. Then when he made love with her, it had been under the banner of darkness, communicating with touches, and soothing murmurs. They had gone so slow, sweat had beaded his brow and his arms had trembled from holding back.

It had been like that for the first few weeks, before she lost her shyness. A wry smile twisted Edmond's lips. When he had received Adel's summons, he'd only intended to put her at ease, and provide the relief he thought she would crave at the knowledge he would not expect marital relations when she still had love for another. Instead he'd been consumed with the need to pound his lust inside of her because of the visceral desire she elicited.

Bloody everlasting hell.

He wrenched opened the library door and slammed it with much more force than he'd anticipated. How it had all shot to hell so quickly, his muddled brain still had to figure out. Worse, not once had the dangers of bedding her entered his thoughts the second she had tumbled into him. What if he'd lost control, took her, and she'd fallen pregnant?

He swallowed down the sick feeling rising inside, stalked to the side mantle, and poured brandy into a glass. With three swallows he consumed the fiery drink. It did the job. The queasy feeling had been replaced with the harsh burn of the liquor.

Edmond strolled over to a wing-backed chair by the fire and sank into the chair's plush depths. He needed to analyze their situation and find a way to resolve the raw emotions bubbling in his gut. Since his loss of control and his sense of self when Maryann died, he'd prided himself on his cool emotional state that he had worked with a ruthless will to attain.

He was now married. *Fact.*

He had no need for another child. *Fact.*

His new wife seemed to desire marital relations. *A distressing fact.*

And he could not get the taste and feel of her out of his head. *A disturbing fact.*

He had barely touched her and she had been so wet. *An enticing fact.*

Edmond scrubbed a hand over his face and laughed ruefully. He should have left the chit to her ruin and disgrace and wed lady Evelyn. He was certain *that* lady would have been thrilled with the knowledge she would not have to burden herself to fulfill any marital duties. But Lady Adel actually wanted him. Her hot and eager responses had almost bewitched him. His cock stirred, and he groaned.

A knock sounded on the door and he glanced at the clock. It was after midnight. "Yes?"

The door opened and in strolled his mother, Lady Harriet Rochester, the dowager duchess. She was dressed in the height of fashion in a Prussian blue silk gown with pale blue long satin gloves, with a matching turban on her head. The modest bodice trimmed with white silk roses and silver embroidery. A row of silver embroidery continued down the front of the dress and around the hem, which also had small clusters of white silk roses at regular intervals around the edges.

At forty-eight, his mother was still a ravishing woman with generous charms, and many men of the *ton* still pursued her in earnest. Diamonds dripped from her ears and throat, and her gray eyes, so much like his, found him unerringly in the darkened room.

"You are home early, madam."

"I was forced to depart Lady Walcott's soiree early after hearing the most alarming gossip," she said, walking into the room.

Hell. She'd not received his note. "There is no doubt you are eager to tell me, and I, of course, must listen."

She glared at him. "The ballroom was rife with talk that you visited Wiltshire and married your mistress," his mother said with cool aplomb.

"You can rest assured that is a rumor."

She wilted with visible relief.

"I did not marry my mistress. In fact, I've never had a mistress."

Her spine snapped straight. "But you did *marry*?"

Her shocked tone settled into the room, and the alarm in it actually caused him to smile.

"You are smiling," she said faintly, walking to sit on the sofa facing him. "I am not sure if that portends good fortune or something ominous." Yet she looked hopeful and it twisted his heart to see it.

"I did marry Miss Adeline, Sir Archibald Hayes's daughter. They are from Somerset."

At first joy cascaded over his mother's face, but it was quickly replaced by a frown. "Sir Archibald…Sir Archibald," she muttered. "I do not believe I am familiar with the Hayes from Somerset."

"I would think not, they do not move in your elevated circles."

"Then the girl is without connections?"

He merely grunted.

"What happened to the list I created? Those young ladies were highly agreeable in wealth and connections. I cannot fathom why you would not have made any one of them your duchess, but this unknown…miss."

He drummed his fingers on the desk. "The situation was of such, it was best I married Adeline with haste."

"Good heavens." Lady Harriet's hand fluttered to her throat. "So the ghastly rumor of a compromising situation has merit? I never thought you had it in you, Edmond, after…" she glanced away into the fireplace.

After Maryann.

It was curious that the bracing pain he would normally feel when his mother had slipped and mentioned his departed wife was absent. "You can say her name, Mother."

She gasped, and he understood. He'd not allowed any discourse in relation to Maryann since her funeral.

"Tell me about this young miss," she finally said with a birdlike look of enquiry.

He surged to his feet and walked to the windows, tugging the curtains open, they overlooked the lake. The moonlight was reflected on the water in the ripples of a light breeze. The lights that remained still burning in the house sparkled in the surface of the water as an occasional trout surfaced to eat some nocturnal insect. "There is not much to tell. We just met."

"Then at least tell me how you came to be married."

"I visited Lord Gladstone to complete settlement negotiations for Lady Evelyn. She was averse to marrying me and arranged for her friend to enter my room."

"And this Miss Adeline went along with such an outrageous plan?"

Sudden amusement curled through him at their antics. "Adeline thought she was climbing into another man's bed."

"Good Heavens," his mother said faintly. "I cannot credit such assertions. And you took *her*, to be your wife?"

"She would have been ruined otherwise, and I was in need of a wife," he said blandly.

His mother was silent for the longest time, and he was content to simply stand with his hands on the window frame, watching the glow of the moonlight shimmering over the lake and listening to the crackling in the fireplace. It was startling to realize he now felt calmness inside…one that had been missing for months.

"I have known you to be honorable and have good sense, Edmond, but marrying a young miss with such little acquaintance and nothing to recommend her, I simply cannot credit it."

"According to Lady Gladstone, Miss Adeline is an extraordinary young lady in temper, intellect, and manners, at least until she entered my room," he said wryly.

"And what is your opinion of Miss Adeline after she acted with such…wanton impropriety?"

"I think she is a woman to be admired."

He did not turn at his mother's soft gasp. Instead he analyzed his assessment. "She is not a mincing miss. She has courage and a good deal of audacity. Even with the threat of ruination hanging over her head like a sharpened sword, she resisted marrying me. My title and wealth held no appeal for her, and that more than anything showed me her character." Edmond thought of the fire in Adel's eyes earlier, the determination and fury that had flushed her cheeks transforming her from lovely to bewitching. "She is beautiful, bold, and not without charm. Her head barely reaches my chin, and her hair is raven, its thickness and beauty I have never seen, and her eyes…they are honest and exquisite."

He thought of her interaction with his children, how she had strived to make them happy and at ease, despite her own turbulence and anxiety. "She is kind and thoughtful, fearless where she should be wary…and I can see her core of strength. Even if I had not married her, she would not have crumpled underneath society's disdain."

And he had hurt her with his thoughtlessness. A curiosity to know her filled his veins, yet he had no notion how to connect with her. He was not even sure he wanted to, despite the manner in which she tugged at him. How long could he truly avoid her for?

Edmond had done a good job on the ride from Wiltshire to Hampshire, making no effort to ride with her in the carriage. After introducing her to his daughters, he had been relieved when Rosa's tea party dispersed. He had been filled with a vision of taking Adeline to his bed. He had ridden away, desperate to cool the ardor he would not act upon. Perhaps it was better to be in her presence and render himself immune to her sensuality, instead of staying away where whenever he glimpsed her, it would be like drowning in desire and desperation for her touches and kisses.

His mother said nothing. He turned and faced her. Wonderment had settled on her features, and if he was not mistaken, her cheeks were damp with tears. With only the light from the fireplace illuminating the library, it was hard for him to tell.

"She sounds lovely," she finally said. "I am quiet eager to introduce her to our society."

"I am sure she will be happy for your patronage, not that she needs it, but she believes she lacks social polish."

"Well I daresay she is correct, being the daughter of a baronet is a far cry from being a duchess."

He said nothing to that assessment.

"Do you think her a young lady you might come to love?"

"Is there something in the air I am not aware of?"

His mother arched a brow. "Your new duchess has already

spoken of love to you?" Shock and something suspiciously like amusement colored her tone. "I know you are adverse to loss, but I urge you to not be too cold with her. This can be an opportunity for you to be happy again."

Would she ever stop her meddling ways? She'd had a list in her writing desk of women he could possibly marry before he had even asked. "I am content."

"No, Edmond, you are simply existing. They're quite different, I assure you. Your father died eighteen years ago, and sadly I only existed for you, now I am slowly awakening, and the difference is inescapable."

"Have you met someone?" he asked, beyond curious as to who would have captured her fancy, after the ruthless way she had guarded her heart after his father's death. He and his mother had more in common than she realized.

"I will arrange for the dowager house to be opened and staffed, and I will retire there by the end of the month." With that she rose. "Good night, Edmond."

"Good night, Mother."

The soft snick of the latch indicated her exit, and Edmond turned his mind to his duchess. He had been harsh when he ordered her to never visit the chambers that by right belonged to her. But when he had spied her there, his reaction had been instinctive and without much thought. Since Maryann's death he'd not been able to visit the chamber too often. Each instance in which he had crossed the threshold the intolerable memory of too much blood, its metallic scent and the taste, would fill every crevice of his being. Her wail that it had been his desire for an heir, why her life had been jeopardized always haunted him.

It was time to have the room gutted and reorganized for his new duchess.

His heart jolted. Despite the fact he did not enjoy his too visceral reaction to her, he had to make strides to welcome

Adel more thoroughly into his life. It was not as if he could damn well ignore her for the duration of their marriage, where if life was indeed favorable to them, they would have a union of at least another forty years or more.

He chuckled ruefully. Never had he imagined in as little as a few days of meeting her, he would be thinking of the future. Life had been so bleak for such a long time, and he had been content to reside in the mire of grief. The needs of his children had ripped him from that endless cycle, and now it seemed his new wife was awakening another part of his soul.

He wasn't sure if he should be alarmed...or simply embrace the curious fascination unfurling in his heart.

. . .

Adel stirred, kicking off the coverlet that had tangled between her legs. The memory of the night rushed through her, and she winced. How would she face the duke? She groaned, despising the flutter working its way in her heart. She had so many questions and doubts; it was a miracle she had succumbed to sleep so quickly after he'd departed. How would she even go about facing his wall of reserve? She'd not expected this at all. Not that she'd had many expectations when she came to think of it. Being a duchess had never been in her realm of aspirations.

There was a soft knock on the door.

"Yes?" she asked a bit too hopefully.

The door opened and a servant bustled in, bobbing a quick curtsy. If Adel's memory served her correctly, this was Prudence.

"Good morning, Your Grace. Will you be wanting a bath and a breakfast tray?"

A quick glance at the clock on the mantel revealed that it was midmorning. Drat! She had never slept so late unless she had attended a ball the night before. It was tempting to hide in her room, and from Edmond, but she must learn to be in the presence of the wretched man. Last night had been a revelation.

"A bath would be wonderful, Prudence, but I will be going downstairs."

The maid's head bobbed as she disappeared into the adjoining bath chamber and the sound of running water echoed. Adel was pleased to note that Rosette Park had the most modern of plumbing, and no one was required to lug buckets of water up the winding stairs.

An hour later, dressed in a dark blue day gown with long sleeves, her hair caught in an elegant chignon, she was decidedly pleased with her appearance. There was another knock on the door and before she could respond, in came Edmond. She surged to her feet, moving away from the vanity to face him. His gaze caressed over her, and she felt the touch of his eyes on every dip and swell of her body like it was a physical touch. A blush heated her skin, and she tried her best to suppress how flustered she felt. Was he not aware of Prudence in the room to be staring at Adel with such shivering need?

Then he looked up, all traces of admiration dampened.

She strove not to appear disconcerted. "Yes, Your Grace?"

He arched a brow at her decidedly cool tone. "Have we reverted to being formal?"

Adel allowed a smile to touch her lips. "Not at all... Edmond."

He flicked an autocratic glance at the maid and she hurried from the room with her eyes carefully cast down.

"I made a hash of things last night, and I've come to apologize."

She blinked in slow surprise. "Thank you."

"I've ordered the duchess's chambers to be aired and

cleaned for you to take residence."

"I… Thank you, Edmond." She did not need to understand why he had been so angry earlier to appreciate what he was now doing. He had locked up those chambers for years. She wished she could glean what had prompted him to act. Did this mean he wanted more than a vague attachment?

"I give you leave to decorate them as you please, as the rooms are yours. I only ask you to give away every single piece of furniture."

Seeing his black scowl forming, she hurriedly thanked him, lest he thought she did not appreciate the effort he was making. "Certainly."

"A monthly allowance of three hundred guineas has also been set aside for you as pin money. If you need it to be increased, you should inform me. My mother is eagerly awaiting your presence in the drawing room. She has some notion of refitting your wardrobe to be on standards of that of a duchess of the realm. A few modistes have already been summoned. Please send all dressmaker's bills and those for decorating the house to me."

At her silence, the scowl that had been in retreat, came back full force. "Does that meet with your approval?"

"You are being very generous. I am at a loss as to what I will do with three hundred guineas monthly."

"It is a minuscule amount, Adeline."

Oh. She fought the blush. Her allowance from Papa had been a sovereign here and there, and Lady Margaret had thought he was overly generous.

Without much thought to her actions, she strolled over to Edmond, tipped and pressed a soft kiss to his cheeks. "I thank you for being considerate."

He froze. "It is truly nothing," he said gruffly.

She stepped back. "I assure you it is *something*. Not many lords would be so accommodating or kind."

He arched an eyebrow skeptically. Without speaking he withdrew and with a shallow bow exited her chambers. The anxiety she had felt last night shifted, and soft hope stirred in her breast. It mattered not that he had not addressed consummating their vows. Surely, his approachable charm now must mean he was willing to try and make their unorthodox marriage work.

Chapter Fourteen

The meeting with Lady Harriet had gone splendidly, so much so that Adel was still in a daze. She had braced herself to be met with cold hauteur, because of her nonexistent connections and dowry, but the dowager duchess had been charming and welcoming.

Adel's anxiety had fled, as the local dressmaker from the village arrived and they spent almost two hours admiring materials and patterns. She had not balked at the multitude of gowns that were ordered—morning dresses, day and traveling dresses, several ball gowns, corsets, petticoats, and assorted unmentionables. She knew full well how unpolished she was, having spent most of her life in Somerset. With the little she had brought to her marriage, she wanted to appear to be a duchess Wolverton would be proud of, a mother their daughters and future children, if he ever unbent, would want to emulate.

She would be expected to throw lavish balls, dinner parties, house parties, and support a number of charities. From what she gleaned of the duke's politics he was a liberal, and with the call for reform in many sections of society, she would be expected to host political parties. Adel had already made a note to order subscriptions to the magazines his articles had appeared in, namely the *Cobbett's Political Register*, *The Gentleman's Magazine*, and *Transactions of the Royal Geographic Society*.

The dowager duchess had apologized for overwhelming her, and Adel stated firmly that she welcomed her direction within reason. Lady Harriet initially seemed shocked at Adel's forwardness, then the dowager duchess beamed in approval.

Relief filled her at the warm reception of Edmond's family so far, now if only the duke himself would follow suit. Adel made her way to the schoolroom, after knocking briefly she twisted the knob and opened the door. All heads swung her way, and Adel smiled. The room was large and cheery with the walls decorated with bright strange animals such as Indian elephants and tigers. There was a desk and several chairs, a large bookcase, a globe on a stand, blackboard, cupboard, and a rocking horse in one corner.

"Hello," she said softly.

The tutor frowned. "May I be of assistance, Your Grace?"

A desperate flutter wormed its way through her heart. She now had children and from the look on their faces they were uncertain of her. She had hoped their time together yesterday would have dispelled some of their anxiety. Adel was suddenly grateful for the atrocious way Lady Margaret had treated her. Otherwise Adel might not have known when to push and when to retreat. "I thought I would bid Lady Sarah and Rosa good afternoon."

The tutor scowled. He was a short rotund man who seemed like the serious sorts. "Very well, Your Grace," he muttered, clearly wishing she were elsewhere.

"Good afternoon, ladies," she said, walking farther into the room.

They rose from their desks and dipped into elegant curtsies. She was charmed.

"I thought we could have luncheon together today, if it is to your liking."

They peered at each other considerably and seemed to communicate before facing her.

"We would be obliged, Lady Adeline," Rosa said with a tentative smile.

Adel gave them approving smiles. "I will be taking a tour of the house with Mrs. Fields. I shall arrange it so I am in the smaller drawing room within the hour. Does that meet your approval, Lady Sarah and Rosa?"

"Yes!" they said together.

With a nod to the tutor, she exited, and then exhaled a sigh of relief. That had gone much better than she had hoped.

In short order, she met Mrs. Fields below stairs, and her tour of Rosette Park began. With two wings and over one hundred rooms, the hour spent with her housekeeper passed in an exhausted blur.

Adel had to cut the tour short, and hurried to the drawing room to meet with Sarah and Rosa. Walking through the immense foyer she spied a footman, removing a painting that looked a lot like her husband's daughters, only the lady painted had been older, and very beautiful.

"What are you doing?"

The footman paused. "I was ordered to remove the portrait, Your Grace, and mount it in the gallery."

Emotions tightened her throat. She still remembered the day she had entered her home and realized her mother's smiling picture had been removed, to be replaced by a cold and beautiful hauteur. Her mother had been placed in a lesser room, and it was Lady Margaret whose portrait would grace the fireplace in the entrance hall. Oh, how Adel resented her father and his new wife their happiness.

There was a sharp gasp behind Adel, and she did not need to turn to know it was one of the girls. There were several rustles and she deduced both girls were someplace behind her in the hall. "Yes, please take down the painting—"

An inarticulate cry slipped from one of the girls.

"And have the frame thoroughly cleaned and then remount it. I am sure whoever gave the order for it to be removed, meant just that."

The footman's eyes flicked behind her, and then back to her face. Adel was startled at the depth of relief that filled his eyes. But he still hesitated. "And where will your portrait hang, Your Grace?"

Her portrait? He must have spied the confusion on her face.

"I was told the painter Mr. Thomas Lawrence will be visiting later in the week to capture your likeness, Your Grace."

Oh. Even she had heard of Mr. Lawrence, from what Adel could recall he had painted the Queen and even the Prince Regent. And he was coming to paint *her*? *You are now a duchess*, she reminded herself sternly. Affixing a smile to her face, she spoke, "Then we will make room for them to hang side by side."

He nodded sharply and walked away with the painting. She composed herself and then faced the girls. "My goodness, you girls certainly did your sums in a quick fashion. I have not yet taken my morning stroll, would you care to join me?"

"Stroll?" Rosa asked with a frown.

Adel nodded. "I feel a need for fresh air and exercise before I start my day. I normally took very long walks back home in Somerset. Today is glorious, and we must take advantage."

Both girls smiled back cautiously.

"We have history lessons in a few minutes. We must

return to the schoolroom," Rosa said, yearning on her face.

"Well...I am sure Mr. Davenport would not mind if I took over this lesson."

Their faces brightened and right away she knew she made the right decision.

"Come along."

Her heart squeezed when they scampered to hold one of her hands each. As she near the door, their staid butler Mr. Jenkins held it open.

"Please inform Mrs. Fields we would like a picnic basket prepared quickly and delivered to us on the lawn," Adel said to him.

"Yes, Your Grace."

They exited and soon they were walking across the lawn, inhaling the cold crisp air into their lungs.

"We are never outside this early."

"Surely not." It was already past two in the afternoon. Adel would have taken her walk much earlier if she'd not overslept and then conferred with the dowager duchess.

"After breaking our fast, we will go to the school room," Rosa said. "We come outside after all our lessons, but we do not take *long* walks."

"Well we shall certainly fix that, won't we?"

Sarah's eyes rounded, and she nodded eagerly. It felt natural as they strolled along the vast expanse of the estate to simply chatter and laugh, as if she had been in their lives for weeks instead of a couple of days.

They came upon a pond with several stone benches and they sat.

"Our mamma is in heaven," Sarah suddenly whispered.

Adel smiled gently. "So is mine."

They gasped.

"Do you think they are friends?"

"Most certainly."

Sarah's faced scrunched. "Grandma said heaven is not real, but Mamma is certainly at peace," she parroted.

Two footmen arrived with blankets and a basket. They laid them nearby and set out the food, before melting away. Adel and the girls wasted no time tumbling onto the blankets.

"I do not think we can stay with you for luncheon...Mr. Davenport expects us back before three."

Adel winked. "I am sure Mr. Davenport will understand if I take today to learn my new daughters."

Sarah and Rosa fairly glowed, and it finally sank in how starved they had been for attention. How was this possible with the dowager duchess still living at Rosette Park?

After biting into an apple, Adel spoke, "Not everyone believes there is a heaven, but I am certain of it."

"Have you been there?" Rosa asked, munching on grapes.

"No, but just because I have not, does not mean it is nonexistent. I choose to believe my mamma is there...happy, laughing as we speak and making friends with your mamma."

Relief filled Sarah's expression and she nodded.

"What was your mamma like?" Rosa asked almost shyly. "My mamma loved to sing and play the pianoforte."

Adel stretched her legs out, and propped her weight on her elbows. "Those are such wonderful skills. My mother was very unconventional and when she sung, our dogs barked in protest."

The girls giggled and Adel grinned. "And Mamma sang every morning, with the most atrocious accent."

"Was she French?" Rosalie whispered.

Adel winked. "American."

The girls' eyes widened and they glanced at her consideringly.

"Mrs. Galloway told us the Americans are savages."

Adel frowned. "And pray tell who is Mrs. Galloway?"

"Our governess. Father fired her when she smacked

Sarah," Rosa said.

"We put frogs in her bed...and she smacked us," Sarah said giggling.

Adel was happy to see they were not scarred from the experience. "And why would you girls do such a ghastly thing?"

"We did not like her," they said together.

"She was very mean," Sarah said, her lower lip trembling.

"Come here, my darling," Adel said, then "*oomped*" at the force Sarah flung herself into her lap.

"Today is not a day for bad memories. We are going to eat, have some lessons, and have fun."

Rosa shifted closer to Adel's side, but did not hug her.

"Now the first lesson...let me tell you of the red Indians and...dare I say it? They are called savages by some."

They gasped and Adel settled into what would be a glorious afternoon.

Chapter Fifteen

Edmond strode toward the wide pond at the eastern side of Rosette Park, Maximus at his heels as usual. The night wrapped around Edmond in a cool caress, a welcome respite from the sweltering heat earlier. Dinner had passed in a blur, with minimal conversation between him and Adeline.

Amusement wafted through him. She had spent a good portion of it glaring at him, and it was not that he willingly ignored her, he was just too tempted to partake in all she had to offer. Her smiles, her wit and conversations, and the kisses she was hell bent on tempting him toward.

Vexing woman.

He'd been content to allow her and his mother to lead the evening, but had excused himself from joining them in the parlor for reading. That had been over an hour ago. He'd spent the time visiting his girls in their bedchamber and had read to them before kissing them goodnight.

Maximus's heavy body bounced him, and Edmond ran his hand through his thick coat. After a few minutes he reached the cypress tree overlooking the pond and sat on the stone bench, Maximus sprawling at his feet.

There was a rustle of sound and he twisted and spied his duchess walking down the grassy knoll from the opposite direction. He frowned, not sure if he hadn't somehow conjured her. What was she about? Edmond observed in fascination as she ran down the embankment and halted at the water's edge. She tipped her head to the night sky, and a smile curved her lips.

His skin prickled in response to her presence. He fleetingly wondered if he were to bed her and get the deed over with, would he be so aware of her. She started to strip. He slammed his eyes shut and opened once more and his duchess was still removing the pale high waist yellow gown she had worn to dinner. It pooled at her feet in a whispering sigh. A few seconds later she stood in her white chemise, the gentle blowing breeze conforming the material to her body. Rounded hips and buttock, high pointed breasts, and well-curved thighs were revealed in stark silhouette.

Christ.

She dipped a toe into the water, and with a soft yelp retreated. Then she grinned, backed up, and launched toward the water. Edmond watched in stunned disbelief as she jumped into the lake. Despite it being summer, the water would be cold, and larks like this he would expect of himself in his younger days, or from his brother Jackson, not from a young lady.

Seconds later she surfaced and a shout of laughter escaped her, throaty yet incredibly feminine. He stepped forward, and she spun in the water with sleek grace toward the sound, an expression of shock settling on her lovely features.

She peered into the dark toward the cypress tree. "Is someone there?"

A quiet wistfulness filled Edmond. He didn't want to frighten her away…he wanted her to stay. Instead of fighting the desire, he stepped closer. Then the dratted dog lurched forward and bounded to her.

Her eyes widened, but she swam toward the embankment and hauled herself from the pond. His cock jumped and hardened at the sight of such beguiling sensuality. The punch of desire made Edmond lightheaded, and he bloody stumbled. The wet chemise pasted to her form left little to his imagination. From where he stood, he fancied he could see the dark duskiness of her nipples that stabbed against the wet material, and the dark curls at the apex of her thighs. Her skin glowed like smooth ivory under the moonlight, her raven hair a rousing contrast.

Bloody hell, he couldn't tear his eyes from her.

Her elegant fingers stroked Maximus' fur, and his great brute of a dog, fairly melted in a puddle at her feet. Her laughter, husky and lyrical floated on their air. "You are just a big puppy, aren't you?" she crooned.

Edmond scowled. She was turning his dog into…into… He snapped his teeth together when the word eluded. But he did envy his damn dog its position.

"Where is your master?"

As if he understood, Maximus's head lolled toward Edmond's direction and a great *woof* rumbled from the beast. She lifted her head and peered toward the shadows of the cypress trees.

"Are you there, Edmond?"

"Yes," he said, after an awkward silence and moved from the shadows, sauntering toward her.

Her face lit with a smile of welcome. She shivered. "This is one of my more ill-advised ideas. It did not occur to me to bring a coat or blankets. I simply saw the brightness of the moon, and admired how the light shimmered on the surface of the pond and followed the impulse," she ended, with a charming chuckle.

He stepped forward, shrugged from his coat, and held it out to her.

She smiled uncertainly. "It will be soaked."

"It does not signify."

She was staring at him with a frown creasing her delicate brows. "I am happy to return inside. I believe I may have intruded on you here."

"Please do not leave on my account, the lake is large enough."

"Thank you." She took the proffered coat and hurriedly bundled herself into it.

"Oh, the warmth is wonderful." She dealt him a considering glance. "Are you chilled?"

"The air is tolerable."

Then silence. Her presence was strangely soothing, and he realized it was her quality of stillness. She was simply gazing about, appreciating the land under the banner of moonlight. He grimaced. Maryann would have been chattering nonstop, and he would have listened to tales of their neighbors and latest fashion with an indulgent ear.

"Maximus is a beautiful dog."

What was he to say to that? Edmond grunted noncommittally.

"Has he any siblings?"

Edmond blinked. "Who?"

"Maximus."

"No, I found him."

She stirred and faced him, looking dwarfed and ridiculously appealing in his coat. "Where?"

He sighed, she was determined to draw him into conversation, and he found he wanted…hell, he wanted to converse. Sometimes it was damned lonely to always be in his own head. "There was a storm a few years ago, and the bridge in the village collapsed with a few carriages. I was there helping to rescue people from the waters when I spied him drifting past on a fallen log. I took him home with me. He was a pup then."

She smiled. "It is hard to imagine such a great brute to be a pup. He is so wonderful I am amazed no one claimed him."

"He was starved and flea ridden. I doubted anyone would have come."

She stuffed her hand in the pocket of his coat, and with a frown withdrew his flask.

"Ah, liquid courage," she said wryly.

"It is whiskey."

She rolled the word on her tongue. "That night at the Gladstone's I was so nervous I drank three full glasses of sherry."

He remembered the sweet tartness on her tongue. Suddenly he was intensely curious about her. "What possessed you to act with such boldness?"

She gave him a considering glance, then a wide smile appeared on her lips. "I think someone is curious about me."

He blinked.

She unscrewed the flask and took a swallow, then spluttered and coughed until her eyes watered. "Damnation!"

Edmond couldn't help but smile at the loud unladylike curse. "No one told you to drink it."

"I thought it would have warmed me like the sherry." She grinned. "And it did."

Then she held out the flask to him as if they were drinking companions. The night was taking on a surreal feel. Yet he gripped it, and took a swallow, welcoming the warmth that settled in his stomach and spread through his veins.

"The Earl of Vale kissed me when I did not want him to," she said abruptly. "It was a soiree at his house in Hertfordshire, held by his sister. Lady Margaret insisted we all attend, and Lord Vale startled me in the gardens and tore my dress, and left bruises on my arms and lips."

The cold rage that stirred in Edmond's gut startled him. He shifted through everything he knew of the man, and made the resolve then that Vale would understand the error he'd made in touching his duchess. It hardly mattered Edmond had not known her then.

"He of course offered for me, and instead of Papa saying no, they thought his offer would restore my honor." She scoffed. "*My honor…*when he had been the one to act in such a frightful and disgusting manner. I knew I could never marry such a man, and Mr. Atwood had offered for me several times. I simply thought being in his room would force Papa to see sense. I never expected to end up in your bed," she said with a delighted smile.

Why she seemed so pleased he had no idea, for her folly took her from a man she had affections for.

He grunted noncommittally, but resolved in his heart that Lord Vale would be made to see the error of his debauched behavior toward Adeline. Edmond held the flask back to her and she pursed her lips.

"I already tasted it once, and I am sure you were appalled at my unladylike manner."

"I do not believe taking a few sips of whiskey to be only a gentleman pursuit."

Her mouth stretched and he was unwillingly fascinated by that crooked smile.

"How enlightened. I daresay I thought I would have been upbraided."

"I was never one to fall in line with society's expectation."

"Very unusual, I thought all dukes were staid."

"I don't give a damn what's proper," he clipped.

She grinned and grabbed the flask, taking another swig of the whiskey and then shuddering at its potency. "The stars are beautiful," she said on a sigh. "Do you know that many people simply never tilt their head back and marvel at the wonders of the universe? I've had three seasons and on some occasion manage to ask several ladies and gentlemen their opinion. They were very affronted I was not speaking on the latest *on-dit*. In fact, I think they found me odd."

Why was he so riveted?

"My father admired the heavens." Why had he offered that intimacy? He rarely spoke of his father, if ever. He normally protected his true sentiments and opinions behind a wall of reserve. A legacy his father had taught him and one Edmond was proud to say was natural to him. He only ever took a few people into his confidence, Westfall, his brother, and, on very rare occasion, his mother. Now he found himself unaccountably compelled to engage in conversation with his duchess, such intimate conversation, too.

"Truly?"

"Yes."

"He sounds like he was a very sensible man."

"I am sure he would have been glad you approve of him," he said with amused irritation.

"I have always wanted to learn the constellations."

His father had taught him, only months before he had died. Edmond's heart lurched. He had been about to thoughtlessly offer to help her.

"I've read Messier's Catalogue, but I am still at loss on how to identify certain constellations."

His father would have fallen in love with Edmond's new duchess for the mere fact she had read Messier's Catalogue.

"I have a telescope," he heard himself offering.

A delighted gasp escaped her lips. "That is wonderful, you must teach me. You do know what to look for?"

How had it gotten to this stage? An hour later, Edmond found himself bemusedly seated by his duchess on the stone bench, the flask of whiskey empty, her cheeks flushed becomingly, soft sighs slipping from her at intervals as they watched the stars through the damn telescope he had quickly retrieved from his study. He was clueless as to what was happening, but he did like her company. He'd hardly had any time recently to simply sit and converse with anyone. There had been no discourse with females save for his mother and employees, in the last three years. He'd avoided the season, despising the thought of inane and pointless chatter. Yet he and his duchess did not partake in any rousing parliamentary arguments or discuss estate matters. They were simply wonderful, ordinary, everyday musings.

What did he think of heaven?

How had his father died? Edmond had told her, and when she offered her sympathy she had glowed with sincerity.

Did he know all the constellations?

Her favorites were Cassiopeia, Taurus, and Sagittarius.

She loved pies.

She hated needlework and playing the pianoforte.

He was also exceedingly handsome, which was also quite unfair.

He was annoying for not consummating their vows.

And Mr. James Atwood had been audacious enough to send her several letters begging for forgiveness and to resume their friendship.

Startlingly Edmond felt a surge of icy anger at that last revelation. "And what did you say to your Mr. Atwood?"

She cleared her throat. "Well he is not *my* Mr. Atwood anymore. But I did reassure him we are friends." She glanced up and her beautiful eyes widened. "Upon my word, your countenance has taken on a decidedly diabolical cast."

Amusement rushed through Edmond at her undisguised alarm. "Has it?"

She tapped her chin with a finger. "Hmm, I think, Your Grace, you did not appreciate me saying I would remain friends with Mr. Atwood. But I assure you, it will be a careful friendship at best. Although I find it outrageous the manner in which he abandoned me, I cannot hold malice in my heart." Then her lips stretched. "I say, was it possible you were a tiny bit jealous?"

The notion so shocked him, he jerked. *Jealous?* "I do not feel such emotions."

She rolled her eyes, and he was nonplussed. Adeline was nothing like any other young lady he had met before. She was different, but in the most refreshing way.

"I do confess I am a bit tipsy," she said with a soft giggle and then exhaled on a gusty sigh. She turned her head to him, and in the depth of her eyes lurked laughter…and desire.

He gathered his scattered thoughts, assisted his giggling duchess to her feet, and guided her across the lawns and into the house. Maximus followed happily along, barking when she started singing. Edmond winced at the atrociously unmusical way she carried a tune, but strangely wanted her to continue. He was relieved to see the butler had not retired for the night, and when they crossed the threshold, Edmond swung Adeline into his arms and walked unhurriedly to the winding staircase. The butler's face was carefully stoic when she *oooohed* about how strong Edmond was, poking at his arms. Their butler choked when she asked if he was just as hard all over.

Christ.

She smiled up at him, and something inside his chest twisted.

He liked the woman, for God's sake.

A few minutes later they arrived at her chamber and he rang for her lady's maid, who threw him a startled glance before ushering her singing mistress into the dressing room. Edmond exited, his heart beating in an uneven rhythm, and he wondered what the hell had just happened?

Chapter Sixteen

A peal of laughter pierced the air, and Edmond lifted his head. He tried to convince himself to remain planted behind the oak desk in his study, but he was indelibly drawn to the sound of such joy. Rosette Park had been so silent and weary, as if it had been waiting for the right moment to come alive. It had slowly done so in the two weeks since he had brought home his new duchess. His daughters seemed more relaxed, fresh roses and flowers had appeared to decorate the house, dinners seemed more varied and frivolous, and even their servants seemed more content. His mother had taken a shine to Adel, and Lady Harriet had even gone as far as to congratulate him on making a fine match. Shaking his head in bemusement, he pushed himself up from the high wing-backed chair and strolled to stand in front of the window that gave him a clear view of his wife and children.

Since their late night meeting by the lake, Adel had slowly been fascinating Edmond, so much so that now he couldn't tear his gaze from her. Wisps of hair escaped her topknot and framed her lovely features. She ran with the children, her form lithe and graceful. When not beset with the society of the polite world, as she had been for the past several days, Adeline behaved without the decorum of a duchess, and his children seemed to be falling in love with her for it. Her shout of laughter rang joyously in the air, and against his inclination Edmond moved even closer to the windows.

What were they doing?

He blinked when his duchess darted around a thicket of bushes and fell on her stomach. In the grass. She came up on her knees and peeked through the thicket, and his gaze dropped to her rounded derriere. *Hell.* She was arched just right. He could see himself loving her in that exact position. He could taste her sighs, hear her whimpers, and feel her wetness… He bit back a groan.

She clasped one of her hands over her mouth as if to prevent laughter, and Edmond found himself holding his breath, hoping she would succeed in hiding her merriment, and not reveal her position.

He was a damn fool, standing there, watching her, waiting for a smile…a laugh…a glance in his direction, instead of tending to his untold responsibilities. A dukedom did not operate by itself despite what others believed, but his feet remained rooted. Staying away from her had been sheer hell. They dined every night, and had even played chess the evening before because of the rains, but then they had taken to their separate chambers. Every night she inspired dreams of tangled sweaty limbs, twisted sheets, and heated cries. But it was more than lust. He liked her, truly liked everything about her, her wit and vivacity, and her strength in the face of his reserve. A reserve he desperately wanted to shed, and had no notion where to start.

It did not escape him that they were not legally bound until he consummated their union. He'd almost entered her chambers last night. He'd thought to be perfunctory and quick, so that part was done. But he'd been unable to do it, remembering the flush of passion when he'd kissed her. She deserved more, yet the thought of such intimacy and where it could lead…

"Your Grace?"

He glanced at Mr. Dobson, his secretary. Edmond had forgotten the man was in the room, awaiting his dictation. A young and upcoming barrister, Edmond had hired Mr. Dobson for his political leanings and his keen intelligence. They had been going through several motions together, and he assisted with writing his speeches for the House of Lords.

Bloody rotten hell.

The man must think he had taken leave of his senses.

"We will resume in an hour."

Mr. Dobson frowned but nodded in agreement and departed from the room.

Another peal of laughter tore through the air, and Sarah came barreling around the corner, shouting some nonsense Edmond was unable to ascertain. He watched them play, a need rising in him to join them. He glanced at the mountain of paperwork he had to wade through, mainly sent by his estate managers. There were many letters to be answered, his stewards had informed him there were repairs required at Kellwich Castle. Ditches needed to be dug on his Suffolk estate and drainage needed to be installed. He would be lucky if he had time to write the article he had hoped to on providing training and education for those orphans who were dependent on parish relief for their nurture.

Both girls spied Adel, and with rousing shrieks, they launched themselves at her. They were all acting like hoydens and Edmond never wanted them to stop. The laughter dwindled, and his duchess said something to the girls. They nodded vigorously, and his heart clenched when she brushed a fingertip over Sarah's cheek with a tender smile.

Only God could have conspired to drop a young lady who was kind and patient with his daughters into his lap. There was no other explanation. He watched in fascination, almost pressing his nose to the glass pane, as his girls tipped their heads back and chortled. How did Adel accomplish such a feat?

After Maryann's death he had lost a part of himself, sinking into a roaring drunken stupor for weeks, then an icy distance to protect himself from the ache. When he had resurfaced, it was as if his daughters did not know him, and he had been at loss as how to reconnect. He'd abandoned them in their grief, and he despised himself for it. How had his duchess achieved so effortlessly what he had been trying to for months?

His girls went in one direction, and Adel stood, brushing grass from her gown, and walked hurriedly inside. He lost sight of her and rocked back on his heels. Unable to help himself, he exited his study, and spied her heading down the corridor, toward the library. He followed, cursing himself for the need to see her face up close, to smell her, to even see a glimpse of the smiles she had bestowed on his daughters.

He was merrily leading himself to his own downfall, and he was unable to stop it.

· · ·

Adel slipped into the library, the most glorious room in all of Rosette Park in her opinion. Mahogany bookcases lined the wall and rose beyond the second floor extending to the vaulted ceiling. There was even a ladder to climb to fetch and return books, and there was a staircase for the higher levels. She bent down and randomly selected a volume, caressing the leather binding with loving care.

The door opened, and she did not need to look to know it

was Edmond who entered. Awareness hummed through her veins, and predictably, her heartbeat quickened.

"You spend a few hours every day in here. Do you enjoy reading?"

Without lifting her head she responded, "Quite so. I find there is no better pastime. Your library is wondrous, Edmond."

"Our library," he said gruffly.

At that, she faced him. He leaned against the doorjamb, looking very casual and disheveled, yet so powerfully handsome her breath caught. How she wished to glide her fingers through his hair and pull his lips to her. "You have been riding?"

"Earlier."

She nodded, at loss of what to say further, but very happy he had sought her company. Many of their chance meetings this past week as she settled into Rosette Park and received a few neighbours' calls, had been filled with very banal and inane pleasantries. Very much like their time by the pond, but she yearned for something a bit deeper. Adel felt he kept their conversation light so as to maintain the wall of friendship he had erected. While she liked the idea of being his friend, she also wanted to be his wife, and it seemed he had no notion of that happening anytime soon. She would have to be much bolder with the unfathomable man. She didn't like that everything she was learning about him was through his mother and even at times through his girls.

He strolled farther into the room. "Riding is one of my favored pastimes. To feel the wind on my face as I leave the cares of the world behind for several minutes…"

"It's a similar pleasure I derive from reading and swimming."

"And what else do you enjoy?"

Adel fought not to show a visible reaction, but she was beyond thrilled he was showing some interest in her beyond the trivial courtesies. "Your kisses, I daresay they are even more thrilling than reading."

Edmond took a deep breath and released it slowly. "You are being provocative, Duchess."

"One must do what one can to tempt her husband to his marital duties."

Amusement lit his eyes, and then he smiled. *Oh, my.*

He fairly reeked of sensuality.

"With you it would not be duty." Then he scowled as if he'd not meant to admit such a thing.

Delight filled her. It was clear storming his defences was not the way to seduce her duke, it must be done with one touch at a time, one suggestion, one kiss, until she shattered his resolve to stay away from her bed. There was a possibility he would come to it for himself. But that could be years, months…perhaps never. "What would it be?" she all but purred.

The way he stared at her…intense and hungry was so telling. Need stirred in her blood, and she was mortified to feel her breasts swelling, her nipples aching. He lowered his gaze to her chest, and a flush of desire swept along his chiseled cheekbones.

She spun, facing the wall of books, her cheeks burning at her uncensored response, and he'd not even touched her! It confounded her, how her body responded and the manner it showed how she was so delighted at seeing him. "I am going to read a story to the girls, do you want to join us?" She said. Stretching high upon her toes, she selected a copy of *Robinson Crusoe* by Daniel Defoe, waiting for his response.

Heat reached out and caressed her, and it came from him. Adel had not heard him move. She could feel the solid, muscled outlines of his chest against her back. Without thinking she leaned into his frame and stifled the gasp at the pleasure she derived from the contact.

"Not today," he murmured, his breath fanning against her forehead. "I could hear Sarah and Rosa's laughter from the study."

"Your girls are wonderful."

She felt his smile.

"Your thoughtfulness does you credit. They are much happier since your arrival."

"Please, I cannot claim credit for it. The girls spend a great deal of time talking about the things you have given them."

"You disapprove."

"No… But I daresay they enjoy my company because, well, I actually spend time with them. Sometimes children do enjoy the society of adult company."

She faced him.

He cocked his head to the side, his expression inscrutable. "Then I am even more obliged to you."

"I am thankful they do not hate me."

"You are too generous with your time and affection for that to be possible."

"They remind me a bit of my stepsisters when I'd just met them."

"How many siblings do you possess?"

She arched a brow. "Are you now curious about me?"

"Are you deliberately bringing to mind my thoughtless behavior at the inn?"

"I do believe I am."

He chuckled, the sound rich and warm, and so very appealing. Then he sobered. "I find I am, Duchess, very curious."

Her heart fairly shivered. "Helena is now fourteen and Beatrix is twelve and they are Lady Margaret's daughters, but I enjoy them as if they were my full sisters. I have a three-year-old brother from Papa and Lady Margaret's union." Adel smiled. "I hated my stepmother."

"I daresay it is the duty of daughters to resent stepmothers when they are presented," he teased drolly.

She wrinkled her nose. "Yes…though perhaps hate is a strong word. We never got along. From the moment my father introduced her, I was made to feel insignificant. Papa always adored me and Mamma, with a similar intensity. However, upon Lady Margaret's arrival it seemed all the affections he had left went to her. There were times I wondered if it was because I looked so much like Mamma with hardly any features from him."

Edmond stiffened, and she could feel the chill forming around him. "My girls favor their mother, Maryann," he said after a small silence.

Adel held her breath, humbled by the faith he was showing in confiding in her.

"They have my eyes, and according to my mother, Rosa and Sarah possess my stubborn chin and attitude."

"They are beautiful children." Adel wrestled with the overwhelming urge to wrap her arms around him. Though he seemed decidedly more approachable, she did not want to overstep too quickly. "They would love to have puppies. Your neighbor, the earl, his spaniel bitch has a litter and they are in raptures at the idea of owning two."

She heard him swallow.

"Then they shall have them," he said gruffly.

"And they also need a governess."

"Will you help me select one?"

"Yes. I will ask Lady Harriet to help me if you prefer. I heard you hired the last four…and well, they are now without a governess."

His lips twitched. "Once again, I am indebted."

"I shall collect a boon one day."

She fought to maintain an air of casual indifference. It would not do to betray how much she desired him. It was already wretchedly intolerable that she brought nothing to the marriage, and in this instance to be the only one to feel desire…insupportable.

"And what would you require of me?"

"I promise I won't be alarmed if you kiss me."

"Are you by chance teasing me, Adeline?"

"I assure you not in this instance. You kissing me is a very serious matter I take to heart," she said softly.

Adel had not known she would respond with such bald honesty. The man's nearness rattled her more than she realized. But what startled her even more was that behind his studied reserve, she detected a flare of raw unbridled heat, in the bottomless gray of his eyes.

Then he stepped closer to her. He leaned down so that his mouth was dangerously close to her ears, his breath a caress against her lobes. Edmond lifted his arms and placed them above her head, effectively caging her. The urge to press her lips against his was strong. What was he doing? Thinking? Would he kiss her, make love to her? She waited, her heart quickening, and anticipation shivering through her. His beautiful, heavy-lidded eyes remained intent on her face. *Oh, please…kiss me, you wretched man.*

But he did nothing, nor did they speak. A blistering need to feel his arms around her, just once, surged through Adel, and she bit into her lips to suppress voicing the desire. He already knew where her inclination lay, and she had too much pride to be so overt in her passion for a man that was doing everything to not want her.

They stayed like that for a long time, his comforting heat surrounding her. Then she slipped from the half embrace, and departed the library to read to the children, but her heart was infinitely lighter than it had been before.

Chapter Seventeen

She had dreamed of her duke again, of being kissed, of him once again shifting her nightgown and touching her in her most intimate of places. Heat surged through her, and Adel chewed on her bottom lip. She wanted to seduce Edmond. Seeing him daily was becoming an exercise in patience, and she was startled to realize that, well…she was the impatient sort.

Adel glanced toward the direction he had ridden in, on one of the most powerful yet graceful stallions she had ever seen. Edmond had appeared so assured and masculine, handling the big bay with a firm hand and skilled thighs. Lifting her face to the first rays of sun peeking from the cloud, she inhaled the cold air. Her walk with the girls this morning had taken her to the southern end of the gardens of Rosette Park, where there were topiary gardens.

She bent to caress the petals of a pink flower growing beneath a shrub shaped to look like an eagle if she were not mistaken.

"This one is our favorite," Sarah said, running up to

several trees pruned and shaped to appear like a small herd of elephants. The designs were truly beautiful and elegant.

Sarah slipped her small hands through Adel's.

"Do you see how loving the mother elephant is?"

Adel smiled. "I do."

The girls nodded approvingly and darted between the various shaped trees, a becoming mixture of animals and plants, chattering as to their favorites and why. Sarah and Rosa scampered off in the distance, and Adel kept a watchful eye on them as they ran across the lawn.

Her father would love Rosette Park's grounds. So would Helena and Beatrix. Adel resolved to write to them in Bath, and invite them to spend a few days at Rosette Park. Though it had only been a little over three weeks since she had wed the duke, she missed her stepsisters and her father. She wriggled her nose before admitting to maybe slightly missing Lady Margaret. The sound of hoof beats had her glancing up. Edmond! She straightened as he slowed to a canter, then slipped from his horse. He allowed the reins to dangle freely and walked toward her in graceful strides.

Once again he appeared disheveled and very casual in dark breeches, riding boots, and an opened neck linen shirt.

"Good morning, Adeline," he greeted, with a warm smile.

"Edmond."

He fell into step beside her.

"I've hardly seen you this week," she said softly.

He grunted, and she glanced at him.

"I have been visiting the tenants and overseeing a few repairs, after the visit I received from Squire Wentworth last week."

The Squire had called upon her yesterday, and he was a handsome and pleasant man in his early fifties who seemed to have a fascination with the dowager duchess. Whenever Lady Harriet entered the room, he became flustered and had been hardly able to remove his gaze from her. Adel smiled at the memory; the dowager duchess had seemed equally attracted.

"There were a number of tenants living in tiny cottages and their families had expanded significantly. They could not afford higher rents, and Mr. Thompson, the estate's steward, had not brought the matter to my attention," Edmond clipped.

It occurred to her he was angry, and a pleasant feeling unfurled inside.

"And what did you do?" Though she had a fair idea.

"All families with several children living in those tiny cottages have been moved to some larger ones that were recently refurbished."

"For the same rent?"

"Of course."

"You are generous, Edmond, not many would be so understanding."

"Many of the families lost their men in the war, and those who returned wounded are not able to take care of their families as they ought to be able to. They are England's veterans, and she is not taking care of them as is due."

"Yes, I've read a few of your articles championing better rights and the setting up of pensions for our soldiers. They were exceptionally eloquent and well argued. We must do more, and I would like to support the local causes who provides for them."

He jerked to a halt and stared down at her.

"Have I said something?"

He cleared his throat. "No…but I find I am pleased you show an interest in my activities."

"You are my husband. Everything you do is of interest to me," she said. "And I would like to walk with you when you visit the local villages sometimes."

A gorgeous smile curved his lips, and the flutter in her stomach actually worsened.

"Then I shall ensure I extend an invitation. I will also inform our solicitors of the charities you wish to support and whatever monies you need will be made available."

"Thank you."

They walked in silence and Adel badly wanted to demand why he sought her presence.

"I visited the girls in the school room yesterday," he said gruffly.

"The girls spoke of little else for hours. It was a momentous occasion, as it was your very first visit in…" She bit her lips.

"Is that censure I detect?"

"Perhaps."

A fleeting smile touched his lips. "I would deserve any recriminations heaped on my head. It was their great misfortune to lose their mother at such young ages, and worse, in battling my grief I neglected my girls. There is no greater crime I could have committed."

Acting on instinct, she gripped his hand and tried to lace their fingers together. His riding glove made it awkward and her breath caught when he released her hand, tugged off his gloves, and pressed their palms together. He stared at their joint skin for a bit, as if fascinated by the contact.

Her heart was beating too fast, too hard. Somehow the simple touch seemed a greater intimacy than his kisses. Her fingers curled through his, and they continued strolling side by side, their hands clasped.

"What happened?" she asked softly, remembering his cold order never to ask about his wife, but she chose to ignore it for his shield seemed diminished.

"For weeks I buried my sorrow in liquor, and the false sense of peace it provided."

"My father… My father also took my mother's death horribly. It was sudden. She was in the gardens, tending to her roses when she collapsed. She was just there…and then gone the next. He had loved her most ardently; their union was a rare love match. It seemed he was soused until he met Lady Margaret." Adel glanced at Edmond. "You must have loved your wife very much."

His fingers tightened briefly on hers. "I did."

Adel admired him more for loving his wife, but the knowledge left a peculiar ache in her heart. Their attachment had been so great Edmond had sworn never to love another… even her father seemed like he adored Lady Margaret.

A gust of wind tried to steal the bonnet from Adel's head, and she placed a hand on top of her head, holding it firm. The girls still ran in the far distance, and she fancied she could hear their chortling.

"The girls told me you've never been to the theater or opera," he abruptly said.

She frowned. "Why, yes that is true."

"Nor on a picnic with a suitor."

Adel blinked. "I…yes."

"Lady Gladstone had indicated you had several seasons, why did you not partake in all London had to offer?"

Adel shrugged quite inelegantly. "My only suitor was Mr. Atwood, and my father strongly objected to his courtship. I daresay Mr. Atwood was unable to afford many of the finer aspects of high society, and that included renting a box."

"I see."

What exactly did Edmond see? That she was not as polished as many other young ladies? They came upon a gazebo with flowers covering the entire structure. There was a stone bench, and he led her to it. They sat, and he angled his body so that he faced her.

"Do you wish to be in London, enjoying the rest of the season?"

Adel laughed. "No, I assure you, I am very contented here at Rosette Park."

Rosa careened around the corner, panting, a wide smile of her face. She faltered when she spied her father.

"Good day, Father," she said politely.

"Rosa."

She glanced at Adel searchingly, then back to her father. It then occurred to Adel this would be the first time his children were seeing them together since their initial introduction.

"I'd intended to ask Lady Adeline if she would like to join us by the lake," Rosa said tentatively.

An air of wariness clung to her. Did he not see it? Adel's throat tightened and on impulse she said, "Would you like to join us instead, Rosalie? You and Sarah."

Rosa glanced to her father, clearly waiting for his invitation. The daft man remained silent.

"No," she said with a curious smile, and then bent and picked up the ball. She glanced at her father. "Good day, Papa."

A charming smile crossed his lips. "Rosalie. How did you fare today?"

The joy that chased her features at such a simple enquiry made Adel wanted to grab a tuff of his hair and pull it from his scalp. His yelp would be so satisfying.

"Lady Adel taught us geography earlier. Then we came outside and observed the workings of the compass. It was rather intriguing."

He arched his brow at the ball, and a sweet chuckle spilled from his daughter, then she lifted a small shoulder in a shrug. "I am unsure how we started playing, Father, but it was fun."

"I saw," he said a bit huskily. "Whenever you and Sarah play, I watch you from my study."

Adel glanced at him from the corner of her eyes, careful to not be obvious in her perusal.

He was gripping the edges of the stone bench in a white knuckle grip.

There were several shrieks and peals of laughter in the distance, and Rosalie turned to the sounds.

"I must return inside with Sarah. We will need to refresh for dinner. Lady Adeline and grandmother have promised to dine with us in the smaller dining room. Will you join us tonight, Papa?"

"I will."

A soft sigh of relief escaped his daughter's lips. Then with a smile, she ran to him and pressed a fleeting kiss to his cheek. She turned to dash away but his hand darted and grabbed a hold of her. Edmond tugged Rosalie into his arms and enfolded her in a fierce hug.

Adel froze.

The naked pain of his features was unbearable to look at. Rosalie did not hesitate; she flung her arms and gripped him just as tightly. Adel felt she intruded on their moment, but was afraid to move and shatter whatever drew them together.

"I love you, Father."

"I love you too, pumpkin," he said gruffly. "Now go wash and change. We will all dine together, then afterwards we'll retire to the drawing room and you can play the pianoforte for us. I heard you play today, and you were excellent."

"Yes, thank you, Father," she said, and Adel heard the pleasure in Rosa's voice.

She drew away and ran in the direction of her sister. Then as if she forgot something, she twirled around and waved at Adel.

With a smile, Adel returned her farewell.

Edmond stood and walked away. She remained frozen, wondering if she should follow. Then he paused.

"Are you coming?" he asked with an imperious wave of his hand toward the lake.

She stood. "Is that an invitation to join you on a stroll, Your Grace?"

His lips quirked in a sensual smile. "Would you do me the honor of taking a turn in the gardens, Your Grace?"

"Why, yes, I believe I shall."

He waited until she caught up with him before continue walking. They strolled without speaking, and she had no wish to break the companionable silence. They passed the gardens, and moved in the direction of the lake. They went behind a copse of trees into a small clearing. He sat on a stone bench beneath the cypress tree, hidden deep in the shadows. Adel sat beside him on the bench, desperately wanting to speak but unsure where to start. She had spied his unguarded response to her and the children cavorting a few days ago. It had been a raw and undisguised longing. He had wanted to join them. The novelty of it had left her bereft only fleetingly, and then she'd realized the improbable.

He was afraid of opening himself up to his own children.

"It would have been wonderful if you'd joined us today."

The man grunted, but she wasn't deterred.

"Rosa and Sarah need you."

His gaze settled on her like a cold caress. "I have given them everything."

Yes. Even a wife he had no intention of ever loving. She pushed past the ache blooming inside her and allowed a smile to touch her lips. "Not everything, Edmond. They need you to play with them again."

A dark frown settled on his face, and he thrust his fingers deep into the pocket of his trousers. He seemed almost lost and her heart ached for him. Had she seen him laugh? Do something for the simple pleasure of having fun? He always appeared dark and intense. A deep curiosity to know all of him welled inside of her. "Don't you ever play?"

Surprised chased his features. "Play?"

"Yes...you know, the art of romping, laughing, and having untold fun?"

"Of course not," he said stiffly.

"How sad," she murmured.

He arched a brow. "I am a duke…we do not cavort in the dirt and grass."

She stood and walked deeper into the shadows and smiled when he followed.

"That is a pity. I think I would enjoy very much you tumbling me into the grass."

Intense dark eyes assessed her and Adel stepped closer to his heat. "Come play with me," she said softly.

Something stirred in the air between them, and her breath hitched audibly.

"Have you by any chance given yourself the task of saving me, Duchess, from imagined darkness?"

"Imagined? Your wall of icy reserve is very real." She gave him a smile filled with delight and daring. "And you're a chicken."

Edmond smiled, then grabbed the edges of her gown and slid it slowly up her legs and bunched the material at her thighs. Adel quivered. The act was so unexpected, she almost fainted.

"This is the only way I want to play with you," he said huskily, cupping the center of her womanhood.

Her breath came in a hard burst at his very surprising and provocative touch. "Then *play* with me," she tempted, hot hope rising inside.

"I will not be weak, no matter how great a temptation you are." With a self-deprecating chuckle he lowered his hands.

Acting on sheer instincts, she felt for the stone table behind her, and slowly sat on its edge, and then she widened her legs in the most lascivious manner. A blush heated her entire body, but she held his gaze.

"You are playing a dangerous game," he murmured.

If he only knew. And the stakes were his heart.

"I am?"

"We are on the estate ground."

"I have a clear memory of you saying you did not give a damn about being proper," she said huskily.

An imperious brow arched.

"We are quite secluded," she added, "And it's dark."

Edmond chuckled, and the innate carnality in the sound enthralled her.

He slid his palms along the inner curves of her thighs until he reached her throbbing core. He ran a finger through her curls and hissed at the wetness he found.

"I ache for you," she confessed, completely without embarrassment. "Since your kiss, all I've imagined is your tongue doing wickedly delightful things to my body."

Edmond's jaw flexed, his eyes darkened, and the sudden tension in him was palpable. "Have you?"

"Yes."

"How wicked?"

"I have dreamed of you touching me…where you are now, *every night*."

There was a pulse of silence.

"Have you dreamed of me at all?" She regretted asking the question and braced herself for his cold rejection.

"Day and night I've imagine you sheathed on my cock."

She gasped, and he laughed, a low, deep vibration that speared heat directly to the aching flesh between her thighs.

"Never have I spoken in such an ungentlemanly way to a lady. But you are not just any lady, are you?" His tone was filled with dark sensuality. "You are my duchess…and I can tell you I do not need to be asleep to think of these plump lips on my tongue." He slid a finger through her wetness, so she was not in any doubt as to what he spoke of.

But surely she misunderstood.

"I can tell you I dream of riding you long and hard until

your thighs tremble from the exertion…even as I dream of worshipping your body with slow caresses and kisses. The temptation to taste you has been truly driving me mad."

A shock of delight shivered deliciously through her body as the explicit images erupted in her mind. *Riding her… long and hard.* Anticipation warred with hesitancy, then she stepped off the ledge. Adel fisted his hair and tugged him closer, so she could peer into the hunger in his gaze. "Then why do you resist when I ache for you similarly?"

With what sounded like a groan of defeat he kissed her, and it was glorious. His teeth tugged at her bottom lip, and she sighed. With a muffled moan she parted her lips, and he stroked his tongue inside, tasting her with sensual greed. He deepened the kiss, his tongue tangling with hers.

He hauled her even closer up against his body, lifting her swiftly off her feet, and laying her onto the large stone bench. The hard surface hardly penetrated the haze clouding her mind.

His touch set fire to every nerve ending in her body. He pressed kisses along her jaw, and neck, down to her neckline where he inhaled deep. With a sharp tug, he pulled down her gown and chemisette and took one of her nipples into his mouth. A jolt of exquisite pleasure lanced through Adel. She arched into him, and he moved his kisses lower even as he pushed her dress higher and parted her legs.

His breath wafted over the curls at the apex of her thighs, and she trembled in shock. Surely he wouldn't? *He is…* She gave a muffled shriek. *He is licking me.*

Good heavens! Every preconceived notion she'd held of what happened between a man and a woman shattered. Vaguely she was aware that she should be shocked, but she could not think beyond the chaotic need rushing through her veins.

She caught her breath and then couldn't exhale. Edmond licked her folds, parting them, and then he covered her nub with his lips, sucking it delicately. Only something wicked could feel this good.

The moan of delight came from deep in her throat.

Her hips arched to him, her thighs quivering with tension. She couldn't help but bury her fingers in the thick strands of his dark hair and hold him closer to her. More… She needed *more* of him. His wicked tongue stroked her to the brink of ecstasy, and then he slid two fingers deep inside her narrow slit. Her core flamed at the sensual pain, and despite the sharp bite of discomfort, sensations peaked in her belly and on a wordless cry she shattered as bliss seared her.

Edmond gently kissed the inside of her quivering thighs and lowered her dress. He helped her to stand and her weakened knees would not allow her to walk. Adel stumbled against him, and with an embarrassed laugh she glanced up, and froze.

His cheekbones were tightened with savage need. The brilliance of his eyes glittered, and it was then she felt the tempered restraint in his touch, and she could almost feel the battle he waged.

She lightly skimmed her fingertip over his cheekbone, and he gripped the tip, then flattened her palm to him and gently pushed it to her side. "It is as if you are in pain, Edmond."

The desire in his eyes dared her. She slipped her hand from his, and not releasing his magnetic gaze, cupped his hardness…and instinctively squeezed.

He shuddered. His eyes drifted shut and he tilted back his head, the muscles of his throat working as he swallowed. He looked so primal in this moment; his face a mask of hard-edged sensuality because of *her* touch.

She squeezed again, harder this time, and a low rough growl of need rumbled from him.

"How do you find release?" she asked softly. If he felt something akin to the sharp painful edge she'd been suspended on before she shattered, it could not be pleasant.

"Tell me how to please you, Edmond."

He finally lowered his head and snapped his eyes opened. *Oh*.

She swallowed. In that moment she was glad he was showing restraint, for she instinctively knew if he took her then, he would be too untamed.

He gripped a loose tendril of hair between his thumb and forefinger, firmly tucking it behind her ear. "I will not deny you pleasure again," he said.

Elation filled her but she directed her thoughts on what he did not say. "But you will not take pleasure with me?"

He cupped her cheeks. "I derived immense satisfaction from seeing you flushed and coming apart on my tongue. I can still taste you."

Her heart tripped.

"You are a passionate and sensual woman, Adel. It would be a sin to not please you when you are in need."

She flushed her body to his. "I am in need now."

He chuckled lightly. "Were you not pleased?"

She was, so thoroughly she felt boneless. But wasn't there more? She was sure they had not explored the *it* as yet. "I want everything, Edmond."

Tension invaded his muscles. "I will not risk you."

"How can you be so resolved that I will be at risk? Every woman is different."

"There have been dozens of deaths every day for women in town from childbed complications since my wife died. Medicine has advanced, yet the rate of death has not slackened."

His voice was blank, devoid of all emotions. It was perverse of her, but she preferred the man who showed rage and pain. Grief could be soothed, pain could be comforted, but this coldness was almost impossible to shatter.

"Then do not risk me," she said softly.

Surprised flared his eyes wide.

Then he dropped his forehead to hers. "I promise you I won't. You are young and vibrant. You have much to live for. You do not deserve to have your life snuffed out because I cannot control my baser needs."

Oh, Edmond. "Are there no ways to prevent me from becoming with child?"

"Yes. But they are not foolproof and some are very unpleasant."

"I am willing to try."

"These are not methods suitable for a lady."

She arched a brow. "Who are they suitable for?"

"Mistresses."

Adel had heard some whispers of Cyprians...fallen women. Was he to take a mistress? Adulterous liaisons were the norm among the *ton* and were even seen to be expected in men with wealth and power such as Edmond had. Anger stirred inside. "Are you implying you have a mistress? Let me be honest, I will not have it, Your Grace."

A fleeting smile touched his lips. "You wouldn't, would you?"

"No!" she growled.

"I would never dishonor you so," he said with sincerity.

The rage that had been climbing dissipated. "Oh."

She tipped and pressed a kiss to the corner of his lips. When he froze she whispered, "Oh, no you don't, no more retreating from me. I am holding you to your promise to please me whenever I need, and I can assure you, after the delight I have partaken in, I will need to be pleasured a lot. I will gladly be your mistress and wife, and that way you can do all manner of wicked things to me without worrying about my sensibilities."

He turned his head and unfathomable eyes ensnared her. Then they warmed...heated, and he gripped her tighter and claimed her lips.

The possibilities just got even better.

Chapter Eighteen

You can do all manner of wicked things to me without worrying about my sensibilities.

The husky dare was still rattling around in Edmond's head, fueling his lurid imagination, which in turn had encouraged his cock to remain in a constant state of readiness. He could still taste Adeline on his lips. Sweet, addicting, and he craved more. Worse, he'd told his duchess he wanted to tup her until she trembled from exhaustion.

Edmond scrubbed a hand over his face. He was losing his damned senses. It did not escape him that he was more relaxed with his sexuality with Adeline in a few weeks than he'd been with Maryann in the years they had been married. Adeline challenged him to be unrestrained with his desires and he hungered to succumb to the cravings erupting from his soul.

If you'd not wanted an heir I would not be dying.

He gritted his teeth against the memory of the pained whisper. If he were to give in to the lust and Adeline fell with child… He sighed. How long would he hold onto this torment for? He had given huge sums to hospitals and spent many hours talking with the leading accoucheurs. It had almost become an obsession to try to discover what he could have done to prevent Maryann's death, and he had been shocked to discover how common it was, and how little doctors and midwives truly knew. Thousands of women apparently died in England annually giving birth or shortly after, and that chilling fact had shook him.

He was growing to like Adeline and to put her at such a risk...he would be a selfish ass to even contemplate making love with his wife. *But there are ways to prevent conception.* His breeches tightened uncomfortably at the mere thought.

When he'd hatched his idea to marry, it was not a decision he'd pondered on for too long. He'd moved very decisively and truly had not given much consideration to what it would be like to have a wife underfoot at all times.

Adeline had been his wife for all of twenty-four days, and she already had him in knots. How the hell he had allowed himself to be trapped in such a state of need mystified him. But it was his own dammed fault. He'd known before he married her how attracted he had been to her dark beauty and the intelligence that glowed in her eyes.

Though the desires he felt now transcended attraction. He found he wanted to please her and bring her delight. It was by mere accident his daughters had mentioned Adeline had never been to a theatre or to the opera. Edmond wanted her to explore all London had to offer, and he wanted to be the one to experience it with her.

He hauled himself from the lake, the cold night air biting deep to his bones, but finally his damn cock had gotten the message. He slipped his shirt onto his still wet body and dragged on his boots, then walked briskly toward the house.

He would leave for London tomorrow for a number of meetings with Members of Parliament and the House of

Lords. Adeline would enjoy society as a duchess. Perhaps. But he would extend an invitation, though she might very well decline because of its suddenness. It did not escape Edmond that a few weeks previous he'd wanted a young lady who was not interested in society and the frivolities it offered. Now here he was thinking of ways to throw Adeline back into the fray because it bothered him she'd not had a grand time during her seasons.

He was truly losing his damned mind.

• • •

Hours later, Adel gave up the pretense of sleep and lay on her back in the dark room staring sightlessly at the ceiling. Soft fire still lingered in her blood from earlier in the day. Dinner had been subdued; the dowager duchess had glanced from her to Edmond several times, a smile playing on her lips. Then after only eating a little, she had excused herself. Adel had been left alone with Edmond, and she had silently beseeched him to invite her to his chambers. The stubborn, dratted man had been unflinchingly polite and cool.

She hated the reserve she could see re-forming, the very notion had anger snapping through her blood. Thunder rumbled in the distance, and she shivered. It would rain tonight, and probably for a large part of tomorrow, forcing them to spend the day indoors. She let one leg slip over the edge of the mattress, and then paused. Perhaps he would reject her if she tried to seduce him. Anxiety seared her, but she pushed from the bed, and hurried from her chamber. She didn't stop until she reached his bedroom. Swallowing down the nerves, she knocked firmly.

There was no answer. Disappointment pricked her. Was he already asleep? She spun to return to her room and hesitated. What if he had not heard her over the rain and thunder? She tested the knob. It was surprisingly unlocked. She walked into his chamber and Adel regretted the impulse that had driven her to seek him out. She froze ensnared at one of the most primal, and lascivious sight she had ever seen.

The duke stood by the windows in his chamber...stark naked. He was...splendidly beautiful. His masculinity was overwhelmingly erotic in nature. Unable to help herself she hungrily drank in his posture, the graceful but powerful line of his body. Muscles corded his shoulders, back and thighs. Even the turn of his calves appeared chiseled. She could only see his side profile, and his head was tilted, the strong column of his throat working, yet no sound emerged. One hand was braced against the glass and she could see the tension in his frame.

His other hand was... She glanced down and had to swallow her gasp. Her cheeks flamed and the throb of heat between her legs was startling. He had his...his...member in his hand, stroking, alternately gentle then hard. She squeezed her thighs together hoping to soothe the throbbing ache in the flesh between the juncture of her thighs. She was at a loss how from simply looking at him, such wanton urges could stir in her blood.

She couldn't stay to watch such an intimate private moment. Worse, she had the feeling he was thinking of his wife. A sob hissed from her in denial, but he did not hear. *Thank Heavens*. She decided to depart and made the error of glancing at his face. Adel faltered. His face was drawn into hard lines of loneliness and yearning—stark and agonizing. A low, tortured groan slipped from him and the grimace on his face indicated he was washed in intense feelings, and she belatedly realized it must be pleasure, and not pain as she'd initially assumed. A whimper of need clawed from the back of her throat and threatened to spill in the room, when he fisted the length jutting from him, and slid his hands up, then down the thick stalk, and her name slipped from his lips like a benediction.

"Adeline," he groaned, the sound reverberating deep in his chest.

It was her! He thought of her!

She pressed her hands low on her stomach, desperate to still the flutter of desire erupting through her body. Her nipples beaded beneath her nightgown, and she ached between her legs in a way she struggled to understand. Drawn to him, it was as if her feet had a mind of their own as they moved closer. Her lips parted on a gasp when he rumbled her name once more and even stroked himself with more...vigor.

· · ·

A soft sound of need filtered on the air, and caressed right around his cock. Without moving Edmond knew Adeline was in his chamber. He did not question the how, or why. Hell, he knew why. The hunger she felt was the same reason he had his length fisted in his palm, urging himself to release — something he had not done in years. As he stroked himself he imagined her...tasting her, sinking inside of her. Turning from her earlier was the hardest thing he had ever done, restraining himself when his body had cried out to take her and slake the tormenting lust.

It had finally occurred to Edmond; he had been a blasted fool, denying them what they wanted most, when he could bed his duchess without releasing inside of her. Though allowing such intimacy was a slippery slope that could well lead to the very thing he dreaded. He would have to be vigilant never to slide so far he lost his common sense. He'd acknowledged it would be impossible to stay away from her any longer. They were married, a state that could not be dissolved, and it had finally pierced him that this hunger would never go away, whether it be for weeks, months, or years.

He turned and his knees nearly buckled. Though she was clothed in a nightgown that covered her from head to toe, it was all the more provocative for he knew the sensual beauty it hid. The cravings he had suppressed for so long surged to life, burning away all resistance. She was raw, earthy, beautiful... unforgettable.

Her eyes widened and then lowered to his cock still fisted in his hands. Edmond *would* consummate their vows, though it had gone far beyond duty. It was a living need inside of him to brand her with his touch. He'd almost visited her chamber, but had restrained himself. The fever of lust that dominated him would make it impossible to be gentle with her.

She stepped farther into the chamber, then she made to remove her gown.

"Leave it on." His order was harsh and she hesitated, hurt flaring in her eyes.

"I do not want to hurt you," he all but snarled, hating the idea that she thought he was rejecting her again.

Her lips parted in soft subtle invitation. "I know there is to be some pain."

Did she have to sound so sensually intriguing? "I cannot be gentle, Adeline, and by God you deserve to be worshipped, to be pampered and savored, not be taken without restraint."

• • •

Thick, fierce tension swirled around them, and Adel's heart was a furious flutter in her breastbone. "You have teased me in the most ungentlemanly manner for weeks. I assure you, I do not desire restraint but how you are now...passionate and without reserve."

His jaw visibly flexed. "Come here," he said, the gray in his eyes darkening dangerously.

The promise of carnal delights gleamed in the depth of his eyes, and it tugged her to him. They stood close, and his rough, deep breathing echoed in her ears. She glanced up, the lines of his beautiful face were taut with hunger. Without speaking he gripped the fold of her nightgown and drew it to her hips. Then he palmed her buttocks and lifted her high. She gasped, instinctively wrapping both legs around his hips, and his strong arms supported her with an ease that was thrilling. Adel had expected him to tumble her into the bed, instead he sank them onto the sofa so that she straddled him. She pressed her knees into the soft cushions bracketing his hips, and she twined her hands around his neck.

He kissed her jaw and throat, and she instinctively arched allowing him access.

"I cannot be patient."

The sound of his voice was a whisper of velvet across her skin. "I do not desire control, Edmond." *Please no control.* She'd had enough.

His lips brushed her forehead with acute tenderness, and she sighed.

He gripped her hips and she felt the tempered restraint in his touch. A simple caress, but it seduced and empowered her…for she also felt the trembling in his arms, the pounding of his heart against her chest. He craved her with a similar intensity.

He shifted one of his hands and trailed his fingers to her core, to that bundle of nerves at the apex, which brought her such pleasure. His touch was firm yet light as he stroked it, and then pressed, sometimes pinching. A moan broke low in her throat from the exquisite sensations. He lifted her slightly, and a hard pressure was notched at her entrance.

The feel of him was both shocking and wonderful.

Yet he did not press his advantage, only slowly continued to work her knot of pleasure with his fingers. Tension peaked in her belly, and she dropped her forehead on his shoulder, shivering.

"Edmond," she gasped, when he pressed hard, and liquid heat rushed from her to bathe his fingers and length, which was poised at her entrance.

"I need you wet…so damn wet you'll soak me."

She bit into his shoulder, and he chuckled, low and deep, the sound rich, heated.

Then the hand gripping her hip tightened. He thrust hard and heavy inside her, and a soft cry exploded from her as he sank past her resistance, burying his length to the hilt. Her muscles strained and quivered around him, fighting to accept the broad length suddenly filling it, her breath puffing in harsh bursts. The pleasure-pain was a fiery cascade of sensations twisting through her, and she couldn't prevent a whimper of feminine distress.

"Shhh," he soothed with kisses along her cheeks, and down to her neck. "The sting will soon pass."

She wanted to point out that the throbbing pain was more than a *sting*, but then he bit into the cord of her neck, then licked the spot he'd just tenderly assaulted, while stroking the pad of this thumb in a deliciously hard caress over her nub.

She almost jackknifed from him so intense were the sensations.

He nuzzled her neck. "Are you well?" his voice was gravelly with arousal.

"Yes…the sting is already passing."

His eyes blazed with a fierce tenderness. "Good."

Then he rocked her on him. He worked her on him, up and down slowly, stretching her to take his length comfortably.

"Grip my shoulders."

With the softest of moans she responded to his urgings. His expression was a tight grimace of pleasure as he repeated his sensual motions. She cried out at the overwhelming sensations—it was bliss and agony in equal measure.

"I need more, Edmond," she gasped, trying to increase the wet glide of his length.

He wrapped his arms around her fully, caging her in his embrace and took her lips. His flavor exploded on her tongue—coffee, brandy, and...the man himself. His kiss soothed and allowed her to focus on his taste, his scent, and not the throbbing ache deep in her center, or the vulnerability she felt being so completely cocooned by his strength. He curled his tongue around hers, stroking, licking, and sucking, consuming all her sighs and moans.

His hands burrowed beneath her nightgown, and slid up and down her back in a heated sensual stroke then around to her front. His palms cupped her breasts, his fingers tweaking at her nipples, plumping them. Adel's moans poured forth and she was unable to stop the encouragement for more from spilling from her lips.

He released her nipples, and trailed his hands down to grip her buttocks. Their mouths still melded together in a passionate dance, he glided her up and then slammed her down hard. She moaned into his slow sensual kiss, which was an erotic contrast to the manner in which he rocked her with depth onto his length.

One of his hands slid around to her front, outlining the shape of her hips and stomach, and then Edmond gripped a fistful of nightgown from inside and ripped. Cool air washed over her chest as the silk parted under his strength. He bent her forward, thrusting her breast into his mouth, the move almost lifting her completely from his length. His teeth raked the sensitive tip of her nipple.

Every tug and lick of her nipple resonated in the ache deep in her core.

A wail of agonized need slipped from her as he impaled her once more. Her hips jerked, a cry tearing from her lips as he seated her over and over on his throbbing thickness with more piercing depth and strength.

"Ride me, duchess." His growl was low and rich.

A broken cry of need escaped her as she responded with wantonness. It was almost too much, the need clawing at her, the broad length stretching her, at times lashing her with a hint of pain to swirl with the intense ecstasy pummeling her.

"Adeline."

No other sound followed the guttural groan of her name, but his grip tightened and instinctively she realized the same exquisite tension peaking inside her, rose in him as well.

Sweat slicked their skins as they slid together in the raw, beautiful and primal rhythm. Waves of blinding sensations stormed her senses and she exploded with such intensity that she couldn't breathe, and seconds later he clasped her to him and lifted her, a hot splash landing on her stomach as he groaned his pleasure.

They remained held like that for a few minutes. Then he raised his head, and the hunger she saw, strangled her breath. Edmond stood with her, and in a few strides tumbled with her to the bed, fusing their lips together, nudged her thighs apart, and with acute gentleness, slid deep inside her.

"Travel with me to town," he breathed against her lips.

"To town?"

"Yes, I depart Rosette Park tomorrow."

He shifted, and she shuddered at the pleasure of him buried so deep.

"It is too soon."

"I will delay my journey for a couple days. Is this sufficient?"

Adel swallowed. She hardly knew what prompted such an invitation, but he truly wanted her company. A grin split her lips. "Oh, yes, quite sufficient."

"Good." Then he lowered his lips to hers once more. And for the rest of the night, Adel knew nothing but bliss.

Chapter Nineteen

Two days later, Adel arrived at one of the most fashionable townhouses she had ever seen in Upper Brook Street, several long tedious hours after departing Hampshire. She was tired, but filled with too much excitement at the thought of retiring. She was never the one to look forward to balls and tea parties, given her dismal receptions these last seasons. But to know it was Edmond she would be making the rounds with filled her with an electrifying thrill.

"You are excited," he observed with a small smile.

"A bit. I have longed to visit the theatres and Vauxhall. Only Papa and Lady Margaret had been able to afford certain social pleasures, since we were practicing economy, and no gentleman invited me."

"They were fools…and I am glad they were, for I never would have met you," Edmond said with sincerity.

She smiled at his compliments though she did not take it to heart. Since he had consummated their vows, he had taken her several times and Adeline would not wish it any other way. But she could still see the reserve in his eyes, and many times, the puzzled look that creased his brows whenever she caught him watching her.

The door to the carriage opened, and he hopped down to assist her out. Large wrought iron gates greeted her, and as they entered, she couldn't help marvel at the elegance of the townhouse.

As they entered she was introduced to the butler and the housekeeper. Meg had traveled with her, and in quick order Adeline was being directed to her chambers. A large pile of expensive papers tied with a ribbon was handed to her by the housekeeper Mrs. Bromley.

"These are for you, Your Grace."

She accepted them with a nod, and climbed the stairs, Edmond right behind her. They entered his chamber and a sigh escaped her as they were finally alone. She walked over to the barouche desk in the corner and set the pile of correspondence on it.

"What do you think these are?"

"Invitations to balls, teas, house parties, and begging letters from charities seeking your patronage."

She glanced at him and heat flushed through her when she saw that he was undressing, his lids lowered with intent.

"Surely you jest, there must be hundreds," she said, and tried to clear the huskiness from her voice. "I had thought the manner in which we wed would have society shunning me."

"Come here, duchess."

She arched a brow, and he smiled.

"Please," he said with warm sensuality.

She sauntered over to him, and his eyes tracked her movements. He untied her bonnet and tugged the pins from her hair, tumbling the heavy coil to her back. With a sharp tug, he made her stumble into him, then clasped her hips with infinite gentleness. Yet there was nothing gentle in his mien when he spoke, only an icy ruthlessness that made her shivered.

"Society will gossip about you—us—always, but you are the Duchess of Wolverton. You cannot be cut, it is you now who decides who will enter your circle."

Cannot be cut.

She withdrew from his embrace and moved to the table and selected a few. After breaking the seal of the first three, she lifted her head. "There is an invitation to the Marchioness of Deerwood's annual ball. That is tonight."

"Would you like to attend?"

"It is truly strange. My stepmother had always wanted an invitation to this much coveted event, and now I am inundated. Perhaps I shall invite them for a visit from Bath, surely Papa and Lady Margaret will be happy to attend."

"If that is your wish."

She glanced at him and grinned. "You are naked, Edmond."

"A state you will soon be in, Duchess."

"We are attending this ball tonight."

"Ah…so that gives us three hours. I have been meaning to make use of that sinful mouth of yours."

"Doing?" she purred, sauntering over to him.

"You shall see, Adeline." Then he took her lips in a kiss, and for this moment all else was forgotten as Edmond's touch roused the unquenchable desire inside once more.

• • •

Adel donned a dark green gown and the bodice was low enough just to show the flush of her décolletage, and the cinched high waist of the empire gown fell in straight lines to her delicate ankles. Her hair had been curled and arranged in a high pile upon her head, with tendrils cascading down her cheeks. A truly exquisite emerald and diamond necklace circled her throat with the matching earrings at her lobes. Edmond had presented to her several pieces of stunning jewels he'd had England's most renowned jeweler make for her. Adel had never felt more beautiful and tonight she would be walking out in society for the first time as the Duchess of Wolverton.

She descended the stairs, and a smile burst from her lips at her duke's regard.

His bold, admiring gaze swept over her. "You are ravishing, Adeline."

"It is kind of you to say so," she said huskily.

"It is not a kindness. You are beautiful, and there are times my heart shudders at the knowledge if you had not climbed into my bed, I would not be so content now. I will be the envy of many men tonight, and if any those jaded rakes looks at you for more than a few seconds, I foresee having many duels to fight in the upcoming months," he teased.

She laughed. "With my too-dark hair and pale skin, I know I am only passably pretty, but I welcome the words ravishing and beautiful from your lips always."

His mood turned serious, and his eyes blazed with possessiveness and something more heated than she was unable to identify.

"You are very dashing yourself, Your Grace."

He was sinful. The cut of his evening clothes was impeccable. Edmond was dressed in stark black and white, with a very elegant and intricately tied cravat. His dark hair was tamed almost severely, the cut highlighting the savage beauty of his face and his nose, which was chiseled sharply, aquiline and proud.

He helped her with her cloak and in short order, they were whisked away in their town carriage.

"I must prepare you. Though you've had three seasons and have endured some gossip, tonight will be nothing like you have experienced before."

Her heart jolted. "It won't?"

"You are only second to royalty. You will be fawned over and hated in equal measure. The eyes of the world will be upon you, waiting eagerly to declare in the scandal sheets tomorrow, if you are a fraud or an original." He tugged her close. "Let me assure you, Adeline, you are an original, a swan among crows and I want you to only be yourself, nothing less."

She stared at him, transfixed. "Thank you."

He pressed a hard urgent kiss to her lips, and she moaned.

"I am in favor of not attending the marchioness's ball, and returning to our chambers to explore at once."

"That was a kiss meant to inspire confidence, not desire."

She grinned. "I am feeling a decided lack of confidence; I may need a few more kisses for it to reach an acceptable level."

He tugged her even closer.

"Don't you dare muss my hair," she warned on a soft gasp, before he claimed her lips.

The carriage ride passed in the most delightful way, and when they arrived, Adel's lips stung from being kissed so thoroughly, and she ached. From the tension holding Edmond rigid, he suffered a similar fate.

Their carriage joined a queue of conveyances, which were delivering guests to the ball. When they finally reached the door, they descended and they made their way into the marchioness's mansion. "It will be interesting seeing the *ton* through the mirror of power," she said softly as they were announced.

There was a ripple through the crowd as they entered. When they reached the receiving line, the marchioness was eager to greet them.

"Your Graces," she said with a pleased smile.

The silence in their immediate vicinity began to spread

until they had the regard of everyone in the receiving line. Adeline thought it all ridiculous.

You are second only to royalty.

The marchioness was clearly thrilled to be the first host in years to have the elusive duke at a social setting where he would hopefully mingle with her guests.

Greetings were exchanged under the watchful eyes of the *ton*. Adel and Edmond mingled with the guests in the entrance hall, before heading to the more densely populated ballroom.

"It's Wolverton…and his duchess."

The whispers started immediately and echoed through the ballroom.

"They are such a beautiful match."

Several ladies and their lords surged forward, and the trepidation Adel had felt melted. She nodded, responded to polite enquiry, and even had a few occasions to laugh. The entire time, her duke stood beside her, a dark protective force. Then she spied Evie on the periphery of the room observing her. Adel turned to Edmond. "I must speak with Evie."

He glanced down. "Remember to thank her for arranging our downfall."

Adel laughed.

"I will take some air on the balcony."

She nodded, and he strolled unhurriedly through the fringe of the crowd to the terrace windows. She turned with the intention of moving to her friend, but Evie was suddenly there.

Adel embraced her, uncaring of the throng's rabid notice. "Oh, Evie, forgive me for not writing you."

"Not at all," she gasped, with a watery smile. "I am very pleased you are even speaking with me now."

"I…I do not resent you for your actions, Evie. In fact I would like to thank you."

Her friend's eyes widened quite comically.

"While Edmond does not love me yet, I find our marriage has a comfortable feel…and we have passion, a thing many marriages lack. I am certain I would not have felt such rousing emotions being Mrs. Atwood." Adel ignored the pinch in her heart that hinted she wanted much more from her duke. She wanted his love, his child…his unconditional acceptance.

"Oh!" Evie smiled. "I am so relieved. I have been tormented, fearing for your unhappiness."

Adel chuckled. "I am very content, actually."

Evie glanced through the terrace door at where Wolverton leaned casually on the balcony railing, a cold imperious duke who held himself aloof from the glittering whirl of society, the facile chattering, and the frivolity of the entire ball. It was very apparent he was there only for his duchess. Pleasure warmed Adel.

"So he improves on closer acquaintance," Evie said, a soft smile playing on her lips.

"Indeed he does, my opinion of him has improved."

I fear I am falling in love…

"So under that severe austerity lies a man of sensitive sensibilities?"

Now Evie's tone rang with such incredulity that Adel laughed.

"I fear he is as reserved as he ever was…but there is a keen consideration for others, and I find I much prefer his passion to poetic sensibilities." *Such passions…*

"I must say I cannot imagine Wolverton as passionate. But his eyes have not left you since you started the rounds. He is besotted."

Adel blushed, and Evie eyes widened even more. Then they both laughed. Adel noted her friend's laughter lacked true merriment. "Are you truly well, Evie?"

For a brief moment despair clouded her gaze, before she

looked away. Then she spoke. "Rumors mention Westfall as having an attachment."

"Westfall!"

Evie swallowed. "Yes, with Lady Honoria, Viscount Tehran's daughter."

"Certainly there is a mistake; the *ton* knows he has sworn never to marry."

Evie faced her and the misery on her friend's face was a blow.

"I asked him, and he confirmed he will be offering for her."

"Oh, Evie, I am so sorry. What are you to do?"

An elegant shoulder shrugged. "I will dance the night away as always and not give another thought to a certain marquess." Then she flitted away.

"I have it on good authority the waltz is about to be announced. I shall have this dance, duchess," a low voice said behind her.

Adel grinned. "How *unfashionable*, are you intending to only dance with your wife?"

As if on cue, the musicians started the rousing strains, and she walked into Edmond's arms.

"And who else would you have me indulge in such frivolities with, if not my duchess?"

"There are many young ladies that society deems to have little distinction, and the gentlemen are not courteous enough to dance with those without obvious partners. I know, for I endured several balls with only Evie's brother, Viscount Ravenswood, asking me to the dance floor."

"I will ensure I offer my feet to all the slighted young ladies for the duration of the night."

They spun in elegant twirls, soaring around the ballroom. She had never felt more contented.

"It's the mad duke."

Nothing in Edmond's face indicated he heard the whisper

as a couple floated past.

"They said he's fought several duels!"

"You must tell me," she teased.

Her duke arched an imperious brow. "Are you asking me why society calls me mad?"

"Hmmm…"

He dipped his head so close, their lips brushed.

There were several shocked gasps.

"They are outrageous."

"Because I did not fit their mould, Duchess. I never took a mistress, I loved my wife…and when I lost her, I traveled to London. For months I took to the rings at Gentleman Jackson and pounded out my rage and pain on any willing participant. I became undefeated and no one save Westfall after a period would enter the ring with me. They would leave with too many bruises, both to their body and pride. I insisted all my matches be bare knuckles, so I could feel every lick of pain, for it would distract me from my inner torment. It was not long before everyone started whispering of my obvious guilt and my supposed madness."

"Oh, Edmond, I am so very sorry."

"It's the past."

"Is it?"

His eyes darkened, and he grounded them to a halt in the middle of the ballroom. He cupped her cheeks, his eyes glowing with intensity. "I am trying, Duchess, I find I hunger to let it all go…"

"What are they doing?"

"Upon my word, I do believe he is about to kiss her."

"Here?"

Laughter bubbled inside Adel at the voices rising in the room. "I fear we will be in the scandal sheets tomorrow."

Amusement glittered in his eyes. "I agree."

Then he kissed her.

Chapter Twenty

A nightmare he had not had in months released its insidious clasp slowly as Edmond woke. The memories were as intolerable as ever, and with icy talons meant to rip and sunder, they seethed within like a devouring monster, stealing his peace.

In a week's time it will be the anniversary of Maryann's death…

Edmond, please save me…save us.

This is entirely your fault… The pained accusation had gutted him.

I wanted to give you an heir…not my life!

Maryann had been ravaged with pain and fear and had hurled the harsh words like a scythe, cleaving him in two. She'd had the presence of mind to even try to soothe him, apologizing, and saying she had not meant it. But he knew the truth, honesty was always more bald and forthright in moments of desperation.

They had both been desperate — and she had been right with every skin flaying accusation. He had failed her by not realizing something had been wrong. Sarah's birth had been difficult and it had taken Maryann weeks to recover. Why had he not been more careful, more assessing, more concerned whenever she paled when he mentioned an heir. There were days he had touched her and she had been stiff, more unresponsive than sensual. She had pleaded melancholy, and he had kept himself from going to her bed for more than a year. It mattered not that Maryann had not gotten pregnant again, until two years after Sarah's birth, he should have noticed the change in her spirits whenever he or his mother discussed an heir.

The blood on the mattress.

The bitter scent as they burned it and all the soaked linens and washrags.

If Maryann had told him the doctor's concern he would never have pressed for an heir.

There was a soft sigh behind him, and he shifted to look at his new duchess. He had taken her several times last night, careful to never release inside of her.

Adel stirred, her lashes lifted, and as simple as that, he wanted to drown himself inside of her kisses, her laughter, her body. It disturbed Edmond that he had never felt such an intensity of feeling with Maryann. He had loved her, he had been certain, but the emotions had always been tempered with gentleness and an awareness of her demure nature. Even how he had made love with her had been different.

Last night he had turned Adel onto her stomach, and had crawled over her, stuffed a cushion underneath her and rode her for what seemed like hours. They had frolicked in the massive bathtub, and he had even taken her there, then against the wall. *Hell.* Adel made him feel raw, desperate, and he made no effort to hold back his passion, or be mindful of her sensibilities. With Maryann, they had always been under the covers, and the one time he had thought to seduce her in the library, she had been beyond mortified. Yet their union had always been sweet and wonderful.

"What has you frowning so?" Adel asked her voice husky with sleep...and desire.

He scrubbed a hand over his face, certain she would push him from the bed if he admitted he was comparing her with his deceased wife, and worse, coming to the more alarming conclusion that Adel made him feel with more intensity. Which placed him on dangerous grounds because if he lost her... The thought wasn't even to be contemplated. Had he been certain he had expelled each time outside of her body? His heart lurched. They had reached for each other so many times during the long night.

He tugged the coverlets from her body.

"Edmond, what are you doing? It is cold!"

He clasped her hips and drew her across the silken sheets to him. She gasped when he nudged her legs apart with one of his feet and placed his fingers against her core.

Her entire body blushed. "Edmond!"

"I am amazed you are still capable of blushing, Duchess."

She scowled up at him.

He stroked a finger deep inside of her...and only felt her heat and wetness. No, he had not released his seed in her.

"What are you doing?" she hissed, narrowing her eyes, slapping his arm away.

"I am ensuring I did not release inside of you."

Awareness dawned in her eyes and she lowered her lids, but he saw the spark of anger.

"Look at me."

Her lips flattened mutinously.

"Duchess."

Anger brought beguiling color to her cheeks. She shoved him, and tried to scuttle away, and he tugged her back with more force than he'd intended.

"*Oomph*" slipped from her as she collided into the wall of his chest.

Immediately his fingers were bathed in liquid heat.

They both froze. She was aroused by his roughness, and the very idea had his cock twitching.

"Remove your hands," she growled. "This is unseemly!" Her cheeks were so red, it was as if they wore rouge.

He removed his fingers from her core, placed another digit under her chin and lifted her head to meet his eyes. He could see the anger, the frustration, the arousal, and the embarrassment in the depth of her gaze. "Never be embarrassed for your passions."

She arched an imperious brow, and hauteur descended on her lovely features. "I was certainly not embarrassed."

"Good." Then he pressed a kiss to her brow.

"But I am angry you thought to check if you had released in me. Would it truly be so bad to have a child?"

He buried his face in her hair.

"Edmond?"

"Maryann died in childbirth."

"I know."

"Then you know I will not risk you."

"This is not your choice to make. We need to have a reasonable discussion."

He withdrew from her, drawing up so he sat on the bed, his back flushing against the headboard. "A logical discussion has been had."

"I am perfectly healthy. You should not believe I will suffer complications."

"My proof is bones beneath the ground; my proof is in the tightness of your passage…"

She gasped and glowered at him.

"My proof is in the narrowness of your hips."

She gathered the coverlet to her, and sat in the center of

the four-poster bed, staring at him with a defiant tilt of her head. "Tell me what happened with Maryann, please."

Her glare intensified at his silence. "I know I was not to ask about her, but surely you can see that is no longer an option. I have kept my silence, but in good conscience I can do so no longer. To be docile will ruin our chance for happiness."

"And if I decline your request?"

"I shall make your life wretched."

He arched a brow. "I fail to see the power you have to do this, madam."

An elegant shoulder lifted. "I will not allow you to bed me."

For a stunned moment he was speechless, and when the import of her words were fully assessed and understood his entire body hardened, tensed. "Are you by chance attempting to manipulate me, Duchess?" he said with dangerous softness, a tone in which many heeded and retracted their offenses with alacrity.

Instead his duchess nodded firmly. "More like encouraging you to communicate with me. I realized last night after you drew me to you for the *fifth time*, that your reluctance to commence your martial duty had been well…bluster, and you are quite unable to resist me."

Grudging appreciation flared inside him.

Then she gave him a sweetly sensual smile. "Upon my word, your mien is once again proud and unyielding. If it is any consolation, I find you magnificent and it will be painful for me to withhold from your touch…and kisses," she said huskily, her eyes glowing with honest need and determination.

"Sarah's birth had been difficult, and Maryann had labored for over twenty hours," he said abruptly.

Adeline's eyes widened with hope and something far tenderer that he was not yet ready to acknowledge. It occurred to him then that his duchess had been bluffing. She had not really thought he would open himself to her. Had he truly been so cold and reserved? He suddenly realized how much he wanted to actually converse with her, so that she could understand his stance even if she did not accept it. He was startled to realize he did not want her contempt or her resentment. When had her good opinion become important?

"Weeks after Sarah was born, Maryann resided in a deep melancholy. I consulted with several doctors, and I was told it was normal for many women who had just gone through the rigors of childbirth. I did everything possible to lift her spirits, and she did rally. The first night I...the first night I tried to take her to bed was eight months after Sarah's birth. Maryann was as stiff as a board and hardly responded to my touch. I did not press an advantage, and I left her be for another several months. But in that time I mentioned on numerous occasions my wish for an heir, after all, what man, especially a duke, was not in need of a blasted successor and a spare."

Warm and concerned eyes held his steady.

"Without me having to seduce her, she came to me, and we resumed intimacy. Shortly after, she became with child." He cleared his throat several times before he continued. "I am not sure what moved her to confide in me, but she finally told me the doctors had advised her to not have any more children."

"Oh," Adeline gasped, sympathy filling her expressive eyes. She made as if to touch him, and then withdrew her hands quickly.

Edmond felt bereft, he wanted—no, craved—her gentle touch, which would no doubt anchor him against the tearing rage and guilt stirring in his gut.

"Why did the doctor not make you aware of the dangers?"

He tipped his head against the headboard, staring at the ceiling. "I was in London, arguing reform motions in the House of Lords when Maryann went into labor. I traveled to

Rosette Park as soon as I received the news of Sarah's birth. It was almost eight weeks later before I would see Dr. Greaves again, and when I questioned him as to her melancholy, for some unfathomable reason he did not see fit to mention the warning he gave her. I am not sure if he thought she had already told me, or if he did not want to remind me I must do without an heir, but he said nothing."

Adel climbed onto the bed, nudging at his legs until he opened them, and then crawled into his lap so that she sat with her back pressed to his chest. He heaved a sigh of relief. Her touching him was highly welcomed. She gripped his arms and tugged them around her front, and brought his knuckles to her lips and pressed kisses on them. Edmond smiled. His duchess was trying to soothe his hurt with kisses. He lowered his nose into her hair and inhaled, wanting to trap her scent into his lungs for a lifetime.

"Then what happened?" she asked softly.

"After Maryann told me, I kept from her bed and watched for her like a hawk. I asked my mother to return to Rosette Park, and we did everything the doctor said for my wife. Maryann displayed no sign of illness, and in fact glowed with health and vitality. Then at seven months into her confinement, she simply woke one morning with blood pooling on the sheets."

Adeline's hands tightened on his.

"I can still smell the blood and feel the heat of the chambers as she struggled to give birth. I had never seen so much blood, or felt such despair. She knew the risk, yet she willingly lay with me, because I had not been able to stop blathering about my desire for an heir. I watched the life drain from her eyes, and I saw the deep regret she felt in loving me."

Adel flinched. "The burden is not yours to carry, Edmond, I would never besmirch—"

"Don't! Do not try and excuse my burden. It is mine

to bear. I should have probed deeper. I should have known something was wrong."

"You are wrong, Your Grace." Her voice was soft, but filled with steel. "It is not only your burden to bear, but mine as well. You made it so when you think to deny me the chance of a child."

The chilled silence was broken only by their breathing.

"I am not foolish enough to believe you will be content with never having a child. But I ask of you to be generous and grant me more time. You are twenty-one. A few more years is all I require." Then maybe the guilt and torment would be a mere phantom caress, and he would be able to look to the future.

She kissed his knuckles. "I agree, Edmond."

Relief scythed through him, and he dropped his chin on her head. They stayed like that for the longest time, until he realized she had fallen asleep in his arms. His duchess was generous indeed, and he would endeavour to make himself worthy of her regard. One day he would be ready.

Chapter Twenty-One

It seemed like every set of eyes in the Theatre Royal, Drury Lane was upon Wolverton's box.

"It's the Duke and Duchess of Wolverton."

Adel was mightily exhausted of hearing their titles bandied about. But Edmond had been correct in his assessment. They were fawned over and gossiped about in equal measure. They had been in town for almost a week, and she had attended several balls and a number of musicales with her husband. Young ladies and gentlemen who had previously ignored her presence flocked to her. She had even been startled to realize that several of the young ladies and misses had started to copy the styles she wore her hair in, and there were whispers that dresses and ball gowns were being ordered in the daring bright colors she wore. The little season had been rather exciting as she was fast making acquaintances, some of which she could see were genuine and she would come to treasure.

"Upon my word, Wolverton has arrived," Lady Deerwood said, raising her quizzing glasses to the foyer.

Adel's heart leaped. She had arrived alone because he'd

had some political meeting to attend. She had not been sure if he would arrive before the opening of the second act. Several ladies had dropped by her box to catch her up on the latest gossip. Adel was more interested in discussing the play they were watching, a rousing tale of unrequited love and revenge. Very similar to another play she had watched with Edmond earlier in the week, but just as entertaining.

"The *ton* is very much atwitter with how many events your duke intends to attend with you," the marchioness said with a sly wink.

Adel gave her a serene smile and sipped the glass of champagne that a footman had delivered to their box.

"Some say it was enterprising of you to trap him. Too many young ladies are admiring your boldness in securing a top match suitor. There have been at least four incidents this week after the *ton* has witnessed how much your duke attends you, my dear."

Before Adel could respond the curtain parted and Edmond entered. He inclined his head to Lady Deerwood, and she rose, dropped into a curtsy, and departed.

Adel grinned. "Your presence always sees my friends scuttling away."

He sat, then leaned over and brushed a kiss against her lips.

"I see you are determined to keep being scandalous."

"Quite so," he drawled. "How are you faring?"

Her skin prickled with awareness. Edmond seemed a bit reserved, and it recalled to mind, his aloofness that morning before he departed for his meetings.

"Never fear, Your Grace, since my arrival I have not spent a minute alone. I have caught up on the latest gossip, and the most remarkable occurrence took place right before the play started."

He lifted a brow.

"The Earl of Vale stopped by our box."

Her duke remained unruffled, and her suspicions were proved correct.

"At first his presence startled me, and I was well prepared to kick him in the shin and cause an even bigger scandal of the year, but he apologized most profusely for his un-gentlemanly and frightful behavior, and even begged my forgiveness."

"As he should."

"Was it your doing?"

"Yes."

Pleasure warmed her. "Thank you, Edmond."

He said nothing further before the light dimmed and the actors came out on stage. Her heart drummed in discomfort.

"Edmond?"

His icy eyes returned to hers.

"Did your meeting go well?"

"It did."

She nodded.

"We return to Rosette Park tomorrow."

Her breath strangled. Though she had missed the girls and the serene beauty of the estate, his words caused a shard of pain to stab her heart. "We were to be in town for another two weeks."

"That plan has been amended."

It did not escape her that he had not thought to consult with her. A powerful voice rose in a melodramatic song, drawing her gaze to the platform, yet her eyes remained unseeing. Adel slid her hand along his and clasped his fingers.

He tensed and ice crept through her. Then he relaxed and she wondered if his returned indifference was simply her imagination.

• • •

Something was wrong. Adeline tipped her head against the padded cushion as the carriage rumbled along the coarse country road with speed. A storm was brewing and the coachman wanted to arrive at Rosette Park before the deluge appeared. She only hoped he did not create an accident in his haste. She shifted the curtain for the carriage and peered into the sky. It was only midafternoon, but the sky had darkened with intent. Edmond rode ahead, glancing back so he did not draw too far ahead of the carriage. But at present, his harsh profile stared straight ahead.

After their several wonderful nights together, and the tender and sometimes fierce way he had loved her, she had not expected his sudden distancing. Their sudden departure to Hampshire was jolting. They had intended to be in London for three weeks. She had no idea what had precipitated his withdrawal, and the annoying man had not made himself available to ride alongside with her so she could probe for his reasons.

They had even stopped at the inn earlier, and instead of resting and spending the night, he had ordered a fresh team of horses, mounting a new horse and leaving his previous mount to be brought to Rosette Park on the following day. After a snatched meal they had continued on with their arduous journey. Adel hated the tension coiling through her stomach, and the ache building in her heart.

A sigh of relief escaped her as the carriage rumbled through the gates of Rosette Park. She had missed the girls. They stopped, and the carriage door was opened. Edmond assisted her descent, but her duke was a veritable stranger.

"Edmond, is all well?"

Distant eyes peered down at her. He smiled, a parody really, for it did not reach his eyes. "I am well, Adeline. I will be back in time for dinner at seven."

"Where do you go?"

"Riding."

She blinked and glanced to the sky which had darkened even further, and the chill in the air had her tugging her coat closer. "You have been riding for hours, Your Grace."

"Then I shall ride some more."

Then with a curt bow, he strolled away and remounted his horse, shouting for a fresh horse rode to the stables. Before she had climbed the steps to the house, she saw him as he tore away from the estate.

Adel hurried inside and with rapid steps moved to the drawing room. She rushed to the windows facing the direction he had ridden in.

"I believe you should go after my son."

She stifled her gasp and spun around. "Lady Harriet, I did not seen you there."

"Of course not, you tore in as if the devil was after you."

Adel allowed a smile to touch her lips, and she hoped it hid the sudden turmoil rioting through her. "Are the girls well?"

"As well as can be. They are at the Earl of Sheffield's estate. Today is one of his girls' birthday celebration, and they had traveled down with their new governess."

"We left London quite suddenly with no time to alert the household of our arrival."

The dowager duchess smiled kindly and rose from the chaise where she had been lounging. "I am sure my son must seem out of sorts today."

"I…yes, he does, and I am flummoxed."

Lady Harriet inhaled. "Foolish of me for hoping he had forgotten. When you departed with him to town, I had thoughtlessly believed he was moving forward."

Adel frowned. "Please speak plainly, for I am at a loss."

"Today is the anniversary of Maryann's death."

Oh, Edmond. Each year on the anniversary of her

mother's death, Adel found it hard to be joyful. She did try for Papa and her sisters, but it had always been a terrible ordeal. "I see."

"I think, my dear, he should not be alone."

"I… He has ridden away."

"Yes, he has gone to the cottage on the eastern side of the estate, past the topiary gardens. He normally spends the night there when…when it comes to this time of the year. He said to me the very first year he disappeared there, that when he is here…he smells the blood and hears her wails."

Adel flinched.

"Go to him, my dear, before the rain comes. He has never had a comforting presence at this time before, perhaps your company will be very welcome."

Then she collected her book and walked from the room.

Adel stood frozen, indecision swirling through her. She wanted to hold him, to be a distraction from the pain that must pummel him. But what if he rejected her?

He smells the blood and hears her wails.

Such a memory must be hauntingly painful, and if she could provide any relief, she would be there for him. She hurried from the room to the parlor where she collected the game of Fox and Geese and a deck of cards. Then she ordered for a horse to be readied while she rushed to her chamber to change into a riding habit and half boots with the aid of her maid.

Less than thirty minutes later, Adel slid from the horse and allowed the reins to dangle. The journey had not been long, and she could have easily walked the distance if not for the inclement weather. As it was, the first cold drop of rain splashed on her cheek as she scrambled up the small steps of the cottage. She had not seen his horse, and she wondered if he was truly here. She rapped on the door with her knuckles and there was no answer. She twisted the knob and strolled inside.

"Leave." His voice rumbled through the small but tastefully furnished cottage.

She found him in the semi-darkened room. He was sprawled in a large armchair, his boots off, his shirt half-open, a crystal decanter in one hand and a glass in another. He brought it to his lips, the strong column of his throat working as he swallowed. Then he refilled it.

"Lady Harriet told me," Adel said calmly as she shrugged off her cloak and tugged off her gloves. She began to unbutton the jacket of her riding habit. "The cottage is cold. Will you start a fire?"

He narrowed his eyes, doing a good job of appearing menacing. But he stood, and placed his liquor on the small center table and walked over to the hearth, which he lit with an efficiency that surprised her.

"I have brought some games if you wish to—"

He stood and faced her. "I am not in the mood for games, Duchess."

She met his eyes and froze. His face was flushed with arousal and something harder that she'd never spied before. It was then she noted the thrumming tension that held him rigid, the sensually cruel slant of his lips, and the dark torment in his eyes.

"What do you need?" she asked softly.

His jaw flexed and his hooded gaze seemed to pierce her. "You could leave."

"Do you truly want me to?"

His throat worked on a swallow, and his eyes glittered with something thoroughly primal and a bit intimidating.

"Would you like to talk?"

"No."

"Then what—?"

"Fuck," he said quite rudely. "That is what I want, Duchess."

She gasped. "You are being deliberately crude."

His left brow arched insolently.

"Are you so afraid of showing me what you feel, Edmond?"

Rage filled his eyes at what he must have perceived as an insult. In that moment she realized he was like the wounded tiger she had seen once in a menagerie, and the slightest imagined infraction might cause him to lash out. He had the power to wound her, deeply. She pushed such thoughts away, and directed her thoughts on what she instinctively knew, that she had the capacity to offer him comfort. When she'd cried for her mother, she had no one. Days of being alone in her room, crippled by the loss that pummeled her anew with each anniversary, she had been frightfully alone. And so had Edmond. He had been woefully alone with his pain...his unreasonable guilt.

She tugged off her riding bonnet and dropped it onto the floor. Then she bent and unbuttoned her boots in silence.

"What are you about, madam?"

"Is it not obvious? You said you wanted to f-fuck." A blush heated her entire body.

"Such crass words from yours lips should not be enticing." His voice was a hoarse rasp. "It is best you return to the main house."

"You need me."

"I need no one."

"Perhaps that has been the problem, my love, you've never had a shoulder to cry on, arms to hold you when you rage."

Shock flared in his eyes, and she frowned. She stiffened. *My love...*

She waited with a pained breath for him to acknowledge her slip. He did nothing, but stare with shivering intensity.

"Get on the bed and await me."

"I think not, my duke." She would offer him the comfort of her body, but she would not allow him to dictate the terms in which she rendered her arms.

She strolled over to him, noting that he braced himself. The rain started in earnest and he shifted his eyes to the small window to their left, peering outside in the dark. The drops slapped against the windowpane like hardened pebbles. When he shifted back his regard to Adel, her throat tightened.

"I can hear her cries with the wind."

"And what do they say?"

His expression shuttered, but she glimpsed an edge of pain and fury in his eyes that had her mouth drying.

"She berates me for not saving her and our son."

Adel stood on tiptoe and kissed his mouth. He trembled. Yet he kept his hands fisted at his sides, not touching her.

She pulled her lips from his slowly. His face hadn't lost the strained look. "And what do they say now?"

He shook his head. "When you touch me…nothing else seems to matter."

She kissed him again, and he closed his eyes, tilting his head. She allowed her lips to trail kisses along the strong column of his neck, down to the powerful muscles of his chest.

"Lose yourself in me tonight. No memories, no pain, only pleasure, Edmond."

"I do not want to hurt you," he groaned.

"Why would you?"

His chest expanded as he breathed deeply. "I am foxed."

Her eyes widened. While his breath held fumes from the liquor nothing about him seemed soused.

She lowered forehead onto his chest. "Then we play cards. My mother taught me how to play piquet."

"Scandalous," he murmured, and it pleased her greatly that amusement colored his tone.

"I know," she said with a smile.

"I wish that I could, but I cannot let you go, not tonight, not when your touch, your smell, keeps it all at bay."

She lifted her head, and he dipped toward her, his mouth conquering. His lips trailed across her cheek to catch an earlobe between his teeth, and he nipped. He grasped the neckline of her chemisette and with one motion, tore open the flimsy material.

Good heavens.

He feathered wet kisses over her neck, down to her collar, and placed his heated wet mouth over a nipple, sucking at it through her shift. The sensation was so sharp she bucked. Everything became a blur as what remained of their clothes were stripped away with haste, and soon they were both naked. He lifted her and strode to the narrow bed, where he tumbled her none too gently. But Adel did not want tenderness. His touch had incited a fever of need in her blood, and she was already wet for him.

They twisted on the sheets, and somehow she found herself, pressing kisses over his chest, down to his stomach, and to the thick length flexing against his ridged abdomen. Desperate to please and drown him in ecstasy, she clasped him and licked around the ridge below his head.

He shouted and fisted the sheets. Pleasure warmed her, and power tunneled though her. Acting on instinct, she licked along his length, before enveloping the flared mushroomed head into her mouth. He growled in approval, a truly lovely sound.

As if impatient for her, he reached down, gripped her hips, and drew her up his body and then flipped her over. His roughness excited her terribly and she moaned.

His heavy weight pressed her down, his hips forcing her legs wantonly wide. He reached between them and slid two fingers over her folds. His fingers moved sinuously over her swollen, wet flesh, and her entire body ached for his possession. He removed his fingers and pressed his blunt hardness to her softness. "You are so wet for me, Adeline."

She shivered and tried to lift her hips. But she was splayed wide and restrained by his strength. She could only grip his shoulders for purchase. He braced himself up on his arms, flexed his buttocks, and drove his entire length deep in one powerful stroke, surging into her almost violently.

"Edmond!"

His face was stark with need. "So right, so damn tight and perfect."

He reared slightly and hooked his arms beneath her knees, pushing her legs toward her shoulders.

"Do you know how beautiful you are, Adeline?" he whispered, his voice low and rough.

Then he drove his length into her over and over, shaking the bed against the wall. Lust rolled through her in a dark hungry tide, and she grasped his head, pulled down, and mashed their lips together. His tongue licked sensually at her lips, sliding deep into her mouth, a provocative mimicry of how he rode atop her. He snapped his hips even harder, his pelvis grinding against her knot of pleasure.

Sweet glorious heavens!

Adel found her release, gasping and shaking, never wanting such ecstasy to end. With a deep groan, and a few more rapid strokes, Edmond shuddered in her arms, gripping her tightly.

Their lips parted, and the heavy pants of their breathing mixed with the lash of rain against the window, and the crackle of the fire. The wind howled around the cottage and thunder cracked as the sky lit up with sudden lightning, yet neither of them seemed to notice.

He dropped his forehead to her, the sweat running from his hairline, down her forehead.

"There are days when I shudder in dread at the thought of what might have happened if you had not climbed into my bed, because I would now be wed to another. I've never desired another woman as I do you, Adeline."

Adel choked, unable to speak. His lips curved in his sinfully alluring smile.

Then he pulled from her and stumbled from the bed.

"Edmond! Are you truly soused?"

"Perhaps, Duchess."

Then he came back over to her and she realized he held his handkerchief. He gripped her legs and tugged her to the edge of the bed, widened them, and cleaned her. A frown appeared on his brow, he shook his head, then his gaze once more traveled to her center.

"You are soft and pink here," he murmured, tracing a finger over her exposed flesh.

She gasped, wanton heat once again stirring in her blood.

"I want to taste."

Before she could formulate a response, he dipped his head and glided his tongue over her.

She cried out weakly, her thighs falling apart even wider at his urging. His lips covered her nub and sucked hard. Adel lost her breath. His tongue flicked over her with firm then light strokes, throwing her into an almost violent release. She quaked, panting. He did not let up, but kept sucking and licking until she writhed with bliss.

"You taste sweet…I could feast on you forever," he said as he rose and flipped her over, drawing her to knees. Her loud cry bounded off the wall as he shoved his thick length into her in one hard move.

"I will never get enough of your taste and the feel of you in my arms."

Desire curled through her body as his words stroked her.

"You're stretched so tight around me," he growled. Then

he proceeded to take her with a roughness she had never experienced before, and she gloried in every pounding thrust until she fragmented under the onslaught of such ecstasy.

Provocative words of encouragement spilled from her lips, and the bed groaned under his loss of control. With a muffled shout, he found his own release, and collapsed onto the bed, twisting her so she fell atop him. Seconds later, his chest rose and fell in a steady rhythm. She covered him with the blankets and snuggled down beside him in the tiny bed.

"I love you, Edmond," she whispered.

Of course he would not respond, for her duke was fast asleep.

Adel had no idea how long she lay on the bed curved into his side, simply listening to his breathing. She shifted and her heart thudded as she felt the wet warmth of his seed pooling along the insides of her thighs. *Oh, God, it is too soon.* He was not ready for this.

She pushed from the bed on trembling legs, containing her wince at the tender ache between her legs. She hurriedly dressed and he did not stir. Adel quickly collected the card pack and the game. The front of her chemisette was torn, but she ensured her riding jacket covered the damage before she left the cottage, throwing on her cloak to protect her from the last raindrops of the storm. The horse was gone, she assumed it had returned to the warmth of its stables at the onset of the downpour, but Maximus was waiting by the door, his tail thumping when he saw her.

Relief filled her at his presence, and with determined strides, she walked away from the cottage and strode toward the main house, uncaring that mud splattered the hem of her riding habit. Edmond had been so passionate and natural—his caresses, his words, they had been everything she wanted to hear and everything she wanted to hold close. Adeline feared he had truly been drunk, but not insensible. What would he do when he realized he had released his seed in her?

Chapter Twenty-Two

Edmond woke with a splitting head and a curse spilling from his lips. Once again he had passed the anniversary of Maryann and his son's death in a drunken haze. Suddenly he despised the notion of liquor and vowed then he would never imbibe to drunkenness again. He pushed from the bed and paused, heat and something elusive slithering though his veins. Something was different. He struggled to remember, and fleeting impressions of Adeline crowded his mind.

Her compassionate smile.

The storm in her eyes that darkened to passion.

Passion… Her lips parted in bliss, her body arching to him, wet heat enveloping his length.

The cottage smelled like his duchess.

He frowned and glanced around. There was nothing to indicate she had been there. He scrubbed a hand over his face as the wisp of a dream roiled though his mind. He glanced down at his flaccid cock, which seemed sticky with the release he'd obviously achieved from dreaming of Adeline.

Hell.

He was like an untired youth. But he was grateful the worst had passed. And he had some explaining to do to his wife. It was hard to explain the guilt that had stirred to know Maryann rotted in the ground, and he was whole, healthy, and without a doubt falling in love with his new wife.

He dressed in a slow manner, mindful of his headache. A few minutes later he exited the cabin to a very dreary atmosphere. When he'd realized it would rain yesterday he had not tethered his horse so that it could return to the stables. It would rain again today. Maximus bounded over to Edmond, getting mud all over his clothes. He chuckled and hugged him around his neck, playing roughly with the great brute. They made their way to the estate, and his steps slowed when he spied Adeline and his girls strolling along a path.

Sarah spied him and with a shriek raced over. He swooped her into his arms, and placed her atop his head, as how his father had done with him many times. His daughter gripped tuffs of his hair for purchase, giggling.

"It is very high from up here, Father."

Rosa ran over chortling and hugged him. "We missed you, Father."

"I missed you both, too."

"Will you come to our tea party in the nursery this afternoon?"

His throat tightened. This was the first time in years that he had received a much coveted invitation to one of his girls' tea parties. They always held them, even invited his mother, and sometimes, he believed, Adeline, but not him. He'd known he was responsible for their wariness but had been at loss for how to mend the hurt he'd caused with his absence. "I would be honored to be on your guest list today, Lady Sarah and Lady Rosalie."

They giggled, and his heart jerked in wonder at the beautiful sound.

He frowned when he noted his duchess seemed hesitant. They walked over to her, and he glanced at the basket in her hands.

"The girls and I took a walk, though it was overcast." She held up the basket. "We picked some berries."

Why was Adeline wary?

"Forgive me for departing with such haste from town."

Her eyes widened and a flush climbed her cheeks. "It is of no great matter. I had been missing the girls and the estate dreadfully. I would have liked to be a part of the decision, however, but Lady Harriet explained what precipitated your actions."

He nodded. "Shall we walk together?"

"We shall."

They moved toward the house in the distance.

"You're beautiful."

She glanced at him, eyes wide, then what he had been waiting for came. A slow smile touched her mouth which was sinfully swollen, as if they had been kissed. Repeatedly.

For a terrible, timeless minute, he could do nothing but stare. The edges of his dream teased his thoughts. "Did you have a pleasant night?"

"Oh yes, I did, thank you, and you?"

"My sleep was restful."

They said no more, allowing the girls to chatter until they reached the main house. All should have been well, yet Edmond wondered at the disquiet lodging in his gut.

• • •

Eight weeks later, Adeline was bent over the chamber pot heaving and looking pale. Her maid Meg held the mass of her hair from her face and pressed a cool washcloth to her brow.

"There, there," Meg crooned as his duchess heaved once

more.

Sympathy filled Edmond. Adeline was having a horrible time of it.

"This dreaded puking will pass in a few weeks."

He felt something freeze in his soul at the maid's words. This was not some random illness. Edmond's mind worked with cold logic. This was the second morning she had been retching before breaking her fast, and last night she had flinched when he sucked at her breast. He had even commented they were delightfully larger and his duchess's eyes had slid away in discomfort. He knew the symptoms, but it made no sense. These past few weeks he had been very careful to always withdraw, even when she tempted him to be reckless.

"Are you with child?" he asked with dangerous softness.

Adeline stilled. Never had he seen her so lifeless, then he met her gaze. They were filled with raw panic. The fear that rose in him was acrid and sharp. With child... *How?* "How?"

She squeezed Meg's hands gently and the maid rose to her feet. She dipped into a quick curtsy to him and darted from the room.

Adeline stood, went to the wash basin and rinsed her mouth, then faced him. Her throat worked but no sound came forth, but he was not mistaken in the anger sparkling in her eyes.

Ice crept over him. "I asked you a question, Duchess."

She squeezed her eyes closed tightly. "You touched me," she said softly as if that would explain her betrayal.

He touched her?

Please do not stop, Edmond... How you make me burn, but such a wonderful delightful burn.

The tide of the dream rose in his head. The heat, the sheer joy of being buried in Adel, the tightness, the wetness, the comfort...it had been *real*. A low groan hissed from the back of his throat and rumbled in the room.

"Edmond," she said on a softly shuddered breath, her eyes glistening with tears. "I know and I understand your fear, but I promise you I—"

"How?" his voice was a hoarse rasp. He knew the night in the cottage was somehow real, but he needed to hear it from her lips. The night that had been haunting his dreams, where deep in the darkest corners of his heart he had been hoping it was true, had been real? The passion he had tasted—never had he feasted on such wonder, such eroticism…and he'd wanted it to happen in the flesh. How foolish he'd been in his desires, forgetting the consequences of his actions.

Her throat worked to swallow. "You rode hell-bent away on your horse and I could not bear the idea of you being alone with your grief. I followed you and…and when you kissed me, I…we…" Guilt filled her eyes, but she tilted her head defiantly. "You consumed me, and I couldn't resist the pleasures I felt in your arms."

The challenge in her eyes nearly felled him.

Silence throbbed in the room like a wound.

"Say something, Edmond."

Somehow the raw metallic scent of blood slinked into the room and filled his nostrils. There had been so much damn blood. Maryann had wept uncontrollably and pleaded with him to save her, save their baby, and he had stood by helpless, *useless*, and unable to do anything as she tired from the exertion of pushing, weakened from blood lost. He had watched the hope die from her eyes, and only fear had remained. He had done nothing…but watch in cold silence, trapped in his own hell and failure.

"Edmond?"

Adeline's soft voice drew him back from the dark fraying edges.

She took a step toward him, anxiety clear in her eyes.

"Edmond, I—"

"Get out."

· · ·

The words were like a solid blow to the center of Adel's chest.

"Are you referring to my chamber or Rosette Park itself?" she asked with a calm that belied the feelings slashing through her veins.

The smoldering rage and contempt in his eyes frightened her.

"You lied to me."

She lied to me. He'd sounded broken when he'd confessed what Maryann had done.

"I did not."

"Now I understand your wariness the morning after. Madam, a lie by omission is deception."

She closed her eyes. "It was not intentional...I slipped from the cottage and returned to the main house. When I saw you later and realized you had not remembered I-I simply did not want your chastisement, so I did not mention that we were together. I never thought I would have fallen with child."

"Why did you not reject me when I reached for you?" he snarled.

"I tried."

He jolted...hard. "I *raped* you?"

Her throat worked. It would be so easy to say he had coerced her, to avoid the heartache about to come. But that would make her such a monster. "You did not," she said softly.

A hiss of relief slipped from him. "It has been eight weeks since, all this time you knew you had been at risk and you said nothing."

"In truth, I had no notion how to broach the topic, Edmond. And I only confirmed yesterday I am with child, and

I am not at risk!"

"You will not give birth in this house."

She flinched. Her gaze captured his, and within his eyes, she saw the absolute truth. He would not yield. The passionate lover she had fallen in love with melted away, as if he had never been, and her cold duke once more stood in his place. "So it is banishment then?" she asked, her lips trembling. She forcefully flattened them, refusing to cry.

"I do not care where you go for your confinement. I have estates all over England and Scotland. Visit any one of them."

She gave him a fulminating glare. "You are being cruel and unreasonable. I will need my family with me…I will need *you.*" There…she was laying her heart bare though he had the power to crush it.

"I will not watch you die!" he snarled. "Nor will I subject Rosa and Sarah to the heartache of losing you."

Her heart was pounding and her hands were shaking. "How arrogant you are. You are powerful and beyond wealthy, Edmond, but it is not you who determines who lives and who dies. Maryann's death was not your fault, nor was it hers. It was simply death…inevitability, in this one a very tragic passing. I am with child—*your* child, and you would think to banish me to some forsaken place without the girls?"

He advanced almost menacingly, and she forced herself to hold her grounds. "If I had not climbed on top of Maryann and rutted until she bred, she would be here today," he said with shocking crudity. "It was *my* desire for an heir…a thing that seems so inconsequential now, that pushed her to accommodate me every time, even knowing the danger to her life!"

How did he live with such guilt? Adel hugged herself and bit back a sob. "It was not your doing, Edmond. Even though the doctors had told Maryann not to have any more children…it was still her choice not to inform you, and I know why she did it. Not because she was being foolish or stubborn, but because she had hoped for a son and loved you. She wanted to grant your desire, and she hoped all might be well."

A cold sneer curved his lips. "And is it that similar hope you possess, Adeline? You, who is slimmer, more petite than Maryann and the hundreds of women that die annually in childbirth. Do you hope you will not perish? Do you hope that the hunger I have for you has not consigned you to an early grave? Is that it, Adeline? *Simply damnable hope?*" His voice was icy with lethal scorn.

She jerked, not at his vulgarity, but the torment that darkened his eyes to ash. "I am truly sorry, Edmond," she said her voice breaking. "I cannot imagine the pain and guilt you have lived with, but I cannot be caged because of your fear that I would have a similar fate."

His gaze dipped to her stomach and lingered there for an inordinate amount of time. "I thought that night with you was a dream…a wonderful, terrifying dream."

The soft words tripped her heart.

"I pray with everything in me, when you birth our babe you are not harmed, that he or she is not harmed. I can live with no other outcome."

Her throat tightened. "I will be well, I promise you."

His expression didn't flicker. "As you said, Adeline, you are not responsible for the hands of fate, nor I. You cannot know if you will live or die. I cannot know, and that is why I had no wish to tempt fate's capricious hand. But this is my fault and I will not hold you to blame. I had known relaxing with you, smiling and enjoying life would lead to this road. If I had been firm in my resolve to never allow such intimacies, we would not be standing here now, debating the possibility of you living or dying when you are brought to bed with our child."

The distance in his voice had alarm shivering through her.

This was going beyond anger or fear. "Edmond, I—"

"No," he said, with such chilling softness that she faltered. "I will never make such a mistake again."

Suddenly she understood what he was about to do.

Perpetual estrangement.

Her eyes smarted with tears. "Stop this," she cried fiercely. "Your unreasonable fear would see us divided forever."

His gray eyes appeared like cold flint. "I am stopping, Duchess."

She absorbed the finality in his tone, his demeanor. If she had thought him cold and aloof before, then the man before her now was a positive glacier...and unknown. All she had been hoping for would now be forever from their reach. Even if she delivered their child safely, he would never return to her arms, never ride with her across the fields, never kiss her, never relax and trust in the attachment strengthening between them with each passing day. His wall of reserve was now absolute, and she would never be able to shatter it.

The loss which scythed through her heart almost brought her to her knees. It took unbearable strength to remain standing and face him. "I will take my confinement at Rosette Park."

"Is that so, Duchess?" he asked chillingly.

"Yes, I will have the consolation of Lady Harriet and our girls' presence."

"Send word when the child is born...if you are alive."

She gasped, and he stormed away.

Chapter Twenty-Three

Edmond swung onto the back of his stallion and powered away from the estate. Blood washing over his vision, and the pale lifeless form of his wife and son crowded his mind. Thunder rumbled ominously, a reflection of his turbulent rage, or was it fear? He saw Adeline splayed in a similar manner, their child stuck, unable to climb into the world and take his first breath, her lifeless, accusing eyes piercing him as her life drained away.

He rode, blotting the emotions until a warning clang sounded in his brain. The rain would be fierce. He drew on the reins and slowed to a canter. When he saw where he had directed them, the breath sawed from his lungs. The cottage. He dismounted, and with long strides walked over the bridge where the river below it was already swelling from the slight rain. His heart pounded as he slammed into the cottage and jerked to a halt.

Hell's teeth!

It was as he had left it. The bed sheets rumbled. He inhaled, and Adeline's subtle fragrance filled his lungs. Surely he was imagining her scent after so long. He moved farther into the room, his eyes drawn to the bed. Distressing lust swam in his veins as the memory of arching her hips and sucking on her soft, wet, womanly flesh, rose in his fevered brain. She had screamed, gripped his hair, and demanded more in her wild passion. She had been fierce and beautiful, welcoming and tight as she offered her body unreservedly. Edmond's knees buckled, and he sank into the lone wing-backed chair in the room.

It truly had not been a dream.

I love you, Edmond.

Had those words been real as well? Edmond's insides turned to ice. Adeline was truly with child, and as sure as the sun would rise tomorrow he would lose her because of it. All of the facts he had studied raced to the forefront of his thoughts.

Fifty in every one thousand women in London died in childbirth. The odds seemed like they could be on his side. Maryann had been taken, and now Adeline could be one of the thousand that would die this year because of that bad luck.

No…not bad luck. Because of childbed fever, convulsions, infection, hemorrhaging.

He struggled to breathe through his nose evenly and to calm the furious pounding of his heart. He would have to leave Rosette Park tonight. He couldn't bear to see her swell with his child and then watch the light dim from her eyes, as the monster named death came to claim her, like it had claimed Maryann and his father.

He braced his forearm on his thighs and lowered his head, ruthlessly building the wall around his heart, for without a doubt, from the terror now tearing through his soul, he had been on the cusp of falling in love with his wife.

What a damn fool he had been. To allow himself such sentiments when his children depended on him. He could allow nothing to plunge him back into that roaring demon riddled with guilt and pain.

When Edmond lifted his head, dusk had fallen. It seemed hours had passed since he'd been sitting in the chair. Rain had lashed the cottage, and thunder had shaken its frame and he'd hardly been aware. When he stood, he felt no tender stirring in his heart for his wife. Only a simple appreciation that she was alive, that she was a kind woman who seemed to cherish his daughters as much as he loved them. That was all he'd wanted. When she died, whether it be in nine months, or several years from now, he would certainly feel its sting, for Adeline was a wonderful woman. But he would not be crippled by torment, haunted by empty, lifeless eyes, and taunted by pleading tears to save her life, nor shredded by wails that accused him of killing her and their child. No…for he did not—*would not*—love her.

• • •

It had been six weeks since the duke had departed Rosette Park for, she believed, London. There was a squeal of joy from below the stairs, and Adel tried to drum up a smile. It seemed Sarah and Rosa had received another letter from their father. A messenger had arrived every morning on horseback, with a long letter for them both. Sometimes, parcels of presents, and even a few books had come. There had been nothing for Adel. The children allowed her to read the letters to them, and the duke regaled them with sights seen in London, and what he did with his day. But not once had he asked how she fared. Like a fool she kept reading the letters daily, hoping for a sign of something.

Why had she not told him what happened in the cottage the minute she realized he'd not remembered? Regret sat in her stomach like rotten food. Though she had come to realize it would not have mattered. It was not her omission he hated, it was the very fact that she was with child. And that would have still been true even if he had known about their night of untamed loving from the beginning. He had retreated back to his old self, and she would simply have to find happiness where she could in their marriage, without him. For now, she could not contemplate the loneliness that would eventually descend. For now, she concentrated on her children and not the crushing pain she woke with daily.

She rose from the bath water, and Meg gently toweled her dry. With mechanical motions, Adel sat in front of her dressing table as Meg tamed her hair. Then she dressed in a simple white muslin day gown, donned her emerald green redingote, and added her bonnet. She would go for a walk this morning, and try to lift her spirits.

A few minutes later she strolled through the gardens, the fragrance of lily and roses filling her lungs. Dr. Graves had said exercise would be good for her health and it was time she took measures to ensure she took her daily constitutional.

The wind tugged at her bonnet, and the air smelled crisp and clean. After her walk she would direct her attention to the few letters she had. Adel had become the patron to several underfunded and much ignored charities in the nearby villages, and a few in town. She had been appalled to learn the closest village to Rosette lacked both a proper school and had no bookstore or library. A few of the children in the village traveled for miles for some sort of an education but most went without and remained unlettered. A school was now being constructed, and it was being overseen by the vicar and his kind wife. One of the local shops was falling vacant in a few months and she had bought the lease intending to turn it into a bookshop. Though she immersed herself with such activities, every night she still ached for Edmond. But she was determined to exorcise the wretched man from her heart.

In the far distance the dowager duchess was strolling with Squire Wentworth. Adel smiled. She could see the affection developing between the two when they thought no one was observing.

Lady Harriet saw her and waved. A few minutes later, she reached Adel.

"It is wonderful to see you up and about, my dear. Is my foolish and stubborn son home?"

A startled laugh jerked from Adel. "No."

The dowager duchess sighed and linked their hands together in companionable silence.

"Why have you not followed him to London? A wife's place is beside her husband and it has been two weeks since your stomach has settled. You are fit for traveling."

"Edmond does not love me."

The dowager duchess froze, and then faced her. "My dear, he worships the ground you walk upon. It is fear that drove him away."

"What utter rubbish. I told him I carry our child, and he ran away to London without writing a single word to me for six dreadful weeks. When I came to this marriage I had nothing to offer him but my eventual love. I gave it to him even knowing he would never love me in return, and now I have never felt more a-alone."

Adel burst into mortified tears. "Oh, forgive me; I've been such a watering pot lately." She swiped at her face angrily. "Did he ever tell you how we met? I *snuck* into his bed at Lady Gladstone's house party. It was quite by accident I assure you, for I'd only intend to comprise Mr. Atwood. Edmond insisted we wed to avoid scandal. Before I even said yes, he told me all the love he had to give was bu…buried with his wife. He avoided my bed with a single minded purpose that even I had started to admire, and the only reason I am with child now is because he had been drunk," she ended on a sob. "He does not want *me*...no gentleman has truly ever wanted me, for I have nothing to offer! Can there be any other opinion?"

Embarrassed at her emotional outburst she marched away. Edmond loved her? As she loved him? Adel faltered.

You are beautiful. You taste sweet...I could feast on you forever.

There are days when I shudder in dread at the thought, of what might have happened if you had not climbed into my bed, because I would now be wed to another. I've never desired another woman as I do you, Adeline.

The heated and sometimes tender words he'd expressed wafted through her mind. It probably should not have, but the memory quieted some of the pain pricking at her heart.

What if he truly loved her? Would he really have felt such fear if he only felt mild affections?

Oh!

Lady Harriet regarded Adel for a lengthy moment. "Come, let us retire to the parlor and ring for tea."

Adel glanced toward the lawns. "And what of Squire Wentworth?"

"He'll keep," she said on a light laugh. "He knows I will not be long, and he may do a spot of fishing in the lake."

A few minutes later they entered the main house, and Adel rang for tea and cakes. They entered the warmth of the parlor and sat on separate sofas. A footman arrived in short order with a tea tray and several pastries.

The dowager duchess faced her. "I've been meaning to thank you for weeks now," she said softly.

Adel lifted startled eyes to her. "I have done nothing."

"Since your marriage to my son, he has laughed." This last bit was said so wistfully Adel's heart ached.

She had thought his icy reserve had only been for her. Had he always been like this? "Is Edmond not a man to laugh?"

"Hardly."

Not even with his first wife? Adel ached to know. "I take no credit for it, but I thank you for the sentiments."

"My son abhors grief," she said, surprising Adel.

Lady Harriet retrieved the cushion she had been embroidering earlier and resumed her task with dazzling skill. "I witnessed something in my eldest son I had not observed in years. Peace. It made me feel hope and fear for my sweet boy in equal measure."

A small smile curved Adel's lips to hear Lady Harriet refer to a man so virile and ruthless with his power as sweet. "I have yet to uncover this sweetness." Though if she admitted it, there had been nothing experienced in her life as heavenly as the sweet bliss of his kisses. The way he watched her sometimes, the intensity in which he loved her had given her hope. The mere memory was enough to make the flesh between her thighs ache. Heat crawled up her neck, and she hastily poured tea into a cup and raised it to her lips, praying Lady Harriet would believe it was the steam from the tea that would account for her flushed appearance.

"Edmond lost his father, a man he idolized, at the tender age of twelve. I was selfish in my grief." She lifted pain eyes to Adel. "I almost lost my son because I was caught up in my own despair."

A drop of blood stained the cushion, and with a gasp, Adel clattered the teacup onto the table and rushed over to the dowager duchess. Adel gently withdrew the cushion and the needle from her.

"Please do not speak of it, for it causes you pain."

Adel understood, it had been four years since her mother had passed, and she could hardly think of her without her throat burning from the need to hold back the tears. There were days where her heart seemed to split in two, and she wondered when the void would ever be filled. Reading had only delayed the inevitable return of dreaded grief. Though since her marriage, life had been mostly pleasing, and she had thought little about the loss of her mother.

"Sit my child," Lady Harriet said gently. "Though it pains me, I wish to speak of it, for I want you to win."

Win? "I was not aware I was vying for a prize."

The dowager duchess's intensity finally penetrated, and Adel's heart beat an alarming thud. She sank to her knees beside her, uncaring of the unladylike position. "Then tell me, quickly."

Lady Harriet closed her eyes and spoke in a clipped voice. "I was so lost in my own grief I did not realize Edmond was wasting away. He'd cried himself to sleep every night, and was barely eating. I'd given orders for his tutoring to be paused, and for his friends to give him space. I did not help him, I allowed him to create a haven in which he could grieve and rail unrelentingly. And he did so for weeks, months. When I came out of my own stupor my boy was skin and bones. I called for the doctor and he gave me the alarming prognosis that Edmond's heart had been weakened from the weight loss, and he needed special attention to encourage eating. A few days later he contracted a fever, and in his weakened state it was a brutal battle. The fear I encountered I never wanted to endure again."

She took a shuddering breath and Adel squeezed her arm. "He recovered. I wanted to cosset him, wanted to keep him close, but he refused. It was as if something had died in him when his father passed. My sweet boy hardly laughed and played. The joy in him had been dimmed. He had been close to his younger brother Jackson, and he pulled from him. Edmond even insisted on returning to boarding school, instead of his tutors coming back to the estates. It was as if he wanted to flee the memories. Then he returned on his eighteenth birthday and met Lady Maryann."

Lady Harriet smiled. "Maryann was beautiful and demure,

and she lit something inside of him. It was a small spark but I was joyful. I encouraged the attachment, and I could sense his reluctance. It was as if he feared being too close to Maryann. But she persevered, and he offered for her. Yet he remained wary. As if he was waiting for something to happen. Though he loved her, he was remote at the best of times. It hurt and confused Maryann, but she coaxed, and he thawed, and it was beautiful to see Edmond enjoying the hope of a happy future. He basked in his beautiful children, and I would dare say he was happy. Then she died."

Lady Harriett pushed from the settee and walked to the windows. "Suffice to say, my child, since he married you, for the first time I have heard my son laugh out loud since his father's death."

Adel flinched.

"I do not care what you did or the why of it…but I thank you. The coldness he exudes now, it is because he cannot bear the idea of losing you, too. I see your unhappiness, and I urge you, do not give up on him."

Then as if embarrassed for her emotional state, she inclined her head and walked with evident false serenity from the drawing room.

Adel slowly gathered herself. Edmond loved her. The assessment felt right, but if he really did, based on what Lady Harriet just revealed, he was truly lost to her.

Chapter Twenty-Four

Weeks of being apart from his duchess had not dulled the agony pounding through Edmond's heart. He rolled his head back against his shoulders, trying to ease the tension. Though when he wrote to his daughters, he was careful not to feed his weakness to learn about Adeline. Sarah and Rosa had no such qualms.

He glanced down to the letters he had splayed on the desk in his library. Dozens of them, and he had taken ink and underlined the phrases that mentioned his duchess.

Dear Papa, Adeline is puking again and seems very low in spirits.

Papa, Adeline smiled today, but then she promptly burst into tears when Mrs. Fields mentioned another letter had come from you.

Papa, Mamma says we must decorate a nursery, but she is unsure where to have it established since Mrs. Fields explained you ordered every trace of the previous nursery destroyed and it has now been made into Lady Adeline's library.

He had read that last letter a dozen times. His girls referred to Adeline as mother. He cleared his throat and looked to the next underlined words in the next letter.

Today was the first morning since you left that Adeline came downstairs to break her fast. She looked so beautiful.

He rustled through the mound and selected his favorite.

Papa, today Mamma took a walk in the gardens. She helped us escape the schoolroom, and Mrs. Fields packed a small hamper for us. We had the picnic by the lake and it was glorious. Sarah and I wished you were here, and Mamma smiled. I think that means she wants you home...we miss you. We also picked names for the baby! Sarah and I are so excited. We are hoping for a brother.

He was a damn fool. For some reason God had found favor in him, and Edmond was squandering it. He should be at Rosette Park with his wife and children. He should be holding Adel, comforting her, rubbing her feet and her back when she was weary. Holding the chamber pot for her when her stomach rebelled.

Instead, he had fled to London, rousing his staff in the dark of the night and setting them on their ears. He had been holed up for days, not visiting the sights as he had been lying in his letters. He did not want his daughters to know he had not been eating and that he was coldly miserable.

The door opened and he glanced up.

Westfall strolled in unannounced, took one glance at the letters spilling all over the desk, some on the floor. The man said nothing, simply moved to the sofa closest to Edmond and sank onto it, tilting his head back and staring at the decorative plasterwork on the ceiling.

"You've been in London for six weeks, and I do not believe you have left the residence," the marquess said.

Edmond grunted.

"There is gossip that you have separated from your duchess."

It had taken Westfall long enough for his curiosity to get the better of him.

"I'd not thought you a man to listen to that kind of rumor."

"I heard it from my valet who seems to have a cousin who is an upstairs maid at Rosette Park."

Edmond arched a brow.

"So what is happening with your duchess? You rested your honor upon marrying her when you did not have to, so why are you mucking it up?"

Edmond leaned back in his chair. "I care for her…deeply."

"Truly?" the marquess asked, with sincere incredulity. "You have truly fallen prey to the same affliction twice?"

Edmond chuckled without humor. Westfall was certainly right in thinking this a damnable curse. Edmond could not sleep or eat without dreaming of Adeline. His first few nights had been tormented with nightmares of losing her, of seeing blood pour from her, and beautiful accusing eyes damming him to perdition. Then they had slowly transformed into dreams of walking beside her on their lake, a child of their own running on the lawn with the girls, seeing the joy on her face. He'd remembered those images, and his fear of losing her had been strangled by the fear of truly never getting to know her in her entirety. If he had only days with her, or months, or years, as he had been praying for, he should treasure whatever time God allotted them together.

Life without Adel was too bleak to contemplate, and it was time for him to return to Rosette Park.

He'd fallen in love with Maryann through the rose-colored spectacles of a young man, who had needed to be awakened. He had seen there was more to life than fulfilling his duty conserving everything his father had left behind. With Adeline… Edmond scrubbed a hand over his face. The depth of emotion he felt for her was truly too frightening at times, but in the midst of the passion, there was a calmness, a joint meeting of souls like he'd never felt before. The realization ached worse than a fist to his gut. He half laughed, half groaned. He was becoming a damned poet.

"It seems I have," Edmond said dryly. "I cannot sleep or work, I do nothing but think of her. Every damn day I write her a letter that I have not posted. Sometimes I write a note in the morning, and there are days I still write to her before I sleep."

"If you care for her, why have you been holed up here for weeks? I confess my ribs do not wish to meet with your fists again."

He'd chosen to work off the raw edginess—both of body and of mind—by bare knuckle boxing with Westfall. Edmond had refused to even swallow a drop of liquor, he would not drink again to bury pain. Perhaps he would for pleasure, or when he entertained, but never to drown his sorrows again. Westfall had simply raised his shoulders at Edmond's pronouncements, carefully peeled off his skintight coat and waistcoat, and joined him on the mat in the exercise room.

That morning's session had been grueling, brutal, and freeing. He fully understood Westfall's desire not to step on the mat with him again for some time. Edmond had been sparring with him almost every evening, ruthlessly striving to detach himself from the torment he'd put himself under. His friend had been constant, even going as far as to take up residence in one of Edmond's guest rooms and he had realized Westfall had his own demons to work through.

Then during the day, Edmond would spend hours buried into writing articles and motions for the following year's debates in the House of Lords. He was dissatisfied with everything he had written and it had failed to distract his heart and mind from being totally obsessed with missing Adeline.

"She is with child. Four months along by my calculation."

"Congratulations to you and your duchess." Westfall rose

and went to the sideboard pouring brandy into a glass. He raised it to Edmond. "Here is to hoping for an heir!"

Dread coiled through him.

"Good God, man, I wished you an heir, not to be roasted on a devil's spit."

"The last time everyone wished for an heir, Maryann died."

"Hell," Westfall said softly. "I wish you nothing but good fortune. All Saint's Eve is next week. I daresay you should be at Rosette Park."

Edmond frowned and rubbed a hand over his chest. "I confess this is the first time I have thought of Maryann and our son without the bitter taste of guilt on my tongue. Thoughts of Adeline simply bring peace, and I have been a bastard to her."

"What have you done?"

With clipped words, and for the first time in years, he unburdened himself to Westfall.

Shadows shifted in his friend's gaze. "I understand your fear, but it is better to hold onto her with everything you have, instead of wasting even a second of time spent with her and lose her forever."

Edmond smiled to hear his friend echo such sentiments. Westfall was a hardened rake, and society gossip suggested he had not an ounce of feelings for anyone but himself. Despite his friend's sometimes cruel, sarcastic tongue, Edmond knew otherwise.

He surged to his feet and strolled to the window facing the gardens. "I should not have left her. This is her first child… and I cannot imagine how uncertain she must feel. I shall go to her."

"And will you tell her how you feel?"

Edmond despised emotions, especially those exercised to excess. Fear and grief were the ones he found hardest to deal with. Even now, the idea of being overly affectionate with his duchess made him feel distinctly uncomfortable. "My presence will be enough to show I care."

Westfall grimaced. "I have never known you to show sentiment, but how you spoke just now…" He said nothing more, only taking several sips from his glass. "There is also a rumor Mr. James Atwood was seen traveling to Rosette Park."

Edmond froze. "I beg your pardon?"

Westfall's lips twisted. "It seemed the man was very happy to hear of your estrangement."

"And how has he heard such rumors?"

"You and your duchess have become a reigning toast, everyone is interested in your lives."

Edmond dismissed Westfall's words. "It does not signify if Mr. Atwood visits Adeline. My duchess has honor."

"A thing I have never witnessed in a woman. Either way, honor is a cold bedfellow. What she needs is passion and—"

"Hold your damned tongue," Edmond snapped. He would not even think of his duchess in another man's arms. "How is your daughter?" Edmond asked, needing to change the subject matter.

Westfall tensed. "She heals as we speak. I swear she will want for nothing, and if society thinks to cut her when she is older they will bleed, Edmond. She has suffered enough." Rage and icy ruthlessness throbbed in his voice.

Edmond understood. Westfall's daughter was a bastard, and he had discovered her existence just before it had almost been too late. His father, the Duke of Salop, had refused to speak with his own son, for doing the unimaginable—acknowledging his bastard so that all of society knew of her existence.

"And her mother?"

"That damnable bitch abandoned her to a baby farm in Willesden Green and pretended Emily did not exist. Do you think now that she is a countess, she would risk her reputation to visit my dwelling to see the child or even acknowledge her?"

No, Edmond supposed not.

"My duchess told me you had formed an attachment."

A tic jerked in Westfall's cheek, and his golden eyes went blank. "It is you we are talking about Edmond, not my affairs."

Edmond grunted. "I saw the way you watched Lady Evelyn at the last soiree I attended with my duchess. If the *ton* had observed the hunger I saw, they would have called for a wedding, surely believing you had already debauched the girl. Yet the attachment you have formed is with Lady Honoria. Please explain yourself."

The marquess downed his drink in one swallow. "Go grovel to your duchess and take your nose out of my business, Wolverton." Westfall slammed the glass on the mantle and stalked from the room.

Edmond sighed. Westfall would speak when he was ready, but Edmond hoped he did nothing foolish when his heart, or his damn lust, was so clearly engaged with another. But the man was right, Edmond had to travel to Rosette Park and visit his duchess. But what would he say? He couldn't bear to be from her? Her death, whether he was with her for several months or seventy years, would shatter him when it arrived, but he needed to spend every last moment with her. *Hell*. He had no notion where to start, but he had to see her.

Edmond launched from the chair and strode from the room, tersely ordering his valet to pack a saddlebag and his groom to ready a horse.

Chapter Twenty-Five

Almost twelve hours later, Edmond arrived at Rosette Park. He had no notion of what he would say to his duchess, only knew he could not stay away from her or his daughters any longer. He swept from his horse, and handed the reins to the footman. The quietness of the estate unsettled him. The last letter he had received from his girls the day before had indicated all was well. He strode up to the front door, and Mr. Jenkins held it open, his face a smooth mask, but Edmond swore he could see an accusation dwelling in his butler's eyes.

Edmond strode through the entrance hall and grounded to a halt.

A maid bustled down the corridor. "Mr. Jenkins, the remainder of her ladyship's and the girls' trunks have been readied to send down…"

The maid's words trailed off when she spotted him, and it was then Edmond realized that the two footmen had frozen with trunks in their hands, and the butler stood stiff, eyes staring straight ahead as he'd been trained to do. Edmond's gaze remained on several trunks, which were already standing in the hall. Their import slammed into his gut like an iron fist. His duchess had left him.

Footsteps sounded behind him, then the housekeeper appeared with a letter.

"Her ladyship left this for you, Your Grace," Mrs. Fields said.

"Thank you." Edmond took it and with clipped strides walked away to his study. He entered and strolled over to the window, almost afraid to open the letter. He realized what an arrogant idiot he had been, thinking he would simply ride to Rosette Park and Adeline would be waiting for him. Unable to wait any longer, he unfolded the paper.

> *Dear Edmond,*
>
> *I have retired to the Somerset Estates. It grows unbearable to live at Rosette Park with the memories of us, and I've finally conceded to the estrangement you desire. It has been weeks since we've last spoken, and I've come to realize you will not look beyond the past to the future with me. I cannot say I regret accidentally compromising you, for you have given me a great gift and I will treasure our child. The girls and Lady Harriet insisted on traveling with me, however I expect you will send word when you wish for their return. My father's estate is only a few miles away, and I will find comfort there when I need. I only ask that you allow the girls to visit me as much as they desire, and when our child is born, you will meet him or her.*
>
> *Adeline*

Edmond hated the weak feeling that overcame him. She did not believe she could get comfort from him, and why should she, when he had been so foolish? She mentioned nothing of loving him, in fact her words seemed so final, his soul ached. He knew then that words would be inadequate. He loved her, and he needed to show her he was more than ready to be a family and do away with fear, that had held him for far too long. Dropping the letter on the desk, he stormed from his study calling for the housekeeper and his butler.

"Your Grace?" Mrs. Fields said, hurrying toward him, with Mr. Jenkins right on her heels.

"Send word to the village. I want carpenters, painters, and all the necessary workers here to build a nursery. Hire as many as possible, for I want it done in less than a week."

Delight crossed Mrs. Fields face, and what appeared to be approval glowed in his butler's eyes.

"And which room shall be converted?"

"The chambers beside the duchess's chambers."

With quick bows and curtsies, his servants departed. Edmond scrubbed a hand over his face. He would build their child a nursery, and then travel to Somerset and plead his case, and pray he had not completely killed her love for him.

• • •

A shout of laughter filtered from the entrance hall, and Adeline smiled. It had been a week since they departed Rosette Park, and the girls seemed to be enjoying Somerset, and she even felt a bit more at peace. In the two months Edmond had been absent from Rosette Park without even scrawling a note to her, something inside of her had withered. If he truly loved her, regardless of his fear, should he not fight to be with her? Adel had pushed past the pain, and resolved to find happiness with her children. There was a brief knock on the drawing room door, and then it was opened to admit Lady Harriet, and her husband's man of affairs Mr. Dobson.

Adel stood frowning. "Mr. Dobson?"

He bowed slightly. "Your Grace. I've been sent down by the duke to make arrangements for a nursery to be constructed here."

Pain almost made her knees buckle. He was truly relieved she was gone from Rosette Park and his life. "I see."

"Tell her the rest, Mr. Dobson," Lady Harriet said with a smile.

"The duke has given instructions that all his estates be equipped with nurseries, Your Ladyship."

"All of them?"

"Yes, Your Grace."

Adel's heart jolted. "Even at Rosette Park?"

"Yes, Your Grace, and also the estates in Scotland."

Oh. What did that mean?

"There will be some knocking and hammering for the next few days, Your Grace, we are begging your pardon for the noise."

She nodded, and Mr. Dobson exited.

"Why is he doing this?" she asked, still in a daze. What did it mean?

"It seems my son is awakening," Lady Harriet said.

"But he still has not written to me."

The dowager duchess walked over to her, and clasped Adel's hands. "I never thought you were the one to sit and wait. You, my dear, are very decisive and bold, traits my son admires. Go to him."

Adeline smiled and rushed from the drawing room. Hope was stirring in her breast, and she did nothing to suppress it. Was this Edmond showing her he wanted her with him? She'd already realized she loved him, and now she had to know if he loved her and was willing to fight for their family, despite his fears. For if he didn't, she would walk away forever.

• • •

A noise alerted Edmond, and he glanced up. Adeline stood at the entrance of the nursery, perfectly still, looking at him. She was dressed in a dark green gown that flowed gently over her rounded stomach. He swallowed. Her stomach was much higher, and more rounded than how Maryann had been when she was sixteen weeks pregnant. "Adeline, I…" His mouth was suddenly dry.

Hell, he had practiced his apology for days, and now that he was face to face with his duchess, words deserted him. He stared at her face which stared back coldly aloof. It was an expression he had never seen her display before and it chilled him. "You came back," he said, at loss for any other words.

"Yes."

His heart lurched. The distance in her tone was inescapable. "I see."

He placed the lion he had been carving on the carpet. What the hell was he to say? He had always been a man of few words, and frustratingly, now the few words he needed had deserted him. All he could think of was how radiant and beautiful she appeared. "I can't work. I can't think. I can't sleep." The words slipped from him, as if from their own volition.

"And what does that have to do with me?"

He distantly became aware of a few servants lingering in the hallway, including the housekeeper and the butler. Didn't they have duties to attend? Though they did not look directly at him, he could feel their keen attention to his conversation with his duchess.

"I have been an unmitigated fool."

She inclined her head with icy civility. "That you have been, Your Grace." There was no give in her tone, she simply agreed with him, noticing his existence in passing, with what appeared to be mild curiosity, as she might give an unusual insect found in the gardens.

The woman standing before him was cloaked in icy

sternness, which he doubted he would be able to ever pierce. Nothing glowed in her eyes, none of the warmth, the passion, the love he had seen before. Nothing remained of the kind, generous lady she had been, and he had been the one to reduce her to this…marble effigy of her former self. Sudden, fierce pride burned in his veins, and he smiled in amused self-mockery. He was so proud his duchess was not weeping and rushing into his arms. With an effort that was almost painful he prevented himself from going to her and drawing her into his arms.

He'd rehearsed dozens of speeches, explanations, yet none of it truly mattered now. He'd hurt this woman whom he had vowed to protect and cherish, and he truly had no notion how to atone. "Adeline, have you ever wanted something very badly, something that was within your grasp, and you only needed the courage to reach for it?" he asked, raking his fingers though his hair.

Her eyes widened, and he witnessed the hope that flared before she buried it once more. Her eyes darkened momentarily then cleared. "Yes," she said.

"That is how I feel about you. You are everything I'd ever dreamed of and more, and I have been so afraid that I will lose you, but I have come to my senses."

A loud exhalation puffed from her lips.

The silence was thick and heavy. She closed the door softly, shutting out their hopeful audience and leaned against it. "I truly despaired of you ever wanting us," she said, resting her hands on her stomach. Her eyes were somber in their depths, and the sadness pierced him.

"The workers arrived before I left. I understand from them that you are making nurseries in all of your estates."

"*Our* estates."

A fleeting smile tugged at her lips. "I fear…I fear that when I need you Edmond, you will not be here. I fear each time I swell with our child you will pull away from me."

"I will never leave your side again. I'm so damned sorry, Duchess. I do not deserve you, nor do I expect you to forgive me. I can only pray your generosity and kindness can extend to me and forgive me for being absent. Even when everything inside me really wanted to be here, I fought against it for fear of losing you, because I love you with everything that I am, Adeline," he said gruffly.

A slow smile stretched across her face. Tender feelings assailed Edmond, holding him spellbound.

"I missed you," she said.

"And I missed you, Adeline."

She patted her distended stomach. "Our son or daughter is very active today."

His throat closed. "How are you feeling?"

His duchess smiled tenderly, and then cocked her head sideways as if pondering a deep matter. "I never knew you carved."

He glanced down at his tools, the lion he had been carving, then slowly rose to his feet. Everything seemed so tentative, and he felt so damn unsure. "I do."

She nodded and met him in the center of the room. Adeline clasped his hands and glided her fingers over the coarseness of his thumb. Her eyes lifted to his. "They are scarred." Then she kissed the small cuts on his fingers.

His throat tightened. "Forgive me, Adeline."

Her lips twitched, and he held his breath waiting for the sweet curve he found himself missing daily. Disappointment lanced through him when the promised smile failed to appear.

"I do."

He drew her to him, clasping her cheeks to press a firm kiss to her lips. She was the most beautiful sight he had ever seen. Her breasts were much heavier, her thighs and hips had a more pronounced curves, but it was her high rounded belly that held all his attention. He lowered his hands to her stomach, tracing the swell. "You are beyond exquisite," he whispered.

The reserve in her gaze melted, and her eyes glowed with a brilliance that made him want to fall at her knees in thankfulness that she still loved him. She did not say it, nor did he press her for the words, but he knew, for he similarly adored everything about her. Her courage in the face of his past coldness had kept her strong with her natural intelligence and her unfailing love and kindness.

He stroked his palm down her spine, from her hips around to her rounded stomach. She stilled, breathing softly. There was a ripple under his palm, and a soft laugh puffed from her.

"That is our baby." Her voice was rife with awe.

Our baby.

And he felt no fear. Edmond cradled her cheeks and kissed her with a desperate passion. She parted her lips and returned his kiss with equal fervour. He wanted the kiss to never end, and more than anything he craved sentiments from his duchess. "Love me, Adeline," he said, kissing the corner of her mouth.

"Can you doubt it?" she gasped.

His chest vibrated with a groan. "No…I truly cannot."

"I love you utterly and completely, Edmond, and I feel I have waited all my life for you." Adeline pressed a kiss to his chest right above his beating heart. "I love you with all my heart, and I thank God every day that I accidentally compromised you."

Edmond felt as though the ground shifted around him, and everything that had been wrong settled back in its right place. She still loved him, and he would endeavor never to lose that love. "Losing your love would destroy me. Never stop loving me, Adeline."

"Never," she vowed, tipping to kiss the corner of his lips.

For the first time since Edmond could remember, he felt whole.

Chapter Twenty-Six

Adeline's shoulders shook with mirth, and with a gasp she wiped tears from her eyes. Edmond was playing a game of charade on the lawn with the girls, and Adel reclined on a chaise longue which the footmen had carried outside for her pleasure, watching them. She was unable to join the game, so she could only make herself comfortable on the chaise, which had been padded especially for her. Today was a rare sunny day, which she had been determined to take advantage of.

Edmond did another hop on his foot and scratched the underside of his arms. Her love looked ridiculous. He was trying to pantomime a monkey, and Sarah should be the one guessing. So far she had put forth several suggestions, the entire time giggling.

Adel reached for the pitcher of water placed on the table to her left, and a sharp pain tore through her back. She drew back her arms, and waited for the sensation to reappear. There was nothing. She had three of the best doctors in England attending her and two local midwives who had come with fulsome references from a number of the ladies who lived close to Rosette Park. It was a concession she had been prepared to give Edmond, for she had no notions of what to expect from the birthing bed.

She had woken in the dark of the night several times to find him seated in an armchair in their chambers watching her, a silent protective force. But her duke had yet to understand that he could not control everything.

He had moved her into his chambers, and on more than one night the torment of nightmares had woken him, but it had been her name he called.

Then he would reach for her, hold her into his arms, rub her stomach as their baby kicked within her.

She slowly struggled to sit and slipped her feet over the edge of the couch. Her back was sore, and she felt she had been in the same position for far too long.

She gingerly stood and stretched.

"Adeline," Edmond said walking over. "Are you well?"

She smiled in reassurance. "I am quite fine, but I do think it might be prudent to stretch my legs a bit across the lawns." Then she stepped towards him.

Horror chased his features, and he lunged for her. It was as her body made the impact on the hard ground, she realized he had been trying to break her fall. She tried to tell him not to worry, but darkness took her mind under.

· · ·

He had failed to keep her safe. The terror winding itself through Edmond's soul was so cold his teeth chattered. When Adeline had fainted, she had hit the ground with an impact that had shriveled his soul. He had only been a fingertip away from reaching her. Why had he allowed her to be out? She was more than eight months pregnant, and had been indoors for days. He'd seen her restlessness and acted, trying to brighten her day. Now he could lose her.

"Papa." A small hand gripped his. He glanced down into Rosa's scared face.

He stooped to her level and drew her close. "Yes, pumpkin?"

"Is A-Adeline going to heaven like Mamma?"

Cold sweat slicked down his back beneath his jacket, and for precious seconds Edmond could not utter a single word. "No."

His daughter searched his eyes frantically and whatever she saw reassured her, for she wilted against him and hugged his neck tightly.

After a moment she spoke, "Do you promise, Papa? Do you promise to save her?"

His damn heart was ripping from his chest. Then he realized what a truly selfish fool he had been. It was not only he who feared loving and losing again. His daughters had fallen in love with Adeline, as surely and deeply as he had. For them it would be just as painful or even more, losing the love, the gentle and the unending support of two mothers.

"Papa, you're squeezing me too tight."

Hell. He'd not even realized.

"I promise you, pumpkin, I will not let him take her."

She rustled in his arms.

"Who, Papa?"

"The devil."

Rosa eyes widened. "I think it is God you should be talking to, Papa. Mrs. Fields says never bargain with the devil."

He kissed her cheek. "Go with Miss Thompson to the music room. Play all of Adeline's favorite songs. I am sure she will love that."

His daughters nodded and then scampered away with the governess waiting by the doorway.

Edmond stood as an anguished wail sliced through the

room. Without hesitation he climbed the stairs and entered his chambers. The slight tang of blood reached him instantly. He waded through the darkness of memory and approached the bed. The first doctor to arrive to his urgent summons had been Dr. Greaves. He and the midwife's heads were bowed closely together, and their furious whispering caused agitation to surge through Edmond's blood.

With a force of willpower, he pushed his doubts and panic aside and concentrated on his duchess.

A smile tugged at his lips when she scowled at him fiercely. "What are you doing in here? I told you to go and be with the girls."

He heard it. Her fear. The crippling unseen power, which had the teeth to render both him and his duchess powerless. "Hush now, nothing you say will remove me from your side."

Despite the pain, pleasure lit her eyes. "Edmond," she whispered his name.

The doctor glanced up, and he walked to Edmond. "May we speak alone, Your Grace?"

"No," Adeline said as she struggled to sit. "Whatever you wish to say, Edmond and I will face it together."

"Your Grace, I…I…the duchess is weakened and the babies are not coming."

"Speak out, man."

The doctor frowned toward the bed.

"Her Grace has had some minor but very worrying convulsions. Before her fall, your wife had been progressing quite nicely, and I did not predict any complications. Now her limbs are swollen and the babies have not turned."

The room swam. "Babies?"

The midwife, Mrs. Agnes, stepped forward, her brown eyes warm and confident. "Babies, Your Grace. From what I can feel, one is already on the way, but he is in breech position. So he may need to be turned…but there is another baby above him."

Edmond checked to see that everything was how he'd ordered it to be. Dozens of jugs with boiled water. Carbolic soap laid out on several clean towels. The fire kept at minimum, so the room was not stifling, and the sheets were fresh cleaned. Several doctors he'd spoke with had insisted it was important that hand washing and general cleanliness was the first order of the day. Beautiful baby clothes had been arranged together with fresh clean towels and bedding.

"Edmond."

He strolled over to his duchess and laced their fingers tightly.

Fierce eyes clashed with his. "I am ready to throw both of them from my room. They tell me nothing, and their silence is not soothing to my nerves," she gritted through clenched teeth.

Her anger filled him with mystifying hope. She was not weeping and muttering that all was lost before hearing their assessment. It gave him some reassurance that maybe she would fight with every breath in her body.

"We are having two babies."

Her eyes widened, and she struggled to sit. The midwife rushed over and aided him in placing well-padded pillows behind her back. At that moment a contraction seized her, and she crushed his hand.

Sweat ran in rivulets down her hairline. Then she smiled at him, and the fear he saw in her gaze almost rendered him insensible. He despaired that she would feel such an emotion. He wanted to rage, and take every pain she felt and be able to give her comfort and love.

"Tell me," she hissed. Her lower lip trembled, then with a willpower he admired, she flattened her lips, and determination glowed from her eyes. "Am I dying?"

Edmond cursed, low and dark in the quiet room.

The doctor sighed and came over. "There is a possibility, Your Grace, that—"

"Hold your damned tongue," Edmond snapped, unable to contain the cold fury slicing through his veins.

He faced his love. "I have spent months scouring books, interviewing doctors on all matters relating to childbirth. The risk, the precautions that might improve the outcome, I was almost mindless in my obsession, and I questioned myself why I should bother to study the subject. Maryann had already died, so why would I ever need the information. But God knew he intended to give me *you*. A hope for a future…of love and peace, and he prepared me to help you in every way possible with our children. I didn't know it then, but I damn well know it now, and if you utter another word or thought about dying…" His throat worked, trapping the roar of denial building in his chest.

"Edmond," she said softly. "I will not perish…not today."

He kissed her wet cheeks, running his hands over her shaking shoulders, trying to comfort her. "I know, for the strength of your spirit is unquenchable. Together we will ensure our babes come safely into the world. I believe you will hold them in your arms. I, madam, would be but a shadow without you."

A watery smile crossed her lips, and a small sob hiccupped from her. "Does this mean, Your Grace, you will stay with me?"

"Nothing will pry me from this room."

Her forehead dropped onto his, her sweat dampening his hairline. "I will not leave you…at least not for another forty years or more."

"Not yet," he echoed. "Neither in this lifetime nor in the next."

Then they faced the demon that had haunted him for far too long.

Epilogue

"You have a wonderful family," Westfall murmured with something akin to envy in his tone.

Edmond moved even closer to the open window in his library, not wanting to miss a second of their delightful romping. His duchess reposed on a blanket with their very active eight months old sons, Jordon Alexander Rochester, the Marquess of Carlyle, and Drake St. John Rochester, crawling over her and cooing. Love swelled in Edmond's chest when his wife chortled and did that very ridiculous talk to the babies that she swore they understood.

Life indeed had been wonderful to him and Adeline. After the birth of their boys, within a couple of weeks his duchess had been back to her exuberant self, refusing to stay abed. Then when he had been hesitant about making love too soon, his duchess had seduced him with shocking sensuality, over and over. Hell, he wouldn't be surprised if she were to tell him soon that she was once again with child, because of how often they were wrapped together in passion.

"I think it's time we joined them," Edmond said.

Westfall frowned, canting his head left and Edmond knew who he searched for. Lady Evelyn.

"You cannot avoid her forever," Edmond said with some amusement. "You are both godparents to Jordon and Drake. I daresay there will be many occasions where yours and Lady Evelyn's paths will cross."

Westfall grunted. "Thank you for inviting little Emily to play with Rosa and Sarah."

There was a throb of emotions in Westfall tone and Edmond consider him. "The circumstances of her birth does not matter to me or my duchess. Your daughter is my daughter, and she will always have my support."

Tawny golden eyes met Edmond's, and then with a small smile Westfall clasped his shoulders.

"Thank you, my friend."

They exited the library and made their way outside. Edmond walked slightly ahead, his heart light, wanting to be in the presence of his wife and children. Rosalie saw him and with a shriek she barreled in his direction. Sarah followed, and then he had his hands full with hugging his girls. Adeline waved, a wide grin splitting her face.

Westfall's six-year-old daughter, little Emily—who was a replica of him with her dark hair and golden eyes—ran into the marquess's arms. Holding their girls, they walked over to the several blankets spread on the lawn. Edmond lowered himself by his duchess and planted a firm kiss on her lips.

"Eweeee!" Rosa shrieked, and Emily and Sarah giggled.

Adeline's answering laughter tinkled like bells, and the love glowing in her eyes made Edmond's chest squeeze. "I love you, Adeline."

"And I you, Edmond."

Then he reached for his sons, who stared at him already

with piercing intelligence. They had stunning hazel eyes like their mother, the only thing they seemed to share with Adeline. Then under the incredulous gaze of Westfall, Edmond proceeded to have a rousing conversation with his sons, who stared at him enraptured. He was as certain as his duchess that somehow from their kicking legs and gleeful chortling, they understood.

Author's Note

I took the liberty of naming my own numbers in relation to the death rate in the Regency era. In truth, there was really no way at the time to be certain of the amount of childbirth death recorded in England because there were no well document records. It was in 1837, the Registrar General's office started to record maternal deaths. This was also encouraged by the Presidents of the Royal Colleges and the Master of the Society of Apothecaries, and people were urged to supply voluntarily copies of certificates of death, if possible with cause. It was not until about 1870, when the registration of cause of death was made mandatory, that rates became reasonably accurate.

Acknowledgments

I thank God every day for allowing me to find my passion.

To my husband, thank you for being my biggest fan and supporter! You are so damn wonderful.

Thank you to my wonderful friend and critique partner Giselle Marks. Without you I would be lost.

Thank you to my amazing editor, Alycia Tornetta, for being so patient when I miss my deadlines and overall a kickass amazing editor.

To my wonderful readers, thank you for picking up my book and giving me a chance! Thank you.

Special THANK YOU to everyone that leaves a review—bloggers, fans, friends. I have always said reviews to authors are like a pot of gold to leprechauns. Thank you all for adding to my rainbow one review at a time.

About the Author

I am an avid reader of novels with a deep passion for writing. I especially love romance and enjoy writing about people falling in love. I live a lot in the worlds I create and I actively speak to my characters (out loud). I have a warrior way "Never give up on my dream." When I am not writing, I spend a copious amount of time drooling over Rick Grimes from *The Walking Dead*, Lucas Hood from *Banshee*, watching Japanese Anime and playing video games with my love — Dusean. I also have a horrible weakness for ice cream.

I am always happy to hear from readers and would love for you to connect with me via Website | Facebook | Twitter

To be the first to hear about my new releases, get cover reveals and excerpts you won't find anywhere else, sign up for my Newsletter.

Happy reading!

Discover a new Stacy Reid series!

THE IRRESISTIBLE MISS PEPPIWELL
a *Scandalous House of Calydon* novel

Dissatisfied with his empty life, Lord Anthony Thornton seeks a deep and lasting connection... and finds himself intrigued by the Ice Maiden of the haute monde. Undaunted by Phillipa Pippiwell's aloof nature and her distaste for the idea of matrimony, he sets out to thaw the bewitching beauty by enticing her with adventures of the most sensual type. But both Anthony and Phillipa hide secrets revealing past scandals best kept buried... and if discovered, could rip them apart.

Get Scandalous with these historical reads...

ENTICING HER UNEXPECTED BRIDEGROOM
a *Lady Lancaster Garden Society* novel by Catherine Hemmerling

Sarah Jardin is far too outspoken and ungraceful to be a lady... until Lady Lancaster invites her to join the Young Ladies Garden Society. But her new life of high-society intrigue is interrupted when she's discovered in a compromising position with the David Rochester—the man she's always loved. They're forced to marry, even as they are drawn into investigating a dangerous conspiracy. With life and love on the line, their unexpected marriage will either end in rapture...or ruin.

HOW TO BEWITCH AN EARL
a *How To* novel by Ally Broadfield

Edward Adair, heir to the Duke of Boulstridge, is more interested in finding a missing family heirloom than a wife. But his parents issue an ultimatum and he reluctantly agrees to find a bride. Instead, he discovers attractive but infuriating Miss Isabella Winthrop offering clues to the location of the heirloom. Isabella finds Edward arrogant, but she works with him to solve the mystery. Their mutual attraction grows, but a secret is revealed that could destroy everything.

One Last Kiss
an *It's in His Kiss* novel by Ally Broadfield

Captain Mikhail Abromovich would rather single-handedly face the entire French army than follow orders to deceive Princess Anna Tarasova, the woman of his heart, by feigning a courtship to hide his covert activities.

The Highlander's Accidental Marriage
a *Marriage Mart Mayhem* novel by Callie Hutton

On a journey to the Scottish Highlands, Lady Sarah Lacey is set upon by misfortune, leaving her without carriage or chaperone, and left to the mercy of the kind and handsome Professor Braeden McKinnon. Whom (in order to secure a room at an inn) she announces is her husband. Braeden can't bring himself to tell her that her proclamation is not only legally binding in Scotland, but sharing a room is considered to be an act of consummation. Now they are bound together until death do they part—even if Sarah has no intention of becoming any man's wife.